PONTIFEX MA

Now The End Begins

DAMIAN NORTH

First Published in 2016
by Damian North

1 3 5 7 10 8 6 4 2

A CIP catalogue for this book is available from the British Library.

HB ISBN 978-1-5272-0324-2

Contact:

www.damiannorth.com

Cover Design by Jay Ahere

For Daniel Cunningham

I do not know with what weapons World War III will be fought,
but World War IV will be fought with sticks and stones.

Albert Einstein.

Prologue.

SUNDAY, 23rd March.

In the cool of the evening, Malachy Devine was driven across northern Israel

For three days the contacts and leads he had followed had taken him to farmlands around Teverya, Afula and Rama, but he still had not found what he was looking for. The only thing he knew, with certainty, was that Islamic extremists had already destroyed one and now the Israeli government were taking no chances with the only one they had left. Yet, that evening he felt sure he was going to see it with his own eyes.

His American security contractor, who was driving him, knew exactly where to go. He had the directions Devine had given him taped to the dashboard. Although Devine did not know it, his contractor knew the significance of their journey to Tel Megiddo. Just like Devine, the contractor was under orders to find the proof too.

Three miles west of Tel Megiddo, Devine's car turned off the road and travelled along an old dirt track, towards the farm that was dimly lit ahead of him. Shutting down his tablet, he searched his dispatch bag for his cellphone to record and prove that what happened three months previously was more than just speculation.

Approaching the farm's main gates, the contractor slowed the car once he saw the military checkpoint ahead. As the car came to a complete stop, right in front of the security gates, four armed Israeli soldiers quickly surrounded them and ordered them to step out of the vehicle with their hands in the air.

'What is your purpose here?'

'I have permission, from the office of the Prime Minster, granting me access to the farm,' Devine replied, handing over his papers to the soldier who wore the lapels of a captain.

Taking the documents, the captain read them carefully. 'Mr. Devine, may I see your passport?'

Motioning with his head that it was in the car, he was allowed to fetch it from his dispatch bag and hand it over.

The captain studied it closely.

'Mr. Devine, come with me,' the captain instructed.

Without hesitation, Devine followed him past the security barrier and over to a military jeep that was parked on the other side.

Not permitted to go any further, the contractor had no choice but to wait for Devine to return; frustrated he could not go with him to see it with his own eyes.

Fifteen minutes later, and having nervously smoked two Camel cigarettes, the contractor saw the lights of the jeep as it returned towards the security barrier. As Devine stepped out of the vehicle, the contractor knew that he had seen it.

'Take me back to the hotel,' Devine instructed, as he got back into the car.

Turning the car around, the contractor knew the time had come. Slowly, he drove Devine towards the main road that would take them away from Tel Megiddo. Although he had talked a lot with Devine over the three days, he now found it difficult to speak to him, knowing what he had to do.

When they turned onto the main road, Devine took his cellphone and rang the only contact that was stored.

'I've just seen it. I've sent you the pictures.' Devine said, before hanging up.

The contractor was not surprised with the shortness of the call, but now that Devine had confirmed its existence he knew it was time to carry out his orders. Slowing the car down, he drove it onto the side of the road. Lifting a gun from under his seat he ordered Devine out of the car.

'Give me the cellphone,' the contractor demanded.

As the betrayal dawned on him, Devine knew that his time had come.

'You'll never silence this!' Devine said, as he handed over the phone.

'Who were you talking to on the phone?'

Devine refused to answer.

'Very well then, get on your knees.'

Devine always knew the price to pay would be high, but he was prepared for the moment. Without fear he blessed himself as he knelt on the dusty road, facing the gun that was pointed directly at his head. He closed his eyes.

1.

MONDAY, 7th April.

The bells of the Vatican tolled the midnight hour.

Above Saint Peter's Square the lights of the Papal Apartment, on the top floor of the Apostolic Palace, burned brightly while hundreds kept vigil for the Pontiff in the square below. In respectful silence, old and young alike prayed for his recovery. Even though the Pontiff wasn't in residence, the faithful still felt drawn to the Vatican to keep vigil for their beloved Holy Father, Pope Clement XV, as he recovered from his stroke and battled pneumonia at the Agostino Gemelli Hospital, in the north-west of Rome.

Across from the square, at a balconette in one of Rome's most exclusive properties on the Piazza Pio XII, Dave Mode stood watching the vigil. He could not bring himself to believe that a supernatural power, in some heavenly realm, was actually listening to their prayers. Looking up into the night sky he saw only the darkness; a vastness of infinite eternity in which he felt completely alone. Faith in an omnipresent was a truth to which he could no longer subscribe. He had rejected the lie he once believed. Experience and the rawness of life had convinced him that hope in such irrational belief was for the weak.

Privy to few details of the overall operation, Mode struggled to shift the slight unease he felt. He wished he could kill again that night. Taking a human life had never troubled the depths of his conscience. A bullet to the side of the head would be a more merciful blessing. His unease rested in knowing that the life of the young priest, who lay sleeping on the bed behind him, was not going to be worth living come the morning. His life was to be spared, but Mode was about to leave it in complete ruination.

With midnight upon him, Mode left the balcony and started to look through the bedside cabinets and wardrobes for the document. He had been instructed by his handler that a trusted source, from within the Vatican, had reassured Specialist Operations Command back in Virginia that the priest had a copy of the document. Mode knew he had to find it.

Making his way into the sitting room he searched under the chairs and through the cherrywood bookcases. He was impressed with the lifestyle the young priest was living. With an amazing view of the Vatican from all the windows and the fine furnishings, it was clear to see that the Vatican looked after its senior priests very well. The very grandeur of the priest's accommodation only made Mode wonder how lavish the apartments inside the Vatican were in comparison.

His thorough examination of the sitting room yielded nothing. The bookcases were shelved with well read books of theology, commentaries on the scriptures and a few political biographies. An ornate dresser contained only a few bottles of wine, liquors and spirits, and a collection of crystal wine glasses and whiskey tumblers.

After searching through the kitchen and bathroom, Mode felt a pulsating desperation run through his body. Time was against him. Having searched every conceivable place, he now regretted drugging the only man who knew where it was. Steadying his nerve, he walked back into the sitting room. The once pristine room was now a mess, except for the black cast iron fireplace which caught his eye.

Behind an array of photo frames, which covered the hearth, Mode noticed the arched candelabra with five unlit candles that sat inside the fire's chamber on the grate. Reaching down, Mode rubbed his right hand across the fret which looked like new. He checked his hand. Apart from a small amount of dust there was no sign of ash. Then reaching up inside the chamber he pushed against the flue damper, but it was sealed shut.

From where he was hunkered, Mode lifted his head and looked up towards the gold gilt framed mirror which hung directly above the mantel. Seeing the mirror sit ever so slightly out from the chimney breast he knew it concealed something.

Rising to his feet he reached for the large mirror. Feeling around its edges he felt three hinges under the left edge of the frame and a magnetic latch on the opposite side that kept it flush against the wall. Having already disabled the apartment's alarm system he released the latch and eased the mirror towards him without hesitation. Mode's smile as the mirror swung open before him quickly faded the moment he saw the Meilink vault safe. He pushed down on the handle, but it was locked.

With a dial combination virtually impossible to crack, Mode took his cellphone from his pocket and made a call.

'I think I've found it,' he said, as his right hand touched the dial combination. 'It's locked inside a Meilink vault safe. I'm going to need the code.'

'Leave it with me,' came the curt reply, before the call was terminated.

Turning the dial so that the zero digit rested below the indicator arrow, Mode waited.

Less than a minute later his cellphone began to vibrate.

'Go ahead,' Mode answered.

'It is a group two lock,' came the reply from a male voice Mode did not recognise.

'Who is this?'

'That is of no importance,' the stranger said. 'Do you know how to operate a group two lock?'

Mode hesitated for a moment, curious to know why a stranger was now involved in the operation, but he refrained from enquiring. 'Tell me.'

'Left four. Right three. Left two. Right one.' The stranger replied.

Mode reached for the dial.

'Tu es Petrus,' the stranger continued. 'Sixteen. One. Eight. Repeat the number.'

'Sixteen. One. Eight.' Mode replied.

With his role in the operation at an end, the stranger ended the call.

Placing the cellphone back into his pocket, Mode turned the dial to the left four times and stopped once the marker for the number sixteen was directly under the indicator arrow. Then turning it to the right three times he stopped at the number one. Wondering who the stranger was, he began to turn the dial to the left two times until he was able to stop at the number eight. Finally, with a quick turn to the right, Mode felt the dial pull in on itself as the bolts inside the safe retracted. You are Peter. Pushing down on the handle he successfully opened the safe and found what he had been looking for.

With no time to waste he removed a slim black attaché case, opened it and began separating the dozen or so files inside until he found the pontifical folder he was looking for. Reading the Latin title, *Sola Fide*, he knew it was the document from the description he had been given. Printed on thick cream coloured paper, the Latin document spanned the correct length of twenty pages, and on the last page it was authenticated by the signature and embossed seal of Pope Clement. Secure in the knowledge that this was the genuine thing, he once again took his cellphone from his trouser pocket and rang the handler.

'Got it.'

'Good.'

'Shall I bring the rest of the documents?'

'Yes. I'll meet you in ten minutes outside Babington's.'

'What about the priest?'

'You know what we want you to do,' came the reply. 'Just do it!'

Placing the documents back into the attaché case, Mode took it with him as he went back into the bedroom. As the priest lay unconscious on his bed, Mode reached for the white linen sheet and pulled it away, exposing the priest's naked body. With his cellphone he intimately photographed the priest as he lay sleeping, before sending the pictures to the number his handler had given him. As he left the apartment, Mode knew that his actions would destroy the life of Pope Clement's private secretary, Monsignor Gustave Hasler, forever.

2.

Cardinal Paul Brenard was escorted by a female flight attendant from an executive lounge at O'Hare International Airport, and taken directly to the first class cabin of flight UA79, destined for Rome. Dressed in a pair of black trousers and a plain white shirt, no one appeared to recognise him and without his clerical collar no one glanced his way. Inconspicuous to most, only the most observant of eyes would have noticed the eighteen carat gold Manfrini ring that he wore on the ring finger of his right hand; the ultimate symbol of the Sacred College to which he belonged. An inch in length and depicting the scene of the crucifixion, the ring was the one trapping of his office that he felt duty bound to wear at all times.

Four months had passed since his last trip to the Eternal City, when he attended the consistory in Saint Peter's Basilica to receive the red biretta from Pope Clement; elevating him as the archbishop of Chicago to the College of Cardinals. Tonight, as he boarded the plane he was acutely aware that the contrast between his last and current trip could not have been greater. Taking his seat, he felt a numbing pain knowing that he was heading to Rome to bury his closest friend, Father Malachy Devine.

'Your Eminence, would you like a drink before take-off?' the attendant asked, as she placed his black suit jacket and hand-luggage into the locker directly in front of him.

'You're most kind,' Brenard replied, as he fastened his seatbelt. 'Do you still serve Tanqueray?'

'Let's say we have enough to fuel this aircraft all the way to Rome,' the attendant said, as she closed the locker door.

For the first time in days, Brenard managed to smile. 'Then I'll have a gin and tonic.'

'The perfect serve coming up,' she replied, as she left him and headed to the first class galley.

Paul Brenard hated flying. Apart from the fine dining service and the reclining flat bed, he liked to travel first class so he could escape the irritation of airports as best he could. Aged sixty-five, he had spent most of his life travelling the world and had become accustomed to the better things in life. A lifetime in the priesthood, despite his many personal doubts in the faith he professed, had afforded him a life of enjoyable privilege. In his world there were two types of priests; the spiritual and the clerical. Brenard knew he belonged to the latter, but that had not always been the case.

When he was eighteen, in the fervour of youth, he believed that he sensed a genuine call and began his priestly studies at Mundelein Seminary, Illinois. Yet, it did not take long for his professors and deans to recognise that he was not destined to learn just enough theology to hear confessions, celebrate mass and bury the dead in some city parish. He had certain qualities about him that few young men his age possessed. As he matured into his early twenties, Brenard not only developed in his physical attractiveness, he stood out for all the right reasons. Along with a healthy balance to study and prayer, he was a keen athlete whose energy for life attracted many to him. The perfect student in every way, it was decided after he completed his first degree in scholastic philosophy at Mundelein, that he should be sent to the Pontifical American College in Rome; destined for greater and higher authority within the Church.

It was during his first year studying theology in Rome that he met Malachy Devine; the formidable Irish student who could quote reams of Thomas Aquinas' Summa Theologica and Scripture, word for word and verse for verse. For both Devine and Brenard, 1977 was the year their great friendship was formed, and despite their varied ministries within the Church, it was a friendship that lasted the test of time. Often months, sometimes years would pass by without seeing one another. Nevertheless, whenever Brenard was in Rome they always met up for dinner and sat for hours over a bottle or two of Devine's favourite weakness, Châteauneuf-du-Pape, picking up from where they had left off, content in the companionship they shared.

Being of Irish descent himself, Paul Brenard became fascinated with the Sligo man, as his own grandfather had emigrated from the same rural county after the First World War to settle in Illinois. Their common ancestral connection with the county, and love of soccer, brought them close together, and during the summer of '77, Brenard travelled with Devine to Ireland. From Malin Head to Mizen Head, in an old VW camper, they explored the west of the island for two months as they followed the Wild Atlantic Way, camped in the wilds of Connemara and served as guides to the pilgrims on Croagh Patrick. For Brenard it was the most memorable vacation of his life. Although they had promised to relive the experience, their two distinct vocations, within the Church, meant that it would never happen.

After three years of study at the Pontifical Gregorian University, on the Piazza della Pilotta, near to the Trevi Fountain, both men found that different paths were being carved out for them. While Malachy Devine lived and breathed books on theology and the sacred scriptures, Paul Brenard opted to embrace the Roman way of life and the company of influential clergy within the Roman Curia.

Consequently, Devine never returned home to Ireland to serve as a priest; his intellect was too great. Staying on in Rome after his ordination, he immersed himself in further studies to gain a pontifical doctorate, before following in the footsteps of the priests who guided his priestly formation by gaining a professorship and the Chair of Biblical Studies at the Gregorian.

For Brenard, his path within the priesthood was clearly marked out for him from the very beginning. After his own ordination, he was instructed to complete two further years of study at the Pontifical Ecclesiastical Academy before he was appointed private secretary to Archbishop Van De Putte; the Austrian cleric who served under several popes as the Apostolic Nuncio to London, Sydney and finally Washington. When Van De Putte reached the mandatory retirement age of seventy-five, Brenard received episcopal consecration from his hands and was appointed archbishop of his native Chicago.

'The perfect gin and tonic,' the attendant said, as she sat the drink into the niche of his armrest. 'Is there anything else, Your Eminence would like?'

'I'm fine, thank you,' Brenard replied, as he took from her the menu for that evening's inflight meal.

Relaxing into his chair, he could feel the 747 being pushed back from the terminal. Glad to see that the Mayan prawn starter was still on the menu, he knew from past experience that it would go well with the rib of beef for his main. Sipping his drink he tried to relax, knowing that after his dinner and a brandy or two, he would get a few hours of much needed sleep before the plane landed in Rome. It had been a long week.

As the inflight monitors went through the familiar pre-flight safety checks, Brenard's mind once again drifted back to Malachy Devine. He still could not understand why the past year had seen his friendship with Devine change so dramatically. Although Brenard knew that Devine was working in Rome, he had in recent months become uncontactable. At his elevation to the College of Cardinals, the one person Brenard wanted with him, to share in his joy, failed to even acknowledge his invitation to attend.

There had to be an explanation behind it all. But, now that Malachy was dead, Brenard knew he would never come to understand it or why his friend would end up murdered on some dusty road in Israel. Yet, what troubled Brenard the most was that even Devine's closest colleagues in Rome had no idea that he had gone to Israel until they were contacted by the Israeli police a few days after his mutilated body had been discovered.

3.

Word had spread throughout the Vatican that Pope Clement was coming home to die.

Having confirmed the news to the Council of Cardinal Advisors and then to the nuns of the papal household, Cardinal Jean Guarducci, the Vatican's Secretary of State, was escorted by his two personal protection officers from the Vatican's Gendarmerie, as he made his way back to his own private residence, a floor below the Papal Apartment.

As the second most influential figure in the Catholic Church, answerable only to the Pope, Cardinal Guarducci sensed a new dawn on the horizon. Events over the past two weeks had changed everything. With a diagnosis in recent years of hardening arteries, the recent stroke and the complications of pneumonia, had left Pope Clement's heart terminally weakened, and soon the world would know that his final days were now upon him.

It had been a demanding time for Guarducci since the Pope collapsed and was rushed to hospital. Despite the day to day running of the Vatican State, Guarducci was already feeling the burden of the extra responsibly weighing heavily upon him. Even though he was relatively young, as far as the College of Cardinals was concerned, he envied his younger brother of two years who had recently retired from teaching at a small junior school in Dijon at the age of fifty-five. Yet, as a Frenchman, Guarducci knew that his call to such an office required nothing but his absolute devotion to the call he had given his very life and soul.

Arriving at the entrance of his apartment, shortly after one in the morning, Guarducci felt a surge in energy that dispelled all tiredness when he saw that his personal secretary, Father Tardini, who was waiting for him, had in his hands a brown envelope. Guarducci's brow furrowed with a hesitant hope that the operation had been successful.

'Follow me,' Guarducci instructed, as he opened the door and led Tardini into his apartment. 'When did it arrive?'

'Less than ten minutes ago.'

'Did anyone else handle it?' Guarducci asked, as he took the envelope.

'No. I did exactly as you requested and met the courier in person.'

Opening the gummed seal, Guarducci removed the document from inside and handed the empty envelope back to Tardini.

'Will that be all, Your Eminence?'

'Yes,' Guarducci replied, as a wry smile crept across his face. 'I will see you later in the morning.'

As Tardini left the apartment, Guarducci walked slowly over to his desk, flicking through each page of the document to make sure that nothing was missing or different from the others he had seen. Sitting behind his desk, he reached for the telephone and dialled the number that was written onto a white address card that sat against the small potted orchid.

The phone rang three times, before the voice of the handler answered it.

'Did you get it?' She spoke softly.

'Yes,' Guarducci replied. 'Thank you.'

'I believe that our business should be concluded by tomorrow.'

'Good.'

'I will ring you once we have it.'

Guarducci paused for moment as he searched for the correct words. 'What about our problem friend?'

'It's been sorted.'

'Today?'

'Reuters have caught wind of the story,' the woman replied.

In control of the situation Guarducci smiled. 'Buona notte, signora.'

Ending the call, Guarducci took great pleasure as he began his most cherished ritual of any given day. Getting up from behind his desk, he walked over to a small walnut drinks trolley and poured himself a large measure of Courvoisier. Then lifting the lid of his silver-plated cigarette box, he took out his daily Gauloises cigarette and lit it. As he inhaled he felt the spinning effect of the kick. He began to relax, knowing that the day he had lived had ended well.

Lifting his drink he switched off the lights, before walking over and opening one of the double casement windows. Leaving the exterior shutters closed, he allowed the atmosphere of the vigil below to enter his apartment.

In semidarkness, his only light coming from the illuminated Saint Peter's Square, he listened carefully to the faithful recite the rosary. *If only they knew*, he thought to himself as he took a large sip of brandy before taking another smoke of his cigarette. *If only they knew that the well from which they drank was poisoned.*

With his office came a power few could imagine possible, but it was a power the world's political elite envied. Over a billion people professed the faith he was sworn to protect. Faithful congregations in every country across the world were represented by nuncios, cardinals, archbishops, bishops, priests, brothers, nuns... all sworn to uphold the faith and to instruct the faithful. The power Guarducci held, rested in the structure of a Church in which every member of the clergy was answerable to him and his holy office.

It was not easy. While he preached love he had to rule with ruthless discipline. It was the only way to save the Church from itself. As a junior archbishop in the Secretariat, working under the late Cardinal Traveris, he recoiled in constant horror as unfolding scandal after scandal engulfed the Vatican. In Guarducci's eyes, Traveris was a pathetic excuse for a man let alone a priest. As Secretary of State, Traveris' grip on order and control was chaotic, as sexual scandals and financial corruption weakened the Church's position within the world.

Day after day, the corrosive drip drip effect of scandal after scandal crucified Guarducci, as he could do nothing but watch; millions lost or laundered in the corruption of the Vatican Bank; papal ushers organising prostitute rings; the so-called revelation of the 'gay conclave', in which senior Vatican clergy who were unfaithful to their promises of celibacy were being blackmailed both from within and outside the Church; the constant allegations of mafia and masonic influences close to the heart of the papacy; the worldwide sex scandals not only against children, but also against men and women lured by clergy who used the power and lure of the priesthood to meet their own sexual gratification; the dramatic fall in worldwide vocations and the questioning of the Church's stance on celibacy and the ordination of women; the constant leaking of classified information from within the Holy See in what the world had dubbed 'Vatileaks'; the weakening of the Church's moral teaching on the family and marriage by a growing vocal minority of priests who publicly challenged orthodoxy. In Guarducci's eyes, corruption and indiscipline had become the two primary cancers of his beloved Church.

This slow and agonising decline ultimately forced the previous Pope to resign, after a select group of cardinals presented him with a three hundred page dossier outlining every single issue and challenge facing the Church from within. With the election of Clement, Guarducci's hopes of reform where quickly dashed when the new Pope reappointed Travaris as his Secretary of State. For Guarducci, it soon became clear that a change of leadership at the top was never going to be enough. What the Church needed was a bloodletting from within the Curia. At the time his trusted friend, Cardinal Boyer told him to let Travaris be. But, Guarducci could not allow the spiralling downfall to continue. All his life he had followed the golden rule within the Vatican - *break whatever commandment and you can be forgiven, challenge the power and they will crush you.*

As he finished his cigarette, Guarducci recalled the night, seven years ago when he made his move and challenged the power.

In a private audience with the Holy Father, Guarducci presented his own dossier of where the problems within the Vatican lay. Without hesitation he placed the blame firmly with Travaris who had sole control over every office within the Curia. In his dossier he also set out a plan for reform from within. That night, Guarducci made it clear that he was the man the Pope needed and to retire Travaris. When he had made his point, he presented his ultimatum when he handed over a signed letter of resignation for Clement to decide.

Less than a week later, his coup was complete when Travaris was summonsed to an unexpected audience and dismissed. Guarducci, the very same day, met the grateful Pope who tore up the resignation letter and appointed him to replace Travaris. Two months later, at his first consistory, Clement elevated Guarducci to the College of Cardinals.

Immediately, Guarducci set to work on his programme of reorganisation; dismissing ineffective men from the Curia and appointing others he could trust. Reform took time, but for the Vatican it was swift. In seven years, Guarducci was a man the Church grew to respect and to approach with fear and awe. Guarducci didn't believe in second chances. If a member of the clergy broke a promise of celibacy, in whatever form, they were to be automatically suspended for causing scandal. Then depending on the seriousness of their misconduct, the processes of swift laicisation was ruthlessly implemented. Seminaries where overhauled and seminarians vigorously vetted before they were ordained. Trials were held for four Vatican officials accused of leaking information to the Italian press; all four were found guilty and were currently serving time in a Roman prison with no chance of a papal pardon. Monique Romilly, a retired Executive Director of the IMF was hired to overhaul the Vatican Bank, resulting in seven more prosecutions, including that of an archbishop for embezzlement. Diocesan files across the world were ordered to be handed over to local prosecuting authorities if allegations were made against any priest.

Guarducci's power was absolute. In all Church affairs he had, in effect, the first and the last say in all matters, leaving Pope Clement free to focus on his mission to teach the faith and to renew it. But now, as he finished his drink, Guarducci could taste the danger. He was sitting close to the edge of his own downfall.

Walking back to his desk he lifted the document, knowing that its very words had the power to destroy everything he had worked so hard to achieve. He felt torn no more. His decision on how to proceed had been made long ago. If the world were to discover the contents of the document he held, if they were to even hear mutterings of its very existence, Guarducci knew that everything he had worked so hard to achieve would be shattered.

Without hesitation, Guarducci took his lighter and set fire to the document before throwing it into the empty fireplace. As the burning light from the flames flickered around the room, Guarducci stood and watched as the papal encyclical burned before him. All he needed, to silence the truth for good, was to find and destroy the fourth and only remaining copy.

4.

Dave Mode examined his watch for the third time in less than a minute. At precisely seven-thirty he made his move. From the online timetable, he knew that the daily routine for the community began in the chapel with lauds followed by mass. Assessing the risks and calculating the odds of success, this was the optimal time to go through with his mission. Everything now rested on the accuracy of the timetable and the hope that every student and priest was obliged to attend morning worship. Making his way along the Via dei Santi Quattro, he turned into the ornate grounds and made his way across the front lawn of the Pontifical Irish College.

Like most colleges and churches in Rome, the main door of the college was open and Mode walked unhindered into the foyer, where he stopped to take measure of the unfamiliar surroundings. From the far end of the building, he could hear the muffled intercessions of the students and priests coming from the college chapel. The main building appeared empty and he sensed no noticeable threat that would interrupt his plans.

Although eager to succeed, he felt no real anxiety or danger. Compared to previous operations in the heart of Syria, he knew today would be without fear of capture or his throat being cut by some fanatic wielding a Damascus steel hunting knife.

Stepping into the vast hallway, he carefully took one final look around him before he started to climb the grand staircase and headed for the residents' rooms.

Reaching the first floor landing he had the choice to turn left or right. To his right he noticed that the corridor had more doors running along its length than the corridor to his left. Sensing which wing housed the resident staff, he followed his gut instinct and turned left. As he made his way along the wing, he read the individual surnames that were engraved on the brass plaques mounted on every door; Cunningham, Murray, McAuley, and then he found the one he was looking for, Devine.

With his gloved right hand he turned the doorknob, but it was locked. Taking a small set of keys from the pocket of his jeans, he unclipped a wrench and wire key. A simple pin and tumbler lock was not going to stop him from getting into the room. With the wrench key placed into the bottom of the barrel he turned it anticlockwise until he felt a slight tension. Then with the wire key he raked the barrel before carefully lifting each one of the five pins. In less than thirty-seconds he felt the tension of the lock give way.

Taking one last look along the corridor, to make sure he was alone, he pushed open the door and made his way inside. It was far from what he had expected to find.

Instead of a suite of rooms and a study crammed with books and academic papers, it was completely the opposite. In the small room he found only a single bed neatly made, a small wardrobe containing a few clothes, a little bookcase with no more than a hundred books, a chair and an oak desk beside the window and a prayer kneeler that stood under the large crucifix that hung on the wall opposite the bed. It was nothing more than a spartan cell.

After thoroughly checking the desk, he started pulling the sheets off the bed and turned over the mattress to check for any cuts or slits through which the document could have been hidden. He even ripped open the pillows, but found nothing. Starting to feel pushed for time, he pulled the bed away from the wall and flipped it onto its side to see if anything was hidden under it, but to no avail. Remembering his discussion with his handler and her certainty that the document had to be in the priest's room, he turned, walked over to the bookcase and started to pull the books out one by one and quickly flicked through them. Frustrated, he finally toppled the empty bookcase onto the pile of books that were heaped on the floor. In a matter of minutes the only other place left to search was the wardrobe. With attentive efficiency, he removed every item of clothing from the rail and checked them thoroughly before tossing them to one side.

'What's going on here?'

Startled, Mode turned around to find an elderly priest standing at the door.

'Who are you?'

Mode's adrenaline raged all the more inside him.

'I think you'd better leave before I call the police,' the priest challenged harshly.

'Has anything been removed from this room?' Mode managed to ask, as dark calculation glazed his eyes.

'That's it,' the priest insisted, as he turned to leave the room.

'Wait!' Mode shouted after him. 'I'm Carabinieri.'

'You sound American,' the priest replied. 'Let me see some identification.'

'Has anything been removed from the room since Fr. Devine's murder?' Mode asked, as he reached for the inside pocket of his jacket to get his wallet.

'The room hasn't been touched,' the priest calmly replied. 'Now, let me see your identification.'

'Absolutely,' Mode replied, as he opened his wallet, making the priest walk even closer towards him to see it.

The moment the priest was within reach, Mode dropped the wallet and with his left hand gagged the old man before he spun him around. The struggle was brief as Mode placed his right hand around the back of the priest's head and twisted it sharply in an upward angle. Death was instant. As Mode let the priest's lifeless body fall to the floor, he heard his last breath escape with a haunting sigh.

Convinced the document was not in the room, Mode decided to leave before he was seen. Lifting his wallet off the floor he placed it back into his inner jacket pocket, then as he closed the door behind him he calmly walked away from the deadly consequences of his actions.

5.

Monsignor Hasler awoke with a thunderous headache and struggled to open his eyes.

Noise from the city flooded the room, and a piercing siren from a passing police car echoed unmercifully in his head. It was not until he realised that he was naked under the bed sheets that he finally found the strength to lift his head to look around. The balconette window was wide open and the lights in his bedroom were still on. At first something did not look right. The room in which he slept looked dishevelled. Then it dawned on him. Someone had been in the apartment.

Throwing back the sheets, he fought against the pain to get up from his bed and to steady himself. All around him his possessions were strewn across the floor. The moment he entered the sitting room and saw the safe lying open, he knew that someone had taken it. Helplessly, he walked over and looked inside the safe hoping that his instinct was wrong; his stomach and the pain in his head tightened all the more with dreaded worry that the document had been stolen.

Suddenly, the phone in the corner of the room began to ring. He ignored it as he frantically began searching the room for his briefcase in a desperate hope.

After the eighth ring his telephone clicked to his answering machine with a single beep.

'Do not pretend you are not there.'

Recognising the voice, he stopped dead in his tracks and turned and stared at the phone.

'Pick up, Gustave!'

With his heart pounding, Hasler grabbed a throw from the back of his sofa and wrapped it around his body.

'Do not ignore me!'

Lifting the receiver, he made a vain attempt to cough away the dryness in his throat, before he could manage to utter the words. 'Good morning, Your Eminence!'

'Finally,' Cardinal Guarducci sneered.

'I am sorry, I seem to have slept in,' Hasler apologised, as he lifted his watch off the coffee table, startled when he realised it was nearly ten in the morning.

'That, is the least of your worries,' Guarducci said bluntly. 'Have you read today's *Corriere della Sera*?'

'No,' Hasler replied, somewhat confused.

'Read it!' Guarducci instructed.

Trying to make sense of what was going on, Hasler lifted his tablet from the chair beside him, switched it on and searched for the *Corriere della Sera*. The moment he opened it, he could not believe what he saw. Such a panic and fear swept through his body. He felt as though his legs were about to give way below him as tears filled his eyes.

Under the bold title of PERVERTITO, he stared at a full length picture of himself lying naked on his bed, with only his genitals blackened out.

'Lord, help me!' He prayed, as he began to read the exclusive story.

An exclusive source, which the paper refused to name, had gone public with a story claiming they had shared a three year open relationship, during which time they had both engaged in promiscuous sexual encounters in gay saunas and even inside the Apostolic Palace. Most damning of all was the allegation that Hasler used his position within the Vatican to grant certain privileged graces to younger clergy for particular services rendered.

A living hell engulfed him, he knew he was ruined.

He tried to remember what had happened to him the previous evening. He could only patch certain events together. He could vaguely recall meeting with an American clerical student for dinner, but as to the purpose of the evening or how it ended he struggled to remember; except for briefly waking up in the back of some car while being driven through Rome.

'Can you even begin to imagine the damage this has caused to the Church?' Guarducci spoke, breaking the silence between them.

'Your Eminence, this story is not true.'

'Enough!' Guarducci snapped, his anger clear to hear. 'The damage you have caused to the Church is incalculable. As the Holy Father prepares to arrive home from the hospital, he now has to face the scandal that his renowned Caro has flung aside his most treasured vow in the most despicable way imaginable.'

Hasler dared not speak.

'I want you in my office within the hour,' Guarducci demanded.

'Yes, Your Eminence.'

'A car is waiting outside your apartment to bring you to the Vatican. At least that way, we will not have to face the embarrassment of the press tailing you across Saint Peter's Square.'

With the Cardinal terminating the call, Hasler fell back onto his sofa; overcome with the swelling emotion of the predicament he now faced. Since entering the seminary aged seventeen he had served the Church faithfully. Not one vow had he broken, but now everything was being taken so cruelly from him. Despite the lies, he knew the cardinal was right. The impact of the scandal was going to be incalculable.

As Pope Clement's private secretary, Monsignor Gustave Hasler knew such a story would travel the world. Furthermore, he knew under Guarducci's absolute rule that he would never work in the Vatican, or have any future public ministry ever again. In the eyes of the Church he was now a pariah. A living scandal to an already scandalised Church. He was Caro no more.

6.

From the moment the Holy See signed the Lateran Treaty with the Kingdom of Italy in 1929, responsibility was inherited by the Italian Republic to ensure the safety of the Pope and senior cardinals as they travelled throughout Rome. While the Pope was being heavily guarded in the Agostino Gemelli Hospital, Cardinal Brenard's armoured limousine was escorted by the Italian police as he made his way from Fiumicino Airport to the Vatican State.

As a cardinal, he was going to be well protected while he visited Rome, especially under the threat from Islamic State militants to kidnap and publicly behead a cardinal of the Church; particularly one of the eleven American cardinals whose heads were prized above the rest.

With his limousine flanked by four Carabinieri outriders, and followed by an armoured protection van, Brenard only wished he had the same ease as he travelled to and from his episcopal residence in Chicago's Gold Coast district, as his escort halted traffic at every junction to enable his motorcade to pass unhindered.

Brenard hardly lifted his eyes from the newspaper as he read the exclusive story of Monsignor Hasler's scandal. Not easily shocked, Brenard found the raw and intimate details of the scandal rather unsettling. Yet, despite the lurid details, he felt genuine compassion for Hasler. Until that morning, he had believed Hasler to be a good and upright man; one the Pope could have trusted with his life. Furthermore, the more he read the revelations in the *Corriere della Sera*, he could only bring himself to imagine the heartache it would cause the Holy Father who would now have no choice but to dismiss him from office and possibly from the clerical state.

Since taking control of the Archdiocese of Chicago, Brenard feared that one day his own past would eventually hunt him down, destroying him like it had destroyed many priests he had personally known. Foremost a priest, Brenard knew that the priesthood was flawed in its humanity. Like many of his brothers, even those who fell by the way, he believed that they all tried to remain true to their call despite the temptations of their own personal struggles with the allure of lust.

For all his time in the priesthood he had struggled with his own vow of celibacy, and he personally knew how difficult the vow was to follow. Despite his desire to live the life of an ideal priest and dedicate his life to the Church, he did fall by the way once and forty years later it still haunted him.

As a young priest working with Archbishop Van De Putte in London, a close friendship with one of the lay secretaries, who worked alongside him in the nunciature, became intimate. Her name was Margaret Black; the media liaison officer for the English Bishop's Conference during the time he was stationed in London. Throughout all his seminary training, he had been warned about the dangers of forming so-called particular friendships. He knew he was expected to walk away if the signs became apparent that a friendship was becoming too personal. But with Margaret he couldn't walk away. Within six months of arriving in London, he had broken his vow. It was a vow so easy to make but nearly impossible to live.

'Do you dedicate your whole life to the service of God, and with His assistance observe the vow of chastity and be bound for ever in the sacred ministry you are about to partake?' He was asked on the day of his ordination to the sacred priesthood.

In his heart he knew he was sincere when he replied, 'Yes!'

But, he was young and his ideals were shaped by old men who taught from dusty commentaries. Once free from their rigour, once free to live amidst the temptation of the world it was a different story. He knew the seriousness of his vow, and he knew the consequences of such temptation. Yet, his spirit and his body yielded the moment he knew that with Margaret he could taste the sin of the flesh. For a long time they fought to keep the boundary between them, but one night after dining out in London, when they went back to her small apartment near Russell Square, they had the first of many intimate encounters.

Their sexual relationship lasted for three and a half years. Never once had he regretted breaking his most solemn vow, because the joy she brought to his life was unlike any other emotion he had ever felt. With every moment they spent together, Brenard found his heart experiencing things he could never have imagined possible. The joy of loving a woman completed him like he had never felt before. He truly loved her, but in the end he could not give up the calling he had to the priesthood.

Eventually, the time they were spending together was not enough for Margaret. She wanted more from life, and when Brenard refused to give up the Church for her, she ended the relationship. Even though he pleaded with her to keep what they had going, he finally came to see that it was not fair on such a beautiful and loving woman. He had to let her go, knowing that his heart would never be complete again without her.

Soon after their relationship ended his nuncio was moved to Sydney. For Brenard the separation became not only painful but eventually unbearable, breaking him down until he finally confided it all in his archbishop. Without Van De Putte, he could not imagine where the heartache would have ended, for it was the old man's gentleness and understanding towards him that helped to heal the brokenness he felt inside. Even as he recalled the memory of the love he once shared, he felt the common numbing pain pull at his conscience and for just a moment he wondered if he had made the right decision to let her go.

Within thirty minutes of leaving the airport his motorcade swept across the Piazza Pio XII as it approached the Vatican. He was nearly there. With his past beginning to haunt him again, he placed it to the back of his mind like he had done so many times before. After all, the task of burying his closest friend was a big enough cross to carry, without the added worry of Monsignor Hasler or the love of a woman he had not seen or spoken to in nearly forty years.

7.

In Cardinal Guarducci's office, a plasma television mounted on the wall, behind his ornate pedestal desk, silently played the rolling news from CNN and their intensive coverage of Monsignor Hasler's sex scandal. From his window, Guarducci could see the numerous news vans on the edge of Saint Peter's Square feeding the world's major networks with live updates and developments of the growing story.

He was not particularly looking forward to meeting Hasler, but such a public scandal needed to be dealt with swiftly and before the Pope returned to the Vatican.

'You may send him in now,' Guarducci requested, as he spoke into the intercom to his secretary, in whose adjoining office Hasler had been waiting.

Walking behind his desk, Guarducci waited for Hasler to enter. Taking a deep breath he gathered himself, adjusted his pectoral cross and summoned an inner strength for what he was about to do.

'Your Eminence, Monsignor Hasler,' his secretary announced, as he led Hasler into the room.

'Thank you. If you could close the door on your way out.'

As Hasler walked towards his desk, it was clear for Guarducci to see that he was a broken man; his face was wrecked with shame and worry.

'I take it this is you?' Guarducci asked in frustration, as he lifted a copy of the *Corriere della Sera* and handed it to Hasler. 'Now we are having to deal with the curse of social media which is freely circulating these pictures totally uncensored. How they got hold of them, God only knows. How we are going to control them, well that is looking near on impossible.'

'It is me, but I….'

'How come someone was able to take a picture of you lying naked on your bed?' Guarducci interrupted.

'I don't know what happened last night, but I am convinced the picture was taken of me as I slept.'

'I think the picture speaks volumes, Gustave. Alone in itself it is damning of your position here within the Vatican.'

'I know how that picture looks and how that story portrays me, but I ask you to believe me. It is not true.'

'What do you want me to do? Release a public statement denying your involvement and association with the person behind this story? Allow you to continue to serve the Holy Father with a big question mark hanging over your reputation?'

'That is not what I am asking for. All I need is for you to trust the truth in what I am saying.'

'Fair enough,' Guarducci replied, as he took his seat behind his desk and looked directly into Hasler's eyes. 'Tell me once again that it is not true.'

'May God be my witness, it is not true,' Hasler truthfully swore, praying for the Cardinal's trust.

'Then explain this,' Guarducci said, as he handed over a brown folder to Hasler.

Hesitantly, Hasler took the folder from Guarducci.

'This is totally fabricated!' Hasler replied, as he opened the folder to find a criminal conviction against him for indecent behaviour. Immediately, his mind was awash with a tsunami of questions as he realised the peril he was in.

'You are denying this as well? Does a criminal record not speak for itself?'

'I swear to you, I have never been arrested or cautioned for anything in my life,' Hasler insisted, not quite believing that he was looking at a copy of a police file that contained a photograph of himself in police custody, a signed confession and a copy of a set of finger prints that allegedly belonged to him.

'How can you expect me to believe you over this damning evidence? Evidence, I might add, that is going to be the main news feature in tomorrow's *Corriere della Sera*.'

'How did you get this?'

'When the story broke this morning, a Vatican press officer contacted a source within the paper and he informed us that they are planning to publish the story tomorrow on your recent criminal conviction. The Inspector General of the

Gendarmerie then managed to get me that copy from the Carabinieri.'

'Your Eminence, it is a fake record.'

'Be silent!' Guarducci insisted. 'The full police report is here in the file. You were caught cruising near the perimeter wall of the Roman Forum.'

'That is not true.'

'Gustave, you signed the confession. In the name of all that is Holy!' Guarducci swore, as he slammed his right palm onto the desk. 'Ordained priests should not be body hunting for sex.'

'I have done no such thing.' Hasler insisted, as tears stung at his eyelids with the false witness that was being drawn up against him.

'I never took you to be a liar.'

'I am telling you the truth!' Hasler cried out, in desperation.

'Watch your tongue, Gustave!' Guarducci rebuked him for raising his voice. 'Remember, that in addressing me you are not only speaking to a cardinal of the Catholic Church, but to the office of the Holy See.'

Guarducci had never felt so aware of his position and the power it held. Despite the palpable tension within his office, there was too much at stake, too much risk of the real truth being exposed that Guarducci knew he needed to bring the torturous saga to a conclusion. Regardless of the cruelty, he knew such a measure was necessary to justify the greater goal of his mission.

'Before I phoned you this morning, I spoke to the Holy Father. He is disgusted by your actions.'

'Allow me to speak with him. I am sure he will understand!'

'Gustave, you will never see or speak to him again. You are being expelled from your post within the Vatican and your priestly faculties have been suspended by the Holy Father with immediate effect.'

'Please do not take my priesthood from me.'

think it is a fair enough measure in light of the contempt e shown to the office and trust you once held.'

As his judgement was pronounced, Hasler began to sob ıtrollably. Within one hour his whole life had been ruined. His world had been thrown into a void of despair, and as he listened to Cardinal Guarducci talk on, he could only wonder who could have done this to him, and even more importantly, why?

'I want you to go back to Munich and present yourself to your ordinary. To be honest, the further you are away from Rome the better. But, before you leave I am going to need your copy of the Pope's draft encyclical.'

'Is this what this is all about?' Hasler innocently questioned, as he wiped away the running tears from his face. With the shock of the scandal that had engulfed him, he had completely forgotten the importance of what really mattered. 'That picture was taken of me last night while I was sleeping, and then when I woke this morning I discovered that the encyclical had been stolen.'

'What do you mean, stolen?' Guarducci snarled.

8.

As Cardinal Brenard's motorcade approached the Vatican, the Carabinieri outriders sealed the public access around the entrance to the Gate of Saint Anne to allow his limousine to drive through unhindered. Under ornate archways and past the museums, he was driven into the Belvedere Courtyard.

As his driver pulled up alongside the Apostolic Palace, Brenard looked on as nine Swiss Guards marched across the courtyard towards Saint Peter's Square for the noon changing of the guard. He noticed they were led by a standard bearer who carried the flag of the Vatican State and not the papal coat of arms; a reminder to everyone that the Pope was not in residence.

Within seconds of his car stopping, the door was opened by the familiar face of Fr. Richard Harrison; the Australian priest who had the responsibility, on behalf of the Prefect of the Papal Household, to welcome English speaking dignitaries and senior clergy as they arrived for formal engagements.

'I hope, Your Eminence had a safe and pleasant trip?' Harrison asked, as he warmly shook Brenard's hand as he stepped out of the limousine.

'One could get used to travelling like this,' Brenard humoured, as the driver got out and carried the one case he needed for that afternoon.

'It certainly has its advantages, especially getting through Rome's traffic,' Harrison replied, as he took the case from the driver. 'I trust you will be residing with Cardinal Boyer for the duration of your stay?'

After Brenard nodded in agreement, Harrison handed a small white card to the driver with Cardinal Boyer's address, and instructed him to bring the rest of the cardinal's luggage to the apartment on the Via della Conciliazione.

'I hear that His Holiness is being discharged from the Gemelli?'

'Yes,' Harrison replied, as he led the way up the steps. 'He's taken the decision to spend his final days back in the Vatican. Cardinal Guarducci is making the final arrangements for his arrival back home. A group of specialist nurses and doctors are going to be looking after him.' Harrison informed the Cardinal, as he led him into the main foyer of the Apostolic Palace.

With its vast marble floors and high vaulted ceilings, frescoed with artwork from Botticelli and Ghirlandaio, Brenard felt a little awed with the very grandeur the palace was designed for. Even the Swiss Guards saluted him the moment they recognised him as a member of the Sacred College. He had travelled through the palace many times before, but since his elevation it was the first time that he walked the marbled floors as a prince of the Church.

'This way, please.' Harrison said, as he opened the door to a room off the main foyer.

Walking into the room, Brenard was impressed, believing it had to be the most ornate cloakroom he had ever seen. Eight large crystal chandeliers hung from the ceiling, and a dozen solid mahogany tables sat in two perfect symmetrical lines across the room, while the walls were lined with thousands of rare books locked behind the glass cabinet doors that contained them.

'May I take your jacket?' Harrison asked, before he placed it in one of the large mahogany lockers.

In the Vatican, it was improper to simply wear the clerical collar and black suit that Brenard felt most comfortable in. Protocol insisted that all clergy had to wear proper full pontificals of their rank while in the Vatican State. So, opening his case, Brenard took out his black soutane, lined with immaculate hand-stitched scarlet trim and put it on, while Harrison took out the rest of the pontifical attire and placed it with great reverence onto one of the mahogany tables before placing the suitcase into the locker.

When Brenard finished buttoning his soutane, he lifted his scarlet fascia and fastened it around his waist; making sure that the drop and fine tassels hung to his left. Then taking his gold pectoral cross from Fr. Harrison, he placed the gold chain around the collar of his soutane before attaching the hook of the cross to the button directly at his breastbone. Finally, he took his red zucchetto and placed it on his head to complete his full attire as a member of the Sacred College.

'If you could carry this on your person at all times,' Harrison said, as he handed him an ID card. 'You'll need it when moving throughout the State.'

'Thank you,' Brenard replied, as he placed it into the pocket of his soutane, knowing that security had become a modern day obsession even for the Vatican.

'If you'd like to follow me, I'll escort you to the Secretary of State.'

When they left the room and walked across the foyer to the lifts, everyone who saw Cardinal Brenard knew why he had come to Rome. Malachy Devine's death, its mystery and the very man himself had been the recent talk of the Vatican.

'I'm greatly sorry for the loss of your friend,' Harrison expressed, placing a hand gently on Brenard's sleeve as they waited for the lift to arrive.

'Thank you, Richard. He'll be greatly missed.'

'He became quite a regular here in the Vatican over the past year or so. A quiet man. Kept to himself and quietly went about his business.'

'Malachy spent the past year working here?' Brenard asked, surprised. 'What was he doing?'

'I'm not too sure, but he was granted top security clearance for the whole State. Authorised by the Holy Father himself.'

'Forgive me Richard you've lost me. Why would Malachy have been given top security clearance?'

'I honestly can't answer that question. But, only two other people in the Vatican are granted that level of unrestricted clearance, Cardinal Guarducci and Monsignor Hasler.'

'Are you sure that your information is correct?'

'Absolutely. Fr. Devine had full clearance to go anywhere within the Vatican and to access the secret archives. Cardinal Guarducci has such a high level of access because he runs the State on behalf of the Pope, and the papal secretary is always entitled to similar privileges because he would often be requested by the Pope to go on his behalf to visit certain departments or retrieve documents from the archives. That's why Father Devine was so recognisable as he walked around the palace, very few people are given such freedom.'

'Was Fr. Devine working for the Pope?'

'I think so. Then again, he could've been working for either Cardinal Guarducci or Monsignor Hasler.'

'Hasler?' Brenard questioned, somewhat surprised as he stepped into the lift with the priest.

'It's possible. As you can imagine, we talked about it a great deal here in the corridors and down in the vaults over lunch. Strange thing was, despite having unrestricted access he only ever visited two places the whole time he was here. As regular as clockwork he would arrive every morning at seven for the Holy Father's private mass in the Papal Apartment before spending the rest of his day working alone in the archives. That really annoyed Fr. Hebblethwaite.'

'Fr. Hebblethwaite?'

'The Vatican's senior archivist,' Harrison explained. 'Between you and me, Fr. Devine's freedom to roam through the archives unrestricted really got on Fr. Hebblethwaite's nerves, as Fr. Devine was allowed access to material that even Fr. Hebblethwaite can't see unless he has written permission from the Holy Father himself.'

'What sort of material?'

'Mostly manuscripts. Some of the earliest copies of the gospels anywhere in the world, and I'm not just talking about the four gospels that the cannon of scripture allowed into the New Testament. He even had access to the complete collection of historical papal diaries and journals that, strictly speaking of course, only the Holy Father ever has the right to read. Then most evenings we would often see him making his way back through the Palace and straight up to the Papal Apartment.'

'Interesting!' Brenard murmured.

'Then several weeks ago he simply stopped coming. Here we are.'

Stepping out of the lift, Brenard noticed the words Segretario di Stato engraved into the ornate Carrara marble that surrounded the official entrance to the Curial Offices.

The dicastery of the Secretary of State was the busiest department within the Vatican. And as Brenard walked through the series of interconnecting rooms, he noticed that the hundred or so staff rarely lifted their heads to look his way as they sat at their desks working on their computers or speaking into phones in languages too numerous to count. Yet, the closer they neared Guarducci's office the calmer the atmosphere became and the more palatial the surroundings. Following Harrison into the waiting room, Brenard heard the argument right away, coming from deep within Cardinal Guarducci's office.

'What do you mean, stolen?' Brenard heard Guarducci shout from within the room, but he was unable to hear anyone answer him in reply.

'I'll leave you in the capable hands of Fr. Tardini, Cardinal Guarducci's private secretary,' Harrison explained as he shook Brenard's hand; much to Brenard's amazement as Harrison deliberately ignored the shouting they could all hear.

'You were entrusted with it,' Guarducci bellowed. 'Do you know what will happen if it has fallen into the wrong hands?'

'Your Eminence, would you like a coffee?' Tardini calmly asked.

'No, thank you.'

'Cardinal Guarducci shouldn't be too long,' Tardini remarked, as he took his seat behind his desk and continued on with his paper work.

'Father, who's in there with His Eminence?' Brenard asked, as he sat down.

'Monsignor Hasler,' Tardini calmly replied.

'You are a disgrace to the Lord and the Church you serve.' Guarducci continued. 'Just, get out!'

Seconds later, the office door opened and just as Tardini had confirmed, it was Hasler. As Brenard sat looking on, he was shocked to see how upset the young priest was as he briskly walked past him and headed out into the main corridor of the department.

The moment Hasler left the office, Fr. Tardini got up from behind his desk and went into Cardinal Guarducci's office, closing the door behind him, leaving Brenard to sit and wonder to himself what on God's earth was going on.

In his forty years of priesthood, Brenard never fully understood the inner workings nor the secrets of the Vatican. Yet, in those fifteen minutes he was left at a loss and with a lot of unanswered questions about the one friend he thought he knew.

9.

'Father, I thought I made it quite clear that I did not want to be disturbed!' Guarducci snapped, when Tardini walked into his office.

'Your Eminence, I thought you should be aware that Cardinal Brenard from Chicago has been waiting outside.'

'How long has he been there?'

'Long enough.'

'Bring him in.'

'There is a serious development I think you should be made aware of,' Tardini said.

'What is it?' Guarducci asked, sensing the seriousness in Tardini's tone.

'Several minutes ago I received a phone call from the Commander of the Swiss Guards. There has been a murder at the Irish College.'

'What?' Guarducci asked, genuinely shocked. 'A student?'

'No. After morning prayer the college rector and the spiritual director discovered the body of the retired vice-rector, Fr. Eugene McAuley.'

'Good Lord! Do they know who murdered him?'

'I am afraid not. A strange, if not disturbing coincidence is that Fr. McAuley's body was discovered in the room of the late Fr. Malachy Devine. It appears that Fr. McAuley disturbed an intruder who was ransacking the room.'

'Jesus!' Guarducci unknowingly swore, as he sat back down behind his desk, remembering the plan to retrieve the fourth and final document.

'Shall I invite Cardinal Brenard into the room for your meeting?' Tardini asked.

Guarducci didn't reply, but simply brought his joined hands up to his chin, as his mind began to race with possibility and concern. For several seconds he sat in complete silence. As he considered the risk of the recent development he felt his frustration grow with the ineptitude of the CIA and their handling of the operation. Then the doubt surfaced once again, and he wondered if he had made the right decision in trusting them with his plan.

'Your Eminence?'

'What?' Guarducci replied, tearing himself away from his thoughts.

'Cardinal Brenard, shall I bring him in?'

'Show him in,' Guarducci said, knowing that he had to carry on with the duties of his office. He could not afford to dwell on the undercurrents that were quickly surrounding him. He had to remain in total control. 'Turn that filth off, I cannot watch it any longer.'

'As you wish,' Tardini obliged, as he walked over to the television and switched off the rolling news of Monsignor Hasler's downfall, before he left the room to fetch Cardinal Brenard.

In those few seconds, as he sat alone in his office, Guarducci could feel a slight sweat break out on his palms as he tried to contemplate the situation as it quickly unfolded around him. He considered ringing the number, but thought better of it. After all, if the handler had the document she would have made contact before now. Clearly, it was still missing. All his plans, everything he had so carefully orchestrated and brought into play over the years now rested on a thin ledge and the growing possibility that the truth could fall into the wrong hands. A truth that could not stop the inevitable from happening, but a truth that could stop him. Yet, what frustrated him the most, in that very moment in time, was the fact that he felt completely powerless.

10.

The Carabinieri wasted no time in cordoning off the Irish College. Across the ornate front lawn, forensic officers carried out a fingertip search of the suspected route the killer had taken to escape. Inside the college, investigating officers were entering the fifth hour of their preliminary enquiries by taking statements; following a prioritised list of the residents and visitors to the college. For no other reason, other than practicality, they began their interviews with the tourists; to free them so they could go and find alternative accommodation for the duration of their stay in Rome. Then, once they had interviewed the priests they finally turned to the students. Sitting among them was Stuart Smith, and when his name was called by an officer he was only too glad to get away from the confines of the dining hall and the rife speculation of the students' conversations.

'Fr. Smith, if you would like to go to the rector's study, an inspector will take your statement.' A junior officer said.

Not wanting to correct her, he simply followed her instruction and went to the rector's study and knocked on the door.

'Entrare!' Someone called from within.

When he opened the door, Smith felt sickened with the cigarette fumes that flooded the room. Although the smoke was thick and heavy, he felt it inappropriate to make his protest known to the middle aged man who sat with authority behind the rector's desk.

'Father,' the inspector greeted him, with a deep southern Italian accent, 'thank you for your patience, please take a seat.'

'It's actually, Mr. Smith,' he corrected, going against his initial judgement. 'I'm not a priest.'

'My apologies. You are the first student I have interviewed,' he replied. 'Your accent, I take it you are not Irish?'

'I'm from Manchester, England.'

'Ah, the home of the United and City men!' The Inspector replied, with a raised eyebrow. 'My name is Inspector Riccardo Pacelli.'

'I'm afraid I'm going to be of little use to you, Inspector Pacelli. I didn't witness anything in connection with Fr. McAuley's murder.'

'If it is alright with you, Mr. Smith, I will decide what is relevant or irrelevant to our investigation!' Pacelli calmly rebuked him. 'Monsignor Magee has provided me with a comprehensive list of everyone who was in the college chapel this the morning. He states that you read a scripture reading during the mass.'

'That's correct.'

'So, that is your alibi covered!' Pacelli said, as he clapped his hands together. 'But, what I would like to know is why you are living here in the Irish College and not residing at the Venerable English College.'

'No reason in particular, other than I was studying under a professor from this college.'

'Studying for what, exactly?'

'A pontifical doctorate in biblical studies.'

'And, what is the name of the priest who is supervising your doctorate?' Pacelli asked, as he lifted a pen to jot down the details into his notebook.

Smith hesitated for a moment, then he gave the name. 'Fr. Malachy Devine.'

Pacelli slowly raised his head, sensing in his gut that he had stumbled across something of significance. Lifting another cigarette from his packet he lit it. 'Tell me about your work with Fr. Devine.'

'I was his student and researcher on work that paralleled my doctrinal thesis.'

'Was the work paid?'

'I've been allowed to live here at the Irish College free of charge, and I'm given a monthly bursary.'

'How much?'

'Three hundred Euros.'

'That will not go far in Rome.'

'It's enough to get by. After all, I don't pay rent, I get my meals and laundry provided free of charge and I don't drink or smoke.'

'I gathered that,' Pacelli commented, as he stood up and opened the window sensing that Smith was uncomfortable with him smoking in the confines of the study. 'Tell me about your research.'

'Fr. Devine was researching the biblical accuracies of the prophet Daniel.'

'The prophet Daniel?' Pacelli quizzed, with a tentative smile. 'Sounds very boring!'

'I find that throw away comment slightly offensive, Inspector Pacelli.'

'Nothing personal,' Pacelli explained, as he leaned back into his chair. 'I am just intrigued as to why a young man in his twenties would be interested in such a field. Why would Fr. Devine pay someone to help him research a biblical prophet?'

'He was writing a book,' Smith lied.

'A book?'

'Fr. Devine was one of the leading biblical scholars of his generation. In his lifetime he'd managed to publish a dozen or so books in his particular field of expertise. I'm sure every time he researched a book he hired a postgraduate student to assist him with the workload. It's common practice here in Rome. Do you have any idea the volume of research that goes into writing a top level book on a biblical subject?'

'I am sure it is very extensive.'

'It takes years, and if you're the one writing the book you can't give up precious time living in libraries looking for some obscure reference in a manuscript or rare book.'

'Forgive my questions,' Pacelli apologised. 'I just find it very strange that after Fr. Devine is killed, someone raids his room and then murders another priest who discovers him looking for something. What do you think the killer was looking for?'

'I don't know.' Smith replied, knowing in that moment that Pacelli could tell that he was lying.

'Do you not think it is very intriguing?'

'That Fr. McAuley was murdered in Fr. Devine's room?'

'There is no such thing as coincidence!' Came Pacelli's cold reply. 'Did Fr. Devine have a personal computer?'

'Yes, he had a laptop. He didn't like paper cluttering up his office.'

'I gathered that,' Pacelli smiled. 'I accompanied the visiting Israeli police on Thursday to his office in the Gregorian.'

'I heard.'

'Do you know what we found when we arrived there?'

'No.' Smith replied, intrigued with whatever Pacelli was going to reveal.

'Nothing. His books were there but everything from his filing cabinets had been removed. Where you ever in his office?'

'Once or twice, but not recently.'

'To get into that room you need an ID card. When we arrived at the Gregorian and found that files had been taken, we checked with security and discovered that someone had deliberately shut down the entry system to gain access to the office on the same day that Fr. Devine's body was discovered. Only a professional could do that. Is electronic espionage your forte?'

Smith felt he had no need to reply to Pacelli, but simply sat and waited for his next question.

'Is there any truth in the rumour that Fr. Devine spent the last academic year working in the Vatican?'

'He spent some time in the Vatican's archives, that's all I know,' Smith continued to lie. 'I would meet him in his room most evenings and he would hand me a list of all that he wanted me to research the following day. I never handed him any printed research notes, he insisted that I emailed everything in attachments.'

'That is the interesting thing,' Pacelli confided. 'We have yet to find his laptop. When his body was discovered he had nothing on his person, not even his passport. We do not even know what hotel he was staying in. Furthermore, we still do not know the purpose behind his visit to Israel. Can you shed any light on that?'

'It's not unusual for a biblical scholar to visit Israel.'

'What about the laptop?'

'When he left for Israel that Thursday morning, I drove him to the airport. He was working on his laptop while he travelled in the car, and he took it with him to Israel.'

'I see,' Pacelli replied, as he dropped the remainder of his cigarette into the cup, letting it extinguish in the thick black remains of his coffee. 'If I need to speak to you again will you be willing to help me with any further enquiries I might have?'

'That goes without saying,' Smith replied, dreading the prospect.

'And what about your email correspondence with Fr. Devine? Would it be possible for us to have a look at your computer hard drive?'

'I can arrange for my laptop to be handed over at a later date,' Smith said. 'I would go get it now but the residents' wing is cordoned off.'

'Would you object to one of my officers retrieving it from your room?' Pacelli asked, looking for the slightest sign of hesitation. 'At most, we will keep it for a few days and have it returned to you by the end of the week.'

'That's okay with me,' Smith replied, knowing that he had nothing to fear. At best, the police would find a few dozen emails that would be of little worth to their investigation. He had himself covered. From the moment he learned of Devine's murder, Smith made sure that any trace of data that could connect him to Devine would never be discovered. His second laptop, the one that contained everything that Pacelli was desperate to find, but would never get his hands on, had been hidden and hidden well.

'Thank you, Mr. Smith. You have been an enormous help to me this afternoon. You are free to go, for now.'

Watching Smith leave the room, Pacelli's intuition told him, without any shadow of doubt, that Smith was now a key link to his investigation. But, time was on his side, and Pacelli knew he would eventually get the truth from him, no matter what it took.

After the shock of the morning's events and Devine's funeral the following day, Smith did not want to stay in the college while the Carabinieri continued with their investigation.

Deciding to take himself for a walk around the city to clear his head, he went into the common room to fetch his coat as it was still raining. As he went to leave he noticed that some mail had been left in his pigeonhole. He lifted it out and started to flick through the letters and periodicals he had ordered. Then as he reached the last piece of mail he literally felt his heart skip a beat.

On a small white envelope, one that was not too bulky, he recognised Devine's unmistakable thick cursive handwriting. When he saw the date of the Israeli postage mark, he knew it must have been mailed before he was murdered. Placing the rest of the mail back into his pigeonhole he slipped the letter into his coat pocket. He was not prepared to read it while the police were still searching the college. So he quietly left the common room, walked to the rear of the building and left the grounds through a discrete side entrance. On the main street he turned left and walked towards the Basilica of Saint John Lateran, the only place he knew where he could read the letter without the fear of watching eyes.

11.

At six thirty in the morning the President of the United States, Patricia Cleary, escorted by her secret service detail, walked along the West Wing's portico towards the Oval Office. In her hand she carried a translated copy of the encyclical, and having read it the previous evening she had found it difficult to sleep.

'Good morning, Madam President,' her staff said, as she walked through the French doors and into the most powerful office in the world.

'Morning,' she replied as she sat the encyclical on the Resolute Desk, before taking a seat with those who had gathered for the morning briefing.

Seated on the chairs, around the carpeted presidential seal, were Christopher Bannon her Secretary of State, Debra Conway her National Security Advisor, Tom Donahue her Chief of Staff, Admiral Markus Lyman the Chairman of the Joint Chiefs, Virginia Moore the director of the CIA and Jared Torrado her Vice-President.

'I trust we're fully rested and recovered?' The President asked with a caustic smile, as she took the briefing papers from her Chief of Staff. 'Following our much heated discussion yesterday morning, I've asked Debra to come up with a national security response to the encyclical and the recent disclosure by British intelligence regarding Azzan Rehman. Last night, she briefed Tom and myself and I thought it best for you all to be briefed on her findings too. Now, I want you all to listen, especially you Christopher, to what she has to say.'

Christopher Bannon nodded his approval that she would have his complete cooperation, even though he still felt dismissive of the entire episode.

'Madam President,' Conway began, as she opened her briefing papers. 'Whitehall has confirmed that Azzan Rehman supervised the controlled production and research of Venomous Agent X at Porton Down. Three months ago, while on holiday in Turkey he crossed the border into Syria and for the past three months it's believed that he's been living north of Baghdad and has sworn allegiance to the Caliph. We should be in no doubt that the Islamic States, although they've struggled to get their hands on a nuclear weapon, would love nothing more than to add VX, the most dangerous chemical weapon ever produced, to their arsenal. A pinhead droplet of VX would be enough to kill us all in this room. Five millilitres, released in an urban environment, would be enough to kill one hundred thousand people within a matter of hours. It's a colourless and odourless agent. Easy to produce with the know how and easily transported and released. It is the poor man's nuclear weapon and all intelligence is now of the opinion that it's the desired weapon of choice for the Islamic States.'

'Sweet Mother of God!' Torrado muttered. 'Do you think we're going to be targeted?'

'Our intelligence agencies have no reason to believe that we are under an imminent threat of attack, however they do believe that with Rehman's knowledge and with the resources of the Islamic States, that it is highly probable that they now have the ability to produce this chemical weapon. In fact, our intelligence sources in Baghdad believe that the production of VX is now a top priority for the Caliph. Whether or not they have already succeeded, we can't be sure. Our concern is, if they have it already it could be easily transported in something as simple as a purpose built thermos flask. Delivered into the hands of a suicidal fanatic, it would be practically impossible to detect let alone stop.'

'Pure speculation,' Bannon interjected, unable to hold his tongue. 'I've read the encyclical for myself. I'm still convinced that we're giving too much credit to the ramblings of a deluded old man.'

'It could well be, but I don't think we can ignore the significance of the penmanship nor the consequences if this document ever became public.' The President spoke out. 'Military and intelligence analysts all believe that the series of events Pope Clement claims he saw in his vision, which he has graphically documented in his encyclical are in theory possible. All we need is the trigger for them to begin to unfold. The release of a chemical weapon against US citizens would be more than enough to trigger the unimaginable.'

'Madam President, can I ask you a direct question?' Bannon asked.

President Cleary gave a nod of her head.

'As a Catholic, do you believe that he saw a genuine vision?'

Silence fell upon the room as they awaited her reply. It was a question they were all thinking but too afraid to ask.

'Until last night,' the President began, 'I was very sceptical. This morning, I feel a great unease. I believe we have done the right thing in assisting the Vatican in silencing this encyclical, and those behind it too. Despite our personal opinions as to whether it should be taken seriously or not, I trust we can all agree on the impact it would have if leaked. That in itself could be enough to trigger religious extremists to play their part in making it a reality.'

'On that, I agree!' Bannon replied. 'But, surely we cannot allow future foreign and defence policies to be based on a document even the Vatican wants silenced.'

'Last night, after being briefed by Debra, I couldn't sleep.' The President admitted. 'We have all been briefed on the procedures to evacuate if the alert is triggered that we are under a direct nuclear attack. Twenty minutes. Twenty minutes warning to get to ground or take to the air. Twenty minutes for the American people to take whatever precautions they can. Twenty minutes to give us a chance to do something. But, this is a whole different ball game. We simply don't have the means to detect a chemical attack. VX, will take less than twenty-seconds to release and no one will know until it is too late. Our battle is on two fronts. Primarily, we need to find and capture Rehman and prevent him from producing such a weapon for the Islamic States. Secondly, we need to make sure that the American people and the world never gets to read what we have read in recent days. Are we agreed?'

All, even Bannon after a slight hesitation, nodded their heads in agreement.

'Good.' The President replied to their support. 'What's the latest from Rome?'

'Our station chief in Rome has reassured us that she is doing everything possible to ensure that we find the fourth and missing copy of the encyclical,' Virginia Moore, spoke up. 'As you have already said, Madam President, those behind this encyclical have been dealt with and should cause us no further problems. If Rome needs more muscle then it can be dispatched immediately.'

'Thank you, Virginia.' The President replied. 'Admiral Lyman, what's your opinion on the matter?'

'I'd like to summon the rest of the Joint Chiefs and together with Debra and her team, put in place several operation plans to outline our response should a worst case scenario in relation to Rehman unfold,' Lyman said. 'We could brief you later this evening, Madam President, on proposed responses, tactical defence strategies and an outline of our military capability if faced with a chemical attack.'

'Should we raise our level of alert?' The President asked.

'We are currently at DEFCON four which has all armed forces under a level above normal readiness, which includes an increased intelligence watch and strengthened security measures.' Lyman replied, 'We could issue an order of standby for a possible increase to DEFCON three, to heighten the possible need for an increased response. What do you think Debra?'

'I think that would be a wise move,' she replied. 'A state of readiness would be a caution worth taking.'

'Admiral, brief the Secretary of Defence the moment he arrives back from the NATO defence summit in Paris.' The President ordered.

'I'd also recommend that we brief the Secretary of Homeland Security,' Conway said. 'At this moment in time, I think we need to ensure that our borders are fully secured and to see what their policies are for the prevention of a chemical attack on home soil.'

'I agree!' The President replied. 'Debra, take care of it. In fact, I'd like the Secretary for Homeland Security to be present at our future meetings. Get him fully briefed too.'

'I'd like to dispatch a heightened security alert to our embassies,' Bannon said. 'If we are contemplating the possibility of an attack and a forceful response, then I need to prepare those on the diplomatic front.'

'As long as you don't cause a heightened panic!' The President cautiously warned. 'In fact, make sure Tom sees any dispatch before it's sent. I want his take on it!'

Bannon sighed his disapproval as his leash was pulled once again.

'The same goes for you all. Everything, and I mean everything must go through Tom. We cannot afford the lines of communication to become blurred.' The President stressed as she stood up from her chair. 'Let's reconvene this evening when I return to Washington.'

With that, they all rose from the seats, bid her good morning and left the Oval Office, leaving her alone with her chief of staff.

'If we win re-election I'm appointing a new Secretary of State!' The President said, as she made her way over to the Resolute Desk.

'You shouldn't let him get to you!' Donahue replied. 'Personally, I blame the drafts from the cold winters of Vermont during his childhood.'

President Cleary smiled, as she took a sip of coffee that her personal aide had sat out for her.

'Are we chasing our tails here, Tom?' She asked, as she sat down behind her desk and opened her copy of the Encyclical.

'It's certainly unprecedented,' Donahue replied. 'But, we're doing the right thing.'

'Are we?'

'Patricia, you can't be entertaining doubts, not now. It's too late to question the decisions that have already been made. We're in this too deep to stop treading water. We have to see it through.'

'I hope we can trust everyone who's involved in this.'

Donahue sat on one of the chairs beside the Resolute Desk. He understood her fears, for they were his own too. But, now she was beginning to frustrate him with the time she was spending in the confusion of doubt.

'Patricia, you really need to stop worrying about what we have done. No one will ever find out. Just focus on today's agenda and let me sweat the small stuff.'

'The small stuff?' President Cleary said, with laughter. 'What we have done would render the world speechless if the truth ever emerged.'

'They won't find out.'

'I only wish I had your certainty and peace of mind.'

'You can still have it. All you have to do is give the word and I'll make sure the problem goes away.'

'No, Tom!' She said flatly. 'I can't believe you've brought that up, again!'

'It's your call, Madam President.' He replied, as he raised his hands. 'I respect your decision.'

'I want him kept alive.'

'I understand.' Donahue replied, as he got up from the chair and made his way to leave the room. 'We're leaving for Andrews in thirty minutes. There's a draft copy of the speech on your desk for your address at the Improved Nutrition Convention later this morning in Milwaukee. Read over it and if there's anything you'd like to change we can do so on Air Force One. Is there anything else, Madam President?'

She shook her head and watched him leave the Oval.

Alone, feeling swamped and powerless, President Patricia Cleary sat in the Oval Office; her only company the dull ticking of the Seymour grandfather clock that stood beside her secretary's door. Directly in front of her, sitting upon the mantle of the fireplace sat the triangular framed flag that draped the coffin of her late husband. Killed in action in Afghanistan, it was his death at the hands of the Taliban that drove her to run for office on a mandate of peace. She'd seen the video of his beheading, and his courage in the final moments of his life. She dreamed of a new dawn in his honour, but the dark night of terror seemed unending.

Ignoring the Milwaukee speech she continued to glance through the encyclical, wondering if it contained any truth or was it simply the writings of an old man, an old friend, who had lost his mind. She hoped and willed herself to believe in the latter, because the truth was something she could never accept. A total annihilation of everything that she held dear, a possible world war and its unknown fallout filled her beyond fear.

As she looked out into the Rose Garden and the dawning sunlight that graced the symbolic power of America, the power that rested in her hands, she prayed for a sign that she had done the right thing in supporting Cardinal Guarducci.

12.

Stepping into Guarducci's office, Paul Brenard felt his own authority eclipsed by the power of the one office that controlled every aspect of the Church. In slight awkwardness, he accepted Guarducci's invitation to take a seat beside the silver and glass coffee table, while they waited for Fr. Tardini to leave. Brenard could see that Guarducci was under a lot of pressure as he watched him take a small handkerchief from the pocket of his soutane and gently wipe the beads of sweat from his brow.

'Paul, let me apologise if you overheard that heated exchange between Monsignor Hasler and myself.'

'I understand,' Brenard replied. 'There is no easy way to deal with such matters.'

'That is why I am washing my hands of the sordid affair. I have sent him back to Munich where his ordinary can deal with his mess. I do not have the physical energy nor the time to deal with another scandal.'

'Will he be returning once it all dies down?'

'Absolutely not!' Guarducci categorically insisted. 'The archbishop of Munich is under clear instructions to find a suitable monastery for him; somewhere remote and far removed from the world's press. Hasler needs time to think about his betrayal and we need the time to come to terms with it. How the Lord dealt with the betrayal in the Garden of Gethsemane, I will never know.'

'How's His Holiness taking the news?'

'Devastated. I broke the news to him this morning. The poor man just lay in his bed and let his tears speak of his heartache. I thought it better he heard the news from myself rather than someone else.'

'I was thinking of paying him a visit while I'm in Rome. I'm not sure of the proper protocol in arranging it.'

'That will not be possible' Guarducci said. 'Forgive my bluntness, but I have taken the decision as the Secretary of State and in consultation with those treating the Holy Father. Visits are restricted. I hope you understand.'

'Of course,' Brenard replied, plainly embarrassed by the reproach. He realised he should have known better. In the Vatican there was a hierarchy and although he was a cardinal he still had his place and was expected to know it and stay in it.

Feeling awkward, Guarducci just gently smiled as Fr. Tardini reentered the room, and placed a tray of coffee and some Biscotti biscuits on the coffee table in front of them. Brenard wasn't the first cardinal he had denied access to the Pope. Just yesterday, he had a full blown row with Cardinal Chiaradia, the cardinal vicar for Rome. With some issue arising, an issue Chiaradia believed should have been made known to the Pope, Guarducci stood his ground and refused him access. He simply could not take the risk; not until the time was ready.

'When he gets back to the Vatican, I will arrange a time for you to see him. He just needs more rest at the moment than visitors. I think you will be shocked when you see him.' Guarducci said, as he lifted a cup and saucer and poured some coffee, trying to make Brenard feel at ease once again. 'The stroke has affected his speech. His words are very slurred and his facial muscles have become paralysed. But, the bout of pneumonia has really hit him hard and he has lost a considerable amount of weight. He looks as though he has aged ten years, or even more.'

'It would be nice to see him,' Brenard replied, as he took the coffee from Guarducci. 'I'd appreciate it.'

'Have you heard about the shocking developments at the Irish College?'

'That's why I'm in Rome,' Brenard replied, before taking a sip of the coffee. 'I'm celebrating the funeral mass tomorrow of Malachy Devine.'

'I am aware of that,' Guarducci replied, as he sat back in the chair with his cup, 'If you do not mind, I would like to concelebrate the requiem mass with you.'

'That's a very thoughtful gesture. It would mean a lot for his family and friends.'

'Unfortunately, there has been another incident involving a member of staff from the Irish College. This morning after morning mass, the murdered body of the retired vice-rector was discovered in Fr. Devine's room.'

'What?' Brenard replied, as he sat his cup and saucer down on the coffee table. 'Do we know who killed him?'

'The murderer still remains at large. The entire events surrounding Fr. Devine's death are so unsettling,' Guarducci manipulated.

'Fr. Richard Harrison just told me that Malachy had been working here at the Vatican in the months leading up to his murder.'

Guarducci was shocked, but composed himself to remain calm. *Typical of the Vatican,* he thought to himself, as he sipped on his coffee. *The gossiping eunuchs miss nothing!*

'For the past year or so I have been unable to make contact with Malachy. So, I was surprised to find out that he'd been working here. What was he doing?'

'I have no idea,' Guarducci replied, allowing Brenard to see his spurious look of surprise. 'It is news to me too. What did Fr. Harrison say?'

'He told me that Malachy had been given unrestricted clearance from the Pope himself, and that he was working for him. Apparently, he was spending a lot of time in the archives and was quite a frequent visitor to the Papal Apartment.'

'Had he been working for the Pope I would have known about it,' Guarducci tried to reassure and cast some doubt. 'I know the security clearance that everyone has within the Vatican and I can assure you that Fr. Devine never had such a high level.'

'I thought it was strange myself,' Brenard admitted. 'Why do you think Fr. Harrison even mentioned it, if it wasn't true?'

'Could be a simple mistake,' Guarducci said, trying to reassure Brenard. 'People come and go through the Apostolic Palace as a matter of course. I am sure Father Harrison has mistaken someone else for Fr. Devine, or if he was working here he definitely was not working for the Pope.'

'Harrison told me that only three people have top clearance for all areas within the Vatican.'

'The Holy Father and myself, are the only two now,' Guarducci added, wondering where Brenard's curiosity was leading. 'Fr. Hasler was privileged to carry such clearance with his position, but after today's sensational revelations I have had no choice but to revoke those privileges.'

'Do you think Malachy could've been working with Fr. Hasler?'

'Why would he have been working for Fr. Hasler?' Guarducci humoured, shocked that Brenard had stumbled across a partial truth.

'Well, if he wasn't working for you or the Holy Father he could have got the clearance from Father Hasler.'

'I want you to take a look at this,' Guarducci said, as he got up from the chair, lifted some stapled sheets of paper from his desk and handed them to Brenard.

'Forgive my ignorance,' Brenard replied, as he flicked through the list of names that were printed in groups of varying colours, 'what is this exactly?'

'Every morning I have the office of the Swiss Guards send me a copy of the security clearance for every given day. At the top of that list there are two names printed in red.'

'The Holy Father's and yours.'

'Correct. So, trust me when I say that Fr. Devine had no such clearance. I would have noticed.'

Sitting back into the chair, Brenard sighed and brought his hands up to his face. 'Nothing makes sense and nothing seems right.'

'I wish I had the answers for you, Paul.' Guarducci replied, as he walked behind him and laid a tentative hand on his shoulder. 'Fr. Devine's murder is something we cannot reason or even begin to understand. We need to accept it and trust that in time the questions we have will be answered, but for the time being we will have to leave the real questions to the police.'

Guarducci could only pat Brenard's shoulder in a sign of concerned understanding. But, as he turned to walk away, he feared the truth that was being spoken by Brenard. He feared that the truth had not been buried deep enough and that someone like Brenard would see the blood on his hands and the untruth of his lies. He knew the answers to the questions that Brenard was asking him, but they were answers he had to keep hidden, at least for the time being.

13.

The smell of incense lingered in the air inside the Basilica of Saint John Lateran and from every crevasse history loomed out of the darkness. Crowded as usual with pilgrims and tourists, Stuart Smith knew exactly where to go.

Walking up the fine Cosmatesque nave, under the sumptuous gilt wooden ceiling and past the statues of the twelve apostles, he headed for the Corsini Chapel. Amid the clamour of the tourists he knew that security maintained a guard outside, allowing only those who wished to spend some time in adoration before the Blessed Sacrament to enter. Indicating that he wanted to go in, the security personnel pulled back the large red curtain and allowed him through.

Counting only seven people praying in the chapel, he was glad that he was going to get the peace he required. Slipping into a corner seat, he felt protected by the shadow of the towering chapel wall. Smith's eyes inspected Galilei's elegant masterpiece. It was the most beautiful chapel in Rome and Smith was no stranger to the place.

Lifting the envelope from his pocket, he looked at it closely for the first time. The ink on the front had smudged a little, but the mint on the top right hand corner was clearly marked - *Haifa, Israel.*

Smith looked around one last time to make sure he was alone. He broke the envelope seal, and with clammy hands took out the folded paper that was inside. It was the same writing he had read every day from Devine's research lists. Scanning overleaf he saw Devine's signature. Taking a deep breath he began to read.

Stuart,

I trust in the Lord, that I will be experiencing the joys of paradise by the time you read this letter. For I know with certainty that my work will ensure that I will never leave this sacred soil alive. The work that I have for so long kept close to my heart is no longer secret. I fear that I will, in the next few hours or coming days, be made to pay with the ultimate price of my life, a price many will eagerly see me pay in the hope that what I know will be taken to the grave.

I swore an oath to the Holy Father himself that I would see this through, and I will. Yet, my heart is troubled with the fear that everything will be silenced. I know the danger my work entails, and I'm sure you'll be able to understand some of its implications from the research you've carried out for me. It is a fear that runs deep, and I am terrified that they will even try and silence the Holy Father himself.

Stuart, I need you to contact Cardinal Paul Brenard. If what I believe will happen, happens, my will and testimony instructs that he should officiate at my funeral. For the sake of the Church, you must tell Paul everything you know about the work I've been doing. Tell him about the encyclical that I've been working on and make sure he knows the reason why I came to Israel. He is the only man I can trust. Stuart, you must do the same, trust Paul Brenard and no one else. Evil forces are at work in the heart of the Vatican.

Soon, the world will be shaken to the core with events that are about to unfold. People must know the truth and perhaps by the time you read this letter, Paul may be the only one able to reveal it.

Pray for me, Stuart.

Malachy.

Haunted with the voice beyond the grave, Stuart slipped the letter back into the envelope. Knowing that Devine had been killed for his work on the encyclical he feared the final outcome, wondering if he would be next. His only reassurance came from the fact that apart from a few within the Irish College and Inspector Pacelli, his work with Devine was very much in the dark.

Leaving the chapel, he walked through the basilica thinking about what Devine had written. Then, stopping near the main doors, he remembered the pictures Devine had sent from

Tel Megiddo and his phone call to inform him that he had seen the truth with his own eyes.

Jesus! He thought into himself, as his stomach churned with the realisation that it all made sense. There could be no doubt. *It's happening. How could I have been so blind?*

14.

Later that evening, Cardinal Guarducci arrived back at the Vatican having visited Pope Clement in hospital. There was nothing more the doctors in the Gemelli could do for him that a palliative care team back in the Vatican could not manage. It was now only a matter of time, and Guarducci knew that the Church expected a dying pope to spend the remainder of his days back in the Vatican, where he could pass into eternity with dignity.

Walking through the Apostolic Palace, he took the express lift directly to the Papal Apartment. No one asked him for his pass, they knew better. Everyone knew Guarducci, and he came and went wherever and whenever he pleased, accompanied as always by two protection officers from the Vatican's Gendarmerie. When he arrived on the fifth floor of the Apostolic Palace, the Swiss Guards that lined the corridor stood to attention and saluted him. At the end of the corridor he came to the entrance of the Papal Apartment; a large blast proof steel door, customised with engraved walnut panelling to fit in with the palatial surroundings. At the side of the door he placed his right hand onto the security screen for his palm to be scanned. When his security clearance was verified, the door slowly slid open and he walked through into the small anteroom, where two officers kept guard to the last door that would take him through into the apartment. Recognising him, one of the officers pinned in the code and opened the door for him to enter.

Once inside, the surroundings completely changed. Under the papacy of Paul VI, the palatial décor of the Papal Apartment had been removed and the apartment reordered. Now, more recent popes lived in quite modest accommodation. Even Guarducci had more palatial living quarters. Walking down the red carpeted hallway and past the Pope's private chapel, Guarducci headed for the kitchen where he could hear the nuns talking.

'Good evening!' he said as he stood in the doorway, startling the four nuns who served as housekeepers to the Papal Household.

'Good evening, Your Eminence,' one of the nuns replied. 'Would you like something to eat or drink?'

'No, thank you.' Guarducci said, as he took a seat at the table. 'I have just visited the Holy Father.'

'How is he?'

'His spirit is strong, but his body is weak. We hope to have him home within a few days.'

'Oh, thank God for answering our prayers. We have missed him.'

'I trust you have. It has been a difficult few weeks and I am sure the news in today's papers has been uncomfortable for you all to read.'

'Is it true?' one of the four nuns asked. 'Monsignor Hasler was the perfect gentleman and devout priest. I cannot imagine him doing such a thing.'

'Sister, what you have read is only the tip of the iceberg. I found it difficult to believe it too. But, I am afraid it is the truth and more is going to be revealed in tomorrow's papers.'

They all gave a collective gasp of disbelief.

'Sisters, I have come with some very difficult news for you all,' Guarducci continued. 'I know your service to the Holy Father has been long and distinguished.'

'We have been serving the Holy Father for twenty-one years,' one of the nuns added. 'Five years here in the Vatican and for sixteen years while he was the Patriarch of Venice.'

'A long time indeed,' Guarducci acknowledged. 'But, I trust you are aware that the Pope's current circumstances have changed. He will need intensive care from the moment he gets home.'

'And he will get it from us, Your Eminence.'

'What I am trying to tell you is, the Holy Father will no longer require your services.'

'Pardon?'

'We can look after his needs.'

'No one will care for him better than us.'

'This is not right!'

'Sisters, please!' Guarducci appealed for silence, as he raised his hands in the air. 'I am fully aware of your loyalty and it will not go unrewarded. I have spoken to the doctors and to the Holy Father, and we all agree that we need professional nurses looking after him. So, I have arranged for a group of nuns who are qualified in palliative care to come here and to serve him.'

'What about us?'

'I know this is difficult, but we need to do what is right for the wellbeing of the Holy Father.'

'Your Eminence, at least give us a chance to show you, to prove to you, that we are more than capable.'

'Sister, this is not up for discussion. The Pope needs more than four nuns who can cook his meals, clean the apartment, make his bed and starch his soutanes. He needs specialist palliative care. I have made this decision in the best interests of the Holy Father. I hope you will all be able to understand that.'

'What about us?' One of the nuns asked again.

'You will have to go back to your convent in Venice.'

'When?'

'I would like you to leave the apartment by lunchtime tomorrow, so we can put in place what the Holy Father needs before he arrives home.'

'Tomorrow?'

Cardinal Guarducci's words had taken the nuns totally by surprise, yet they knew they could not engage with him anymore on the subject. His mind was made up, and as the senior cardinal they knew as mere nuns they would have to oblige his request, even if it meant leaving their home and no longer serving the Pope they loved. Still, they knew they had no right to reside in the apartment as they only served under the pleasure of the Holy See. With the few belongings they had, the physical move was going to be much easier than the emotional thoughts of not serving the Holy Father ever again.

'Now sisters, I still have some work to get through this evening. So, if you will excuse me I will be going on my way. In the morning I celebrate mass for you at seven and then we can have breakfast together.'

‘Your Eminence,’ they replied in unison, as they stood up as a sign of respect while he left the kitchen; leaving them alone to shed their tears, gather their thoughts and begin to pack their belongings.

Yet, for Guarducci it was a night of bitter sweet victory. The nuns had served the Pope well, but they had to go. Things had changed. After Brenard’s questioning that morning about Devine, the nuns were too much of a liability. Even though they did not know the full implications of everything that had happened within the Papal Apartment, they knew too much about Devine’s work and Guarducci could not risk the chance of them turning up at his funeral. A fresh start was needed and having consulted other senior cardinals the right decision had been made. In his heart he knew that with the passing of time, everything would come to pass in his favour.

15.

Tuesday, 8th April.

As the final notes of Ag Críost an Síol bellowed from the pipe organ, the congregation inside the Basilica of San Clemente prayed in silence as they awaited the final commendation of Father Malachy Devine's remains.

It had been a difficult service for Cardinal Brenard to conduct. Burying Malachy was like burying a brother and he struggled getting through the rite, especially delivering the sermon he had penned in the early hours of that morning. When the organist finally drew the hymn to a close, Cardinal Brenard stood up and removed his purple Roman chasuble and dalmatic before allowing the deacons to vest him in a requiem cope. When the deacons had finished, the two cardinals who had concelebrated the requiem mass with him, Cardinal Guarducci and Cardinal Oliveri from the Congregation of the Doctrine of Faith, stood up alongside him, and together they placed on their white pontifical mitres, before being led to the steps of the sanctuary for the final veneration and benediction.

Standing at the foot of his friend's casket, Brenard stood in reflection while he waited for the deacon to bring him the missal.

'Before we go our separate ways, let us take leave of our brother. May our farewell express our affection for him; may it ease our sadness and strengthen our hope. One day we shall joyfully greet him again when the love of Christ, which conquers all things, destroys even death itself.'

As the congregation watched on, Brenard carried out the final acts of the requiem mass. As the book of the gospels was removed from the top of the casket by the assisting Irish deacons, Brenard sprinkled incense onto the white hot charcoal in the thuribile; sending the scented smoke high into the air where the morning light, that shone through the south-east windows, illuminated it as it rose towards the basilica's ceiling.

Taking the holy water sprinkler he blessed the casket as he walked around it, reminding every one of the promise of Christian baptism. Then taking the thurible he began to incense the mortal remains, acknowledging that Malachy's body was once a living temple of the Holy Spirit.

'Let us pray,' Brenard invited the congregation, as he took his place at the foot of the casket for the last time. 'Into your hands, Father of mercies, we commend our brother Malachy, in the sure and certain hope that, together with all who have died in Christ, he will rise with him on the last day. Merciful Lord, turn toward us and listen to our prayers. Open the gates of paradise to your servant and help us who remain to comfort one another with the assurances of faith, until we all meet in Christ and are with you and with our brother forever. We ask this through Christ our Lord. Amen.'

Having completed the requiem mass, Brenard and the two cardinals were led by the master of ceremonies halfway down the aisle of the basilica, where they stopped and turned towards the casket. Then from the sanctuary, six students from the Irish College made their way over to the casket. With help from the vergers they lifted Devine's remains onto their shoulders before following the acolytes as they led the procession towards the entrance of the basilica.

Upon reaching the entrance, the three cardinals and the students carrying the casket processed outside where a hearse was waiting to take Malachy's coffin back to his beloved Irish College for burial in its grounds.

With Malachy's casket placed in the hearse, the three cardinals remained at the entrance to the basilica where they met and consoled the mourners who had gathered along with Malachy's sister, priests and students from across Rome. As each mourner passed, the cardinals expressed their sympathy and offered their consolation, playing the role of shepherds to the mournful flock as they departed one by one.

With their duties fulfilled, the cardinals made their way back through the empty basilica. As they reached the altar a man approached them. They did not recognise him, but they knew he wanted something from one of them.

'Your Eminence, may I speak with you?' the man asked Brenard.

'Absolutely,' Brenard replied.

'In private, if you don't mind,' the man requested, as he looked at the other two cardinals who were content to stay and listen.

'Your Eminences, I will follow you shortly,' Brenard said, letting them know that he wanted to be alone.

Although Oliveri did not mind, Guarducci hesitated. But, in the end he had no choice but to leave Cardinal Brenard and the young man alone.

'Were you a friend of Malachy?' Brenard asked, once the other two cardinals were out of earshot.

'I was, Your Eminence,' the man replied. 'Furthermore I worked for him. My name is Stuart Smith.'

'Pleased to meet you, Mr. Smith,' Brenard said as he shook his hand, noticing that young man appeared a little nervous.

'Your Eminence, I think you should read this,' Smith replied, as he took Devine's letter from his pocket and handed it over.

Just before he walked through the sacristy door with Oliveri, Guarducci looked back at the two men and saw the letter being handed over. He felt his stomach tighten as he wondered what it was about, fearing that the man knew Devine too well. Suddenly, the young man's eyes made contact with him and Guarducci knew he could not stay on watching. So he left them alone in the basilica, convinced the young man was not there just to express his sympathy.

As Brenard read the letter, tears filled his eyes when he realised that Devine knew he was going to be killed. The letter still did not make much sense, but phrases jumped out that made him question everything all the more. *Oath to the Holy Father. The world will be shaken. Silence the Pope.* He felt a great unease as he finished reading it, especially Malachy's warning that *evil forces are at work within the Vatican.*

'Mr. Smith,' Brenard said in an almost whispered tone, as he cleared the emotion from his throat, 'was Father Devine working for the Pope?'

'Yes. That's why he was killed,' Smith replied, as he took the letter back from him.

'Why was he killed?' Brenard asked, with measured scepticism and disbelief.

'We can't talk about it here,' Smith insisted. 'But, I want to tell you everything.'

'When?'

'Will you be attending the wake at the Irish College?'

'Yes.'

'I'll meet you in the college chapel at two while the wake is taking place.'

Brenard nodded his head, as he wondered what Smith would tell him.

'Your Eminence, tell no one about the letter.'

'I won't,' Brenard promised.

'People have been killed and silenced to destroy Father Devine's credibility, and so will many more to stop an important truth from becoming public knowledge.'

Left standing alone in the nave, Brenard watched Smith make his way out of the basilica. He had been left stunned. As he turned to go back to the sacristy, he felt a heavy darkness surround him. The conversation and the events of the previous week now seemed so surreal. Even though more questions filled his mind, he knew he could not speak to anyone about it, at least not until he had heard what Stuart Smith had to say.

What does he know? Guarducci asked himself, when he saw Brenard walk through the sacristy door. The very demeanour on Brenard's face, a look that went beyond the pain of grief, confirmed Guarducci's fear that the revelation had not been silenced.

16.

For Aadam Hamidi, it was the most difficult decision of his life to make, but he knew in his heart that he was following the will of Allah. Sitting on the edge of his bed, he assessed the risks of his plan failing. For his betrayal, he had no doubt that the blood price would be high for his entire family. He knew, from the moment he activated the satellite phone that the intelligence authorities within Baghdad would, within minutes, not only be able to trace the location of his call, but they had the capability to intercept the encrypted secure line. His CIA handler, Usman Khalid, had warned him that he would have less than three minutes to make the call before his safety would be compromised.

As the minarets echoed the call for afternoon salat, he turned to his wife.

'I want you to listen very carefully,' he said, as he took hold of her hand. 'We have to go. I need you to get the two children and put them into the SUV.'

'What's happening, Aadam?'

'Please, just do as I say. Take nothing with you. We don't have much time!'

For a moment, his wife looked into his eyes and could see his fear.

'Go!'

Without hesitation, his wife left him and went to fetch their children, fearful they were being dragged into an unfolding drama over which she had no control.

As terrifying anticipation swept over him, Hamidi got up and pulled the bed away from the wall. As he began to remove the loose wooden paneling, he prayed that his actions could stop the disaster from happening. He still had time. This, everything that was being planned was more than he had signed up for when he joined the forces of ISIS as they swept through Mosul all those years ago. This, what they were about to do, had nothing to do with Allah. It was simply a mass genocide. As he set the wooden panel onto the floor, he reached into the carefully hidden hole in the wall and removed the satellite phone and loose battery.

With trembling hands, he assembled the phone. He knew the chances of getting caught were greater than his family being successfully evacuated to safety in Europe. With no real choice, knowing that an inevitable conflict would see his family destroyed if they remained in the city, he hoped that he was doing the right thing.

'There is none in my heart besides Allah!' Hamidi prayed, over and over again in Arabic. 'There is none in my heart besides Allah! Allah is enough for me! Glory be to Allah!'

Now was the time. If he was going to do it, it had to be now.

Having assembled the phone, he switched it on before selecting the only contact that was stored. He waited for the dialling tone to sound five times before he hung up and waited.

What seemed like an eternity lasted less than ten-seconds, before the phone began to ring. He answered.

'Are you seeking a code red?' Usman Khalid asked.

Hamidi paused for a moment before he answered, 'Yes!'

'What do you have?'

'The Caliph chaired a cabinet meeting this morning. Sleeper cells, loyal to him and based within the United States, yesterday received a batch of the chemical weapon VX which was produced here in Iraq. These cells have been given a direct order, from the Caliph himself, to detonate these bombs simultaneously in New York City, Dallas, Los Angeles and Washington DC.'

'Are you saying that there is an imminent threat of a chemical attack against the United States?'

'Yes!' Hamidi replied. 'That is exactly what I am saying, but I don't know when!'

'Where is your family?'

'We are ready to leave,' Hamidi said, as he walked to the door. 'But, we need to go now!'

'Get to Ramadi,' Khalid instructed. 'Do you remember where you need to go?'

'Yes!'

'Then waste no more time, get moving. You will be safe once you get there.'

For Hamidi, every minute he delayed he knew that the chances of being captured grew. As the Caliph's senior advisor on foreign affairs, he had delivered the ultimate betrayal. Grabbing his attaché case, into which he had placed the relevant documents from the morning's briefing, he quickly headed towards his car. Entering the inner courtyard of his house, he took his SIG Pro semi-automatic pistol from his jacket pocket and shot dead both his security guards at close range. Then climbing into the driver's seat of his SUV, he started up the engine and set off with his family for the CIA safe house in Ramadi. Everything, especially time, was against not only him but also the world.

17.

Cardinal Paul Brenard made a conscious effort to look interested as he engaged with the mourners at the wake. Yet, as it neared two o'clock, he could not stop himself from glancing every few seconds across the reception room towards Stuart Smith. Even though the anecdotes people shared with him, about their relationship with Devine, were heartfelt and personal, the letter Smith had shown him preoccupied his mind. Those who spoke with him sensed that his thoughts were elsewhere, but they all knew of his fondness for Devine and were accepting of his lack of engagement given his personal grief. So, conversations were short and brief while Brenard listened, sipped his tea and smiled obligingly. Inside his impatience grew, for he so desperately wanted to speak with Smith and to find out what he knew. At two o'clock, conscious that Smith was leaving the reception, Brenard made his excuse to leave and follow him.

'If you'll excuse me,' Brenard said, apologetically, 'I'd like to take some time alone in the college chapel.'

'Of course, Your Eminence.' The college rector replied, in his rough Kerry brogue. 'Would you like me to show you the way?'

'I know where it is. I just need to be alone with my thoughts and the Lord.'

'I totally understand.'

'Thank you.'

Every eye followed him as he left the room. Since becoming a cardinal he had become accustomed to being watched in social circles, but with the mystery surrounding what Smith had to tell him, he felt a great unease with the attention he was getting that afternoon. So, leaving his cup and saucer on a table beside the door, he quietly left the reception and left them wondering.

Alone he walked towards the college chapel. Once inside he saw Smith sitting close to the altar on one of the pews.

Blessing himself with holy water, he walked over and took a seat beside him.

'It's hard to believe that he's dead.' Smith said, staring at the sanctuary. 'He knew the dangers, but still it wasn't enough to stop him.'

'Stop him from doing what?' Brenard asked.

Smith knew that the truth would be difficult for Brenard to hear let alone believe. Despite being a cardinal he was just a simple fisher of souls and a shepherd to his own. He belonged to a Church whose mind and reason was so vast that no theologian in one lifetime could consume and understand its dogmas, teachings and traditions. For Smith, the mind of the Church was a living thing, powered and guided by the Spirit of the Divine. While its length spanned thousands of years and touched the depths of eternity, its breadth united one generation to the next in the treasured promise of eternal salvation for all who believed. Yet, the message at its heart was simple. It was to love and to forgive in the name of the Christ who came, who died, who rose to glorified life and who foretold he would one day return to judge the living and the dead. Gazing upon the sanctuary mosaic of the shepherd Christ, Smith knew that the world was capable of accepting the image of the Christ as a good shepherd because of the comfort it brought to their troubled lives. Yet, the true Christ, the radical Christ and not the Christ of ill-informed religiosity, was the paradox who comforted the disturbed while disturbing the comfortable. The truth had to be told and it had to be told now.

'What I am about to tell you is a truth that only four people know,' Smith said, as he looked Brenard in the eye. 'It's a truth you might find hard to believe, but if you trust me I will reveal everything that I know to you.'

Like a priest about to hear the confession of a penitent, Brenard moved closer to Smith and placed his arm along the top of the pew behind Smith's back. No matter what Smith was going to say, no matter how difficult it would be to hear, Brenard needed to hear it.

'Fr. Devine was working as a devil's advocate, tasked to find flaws in an encyclical the Pope is about to release to the

Church and the world.' Smith began, much to Brenard's apparent indifference. 'At the request of His Holiness, the details of this encyclical were confined to himself, Fr. Devine, Monsignor Gustave Hasler and myself. Its content was so sensitive that the Pope didn't even trust members from the College of Cardinals to become consulters.'

'What is this encyclical about?'

'Pope Clement is preparing the world for the end of times.' Smith calmly replied.

To avert a confrontation, Brenard said nothing. But he could not stop a sigh of disbelief from giving away his true feelings. Instinctively, he knew that Smith had to be wrong. The Vatican had its way of working and there was no way the Pope would write an encyclical without the consultation of his cardinals. Furthermore, if what Smith was saying was true, someone would have intervened, especially Guarducci who knew everything that happened within the Vatican walls.

'I thought it was farfetched too,' Smith said. 'When Fr. Devine asked for my assistance I actually laughed at the idea. But, as sure as the air we breathe and the life that is within us, I am now convinced that we are about to see the Great Tribulation take place where everything that we take for granted will be trodden into the earth below us. His Holiness isn't just preparing the world for the second of coming of Christ, he is preparing the world for the imminent coming of the Antichrist.'

'I can't accept this,' Brenard said, as his rational reasoning forced him to stand and to take his leave. 'I don't wish to continue this conversation. Not only are you speaking on matters that you know absolutely nothing about, but you are dishonouring the memory of a dear friend that I've just buried.'

'Your friend was dragged into a gutter and had a bullet put through his head! He wasn't murdered for simply being in the wrong place at the wrong time, he was murdered because of what he had discovered and to ensure that the truth died with him. When he took on this role he was warned, by Pope Clement himself, that his life would be placed in grave danger. He paid the price for the Church and his dying wish was for you to understand the truth, because he feared that dark forces within the Vatican would even attempt to silence the Pope himself.'

Experience had made Brenard increasingly aware of those seduced by the toxic power of religion. All his adult life, his discernment of truth was based on the trust that what his Church taught was authoritative and incorruptible. In his mind he knew he should walk away from the young Englishman, but in his heart he literally felt the pain that perhaps, just perhaps there was a truth he had yet to discover as to why his closest friend had been murdered.

'Let me show you what Fr. Devine was working on,' Smith pleaded, knowing that this would be his last chance to convince the cardinal.

Brenard did not reply, but stood and watched as Smith got up from his seat, walked over to the tabernacle and opened it.

'What are you doing?' Brenard asked in consternation, as Smith lifted out the eucharistic ciborium and placed it on the altar.

'Trust me,' Smith replied, as he reached into the back of the tabernacle and removed the white velvet padding. Then with both hands, Smith lifted out what he had carefully hidden. Walking over to the altar he sat the laptop down, before placing the ciborium back into the tabernacle.

'Fr. Devine insisted on never leaving a paper trail. All correspondence regarding the research was sent electronically,' Smith explained, as he tapped the laptop. 'Although Fr. Devine didn't know it, I saved everything, including the last photographs he sent from Israel. Photographs that will prove to you, that everything I am telling you is the truth.'

Looking at Smith, Brenard could see the flush in his face and the sweat on his brow. Walking away was no longer an impulsive option. With nothing to lose he walked towards the altar. 'Show me.'

'Not here,' Smith insisted, as he lifted his laptop and headed towards the chapel door. 'We need to go somewhere safe and discreet.'

'Where?' Brenard asked, as he began to follow him.

'The Gregorian.'

18.

The archbishop of Munich, Carl Küng, could not stomach the thought of lunch. His years of friendship with Gustave Hasler were suddenly at an end, because as his archbishop the responsibility of imposing sanctions on Hasler now rested in his hands. Guarducci had warned him not to disappoint Rome. Furthermore, to remind Küng of what he personally had to lose, Guarducci disclosed that his name was being discussed at the highest levels for the consistory that was scheduled to take place that coming October. As the archbishop of Munich, Küng was sure to receive the red biretta and his place in the College of Cardinals, the customary rank that came with his archdiocese. He could not face the embarrassment of not getting it.

Having walked his gardens for nearly an hour, Küng stopped when he heard the door from his study open. As Hasler made his way across the white pebbled path, Küng closed his breviary and waited for him to approach. He personally took no delight in what he was being asked to do, but for the sake of Hasler he had decided to act swiftly.

'Your Excellency,' Hasler replied as he approached, only to be surprised as the archbishop stretched out his right hand for him to venerate his episcopal ring.

Kneeling before Küng, Hasler was bluntly reminded that his rank had been stripped from him. As Papal Secretary, he was never expected to venerate any cardinal or bishop, such was the importance of his position. Now, all that had changed.

'How are you keeping?' Küng asked, as Hasler got up from his knees.

'Tired!'

'Well, I am sure you will be glad of the rest. I am sending you to Switzerland and I want you to spend some time with our Cistercian brothers at Hauterive Abbey.'

'Hauterive Abbey? Is that your decision, Carl? Or was it imposed upon you by a higher authority?'

'You will address me as Your Excellency,' Küng replied, as he stepped towards Hasler, forcing him to step back off the path and onto the grass. 'Did you think you were going to be rewarded with some penthouse in the city after the shame you have brought upon the Church and yourself?'

'No, Your Excellency, but I had hoped that in you I would have a friend who would have listened to my side of the story. A friend who would know, in the very depth of his heart, that I am incapable of doing what my accusers say I have done.'

'I was told by Cardinal Guarducci that you would come here protesting as much.'

Hasler stood beside the path, stunned at how another friend like Küng had turned against him. He now felt completely alone.

'I have read this morning's editions of the Italian press online. Serious accusations are hanging in the air.'

'That conviction is a lie conspired by people who want to discredit me,' Hasler insisted.

'Cardinal Guarducci told me last night that it was confirmed by the Italian police.'

'Your Grace, I cannot explain everything to you. In fact, I have not fully made sense of all that is going on, but I have come to the conclusion that Cardinal Guarducci is a man that cannot be trusted!'

'How dare you speak about a member of the Sacred College with such impertinence,' Küng admonished, as he looked angrily at Hasler.

'I am being silenced in the only way they know how.'

'Silenced about what?'

'I cannot say,' Hasler replied, knowing that even in his darkest hour he could not reveal the truth of what he knew, even to the one person who could help him.

'I wish I could believe you Gustave, but I cannot. That is why I have arranged that you should go to the abbey, maybe over time you will come to terms with the truth and then we will consider your future.'

'How long before I can practice my priesthood again?'

'As long as it takes.'

'What if I refuse to go?'

'As your archbishop I am instructing you, under the vow of obedience that you took on the day of your ordination, to go to that abbey and submit yourself to the authority of the abbot. However, you are not a prisoner and are free to go your separate ways from the Church if you desire. If you decide to follow that path then you will be on your own, and you will be walking away from your priesthood. That is your decision alone to make.'

Hasler could not bring himself to give a reply. He was beaten. Walking away was not an option. Yet, as the darkness of his situation engulfed him he forced himself to accept, to feel, to believe that he was standing on the side of truth. He knew, he had even been warned by Pope Clement, that a day such as he was now living, could come in an attempt to silence what they knew. Then again, he was the lucky one, for unlike Malachy Devine he was still alive.

'We are protecting both you and the Church in all of this,' Küng explained. 'If you do what is right you will regain your salvation both within God and with the Church.'

19.

'How are we going to get in?' Brenard asked, as they stood outside Devine's office at the Gregorian.

'Malachy gave me his ID card before he left for Israel.' Smith replied. 'No one knows I have it, not even the police.'

Taking the plastic card from his wallet, Smith said a quick prayer before he swiped it through the card terminal beside the door. Either by chance or Divine intervention, the ID card had not been deactivated. Once the door unlocked they walked in and closed the door behind them.

'They've surely turned this place over!' Smith said, as he walked over the desk and set his laptop down. Then opening the filing cabinet drawers he noticed that every piece of paperwork had been removed.

'Why bring me to the Gregorian?' Brenard asked, as he sat on the leather seat behind the desk.

'I wanted to show you this,' Smith replied, as he took the framed picture of Pope Clement off the wall, sat it on the desk, opened the seals on the back of the picture's frame and removed a folded sheet of paper. Pulling up a chair, Smith sat across from the table from Brenard and handed him the sheet of folder paper. 'This is a list of the twenty prophesies that the Holy Father personally wrote out for Malachy to disprove. These are the Doomsday Prophesies.'

Taking the page, Brenard guardedly unfolded it. On the top of the page was the embossed golden crest of Pope Clement, and below it were the meticulously written biblical references:

The Two Pauline Prophesies:
2 Timothy 3:1-5, 7
1 Timothy 4:1-3

The Six Matthian Prophesies:
Matthew 24:5
Matthew 24:6-7

Matthew 24:8-9
Matthew 24:10
Matthew 24:11-12
Matthew 24:14

The Seven World Sign Prophesies:
Revelation 9:16
Daniel 2:32-33, 40-43
Daniel 12:4
Ezekiel 38-39
Revelation 13:16-17
Revelation 11:3, 7-10
Revelation 13:7

The Five Israeli Prophesies:
Zephaniah 3:9
Zephaniah 3:10-11
Jeremiah 23:7-8
Numbers 19:2-7
Daniel 9:26-27

+Clement XV

Knowing in his hands he either held an authentic papal document or a convincing forgery, Brenard looked at Smith and nodded for him to continue.

'Last Easter, while on vacation in Castle Gandolfo, the Pope experienced a vision.' Smith said. 'In this vision he saw the end of the world. Traumatised, he feared to tell anyone about it. For weeks he kept reliving the vision over and over in his dreams, terrifying him to the point that he could keep it a secret no longer. So, in early May, he wrote his encyclical with the intention of warning the world, and those who desired the truth, that the time was ready for the return of Jesus Christ and his final judgement upon humanity. Yet, before Christ returns the world will be handed over to the terrifying reign of the Antichrist.'

Brenard bit his inner cheek to stop himself from speaking, for he was wary of all visionaries. Only the psychotic had visions. Mad men and women who would fool the many for their own self gain. For example, in his own heart he found it impossible to accept the miraculous apparitions at Lourdes or the stigmatic Padre Pio. At times in his priestly ministry he had preached at Lourdes, and many times on Padre Pio, but at such times when he preached to the faithful who accepted his every word, his skeptical mind always quenched the desire in his heart to believe.

'Once the encyclical was written, Pope Clement sought out Malachy and directed him, under an oath of secrecy, to disprove the vision and what it revealed. The task was too big for one man so Malachy requested help and in turn he asked me to assist.'

'Why you?'

'Two years ago I applied to study for my doctorate. I wrote to Malachy and he accepted me as a student. Over time our friendship and confidence in one another grew and next thing I know, I'm taking an official oath of secrecy and assisting him with his work.'

Gazing at Smith, Brenard fought a swelling urge from within him to object and leave, as the seconds silently passed between them.

'Malachy set out to disprove the Pope,' Smith said. 'Throughout our time together, he was determined to play his role without fear or fault. He was meticulous in his research at the Vatican archives and archives further afield in England, the United States, Istanbul and even Damascus. He held Pope Clement to account in questioning him about every little detail of his vision and in dissecting the encyclical line by line and word for word. No matter how hard he tried he could not find one iota of fault. In the end, like all matters of Divinity, it simply came down to faith, and for Malachy he had enough faith in his own work to know that the signs of the times supported the Pope's vision that we are living in the end of times.

'Everything, and by that I mean every country, city, town, village, man, woman and child is about to experience a true living hell on earth. Already, the true spirit of evil has been incarnated into someone who will bring the world to its knees. This person is what scripture has referred to as the Antichrist, and he will charm the world into a total annihilation. In his rise to power, a power that will govern the whole world, he will trigger a war that will destroy a large proportion of the world's population. In his vision the Holy Father saw a specific nuclear war between the United States, the Islamic States and Russia; triggered by a modern plague unleashed against the American nation. All sides will suffer greatly, but it will be through this war that the Antichrist will unite the remainder of the world under a false peace and rule it for seven years. By his nature he will reflect the true Christ and this will fool many, but for those who are true in spirit they will see him as the one born to harvest the death of many. He will brand those who follow him and persecute those who see him for who he is. In those seven years there will be famine, wars will trigger successive wars, persecution, unparalleled natural disasters and the surrender of the freedom of many to the one they believe will protect them. Then he will rebuild the third and final temple in Jerusalem, in an attempt to proclaim himself as the Lord of all. But, this final action will lead civilisation into the ultimate battle of Armageddon.'

For a few moments both men sat in silence, both unwilling to speak until they knew how the other would react.

Eventually, Brenard leaned forward in his chair and looked Smith right in the eye. 'You said you had proof, show me.'

Taking back the sheet of paper, Smith held it up for the Brenard to see.

'This is the list of every quote in scripture that predicts certain events that will happen just before the end of time. Twenty quotes, all of which but one have already been fulfilled. That's why Malachy went to Israel. He had to see with his eyes that everything was now in place for the fulfilment of the final prophecy. Minutes before his death, he saw the proof with his own eyes.'

Opening the laptop, Smith logged on to the internet and searched for *Numbers 19:2*.

'Read from verse two until verse seven.' Smith said, as turned around the laptop so Brenard could read the screen. 'Aloud, if you could be so kind.'

Guardedly, Brenard began to read:

'You will be given a red heifer without fault or blemish, one that has never worked the field. You will give it to Eleazar the priest. It must be taken outside the camp and slaughtered in his presence. Then Eleazar the priest is to dip his finger into the heifer's blood and sprinkle some in the direction of the Tent of Meaning. The heifer must then be burnt in his presence: hide, flesh, blood and intestines too, must be burnt.

'Then the priest must throw cedar wood, hyssop and scarlet wool into the fire where the heifer is burning. The ashes of the sacrifice must be kept for the ritual use of the sons of Israel for making lustral water; it is a sacrifice for sin. For the sons of Israel this is a perpetual law.'

'What you've just read is the purification right of how the Jewish people must go about building a temple. The lustral water, that was made from the ashes of the sacrifice, was only ever used to purify the foundations of the temple before it was built, and sprinkled upon the Jewish people to make them ceremonially clean before the eyes of God.'

'How is this prophetic?'

'To rebuild the temple today, in the heart of Jerusalem, the people of Israel would need an unblemished red heifer to perform the ceremony of purification. Not only can the temple not be built without the sacrifice of a red heifer, but no one could enter the temple as they would be ritually impure. With the diaspora of the Jewish people by the Romans two thousand years ago and the invasion of the Holy Land, orthodox believers of the Jewish faith believe that the people are ceremonially unclean. The last prophecy, the one yet to be fulfilled is that before Christ returns, the third temple will be rebuilt. Until six months ago, it was an impossible dream. Then in Northern Israel a rare, unblemished red heifer was born. The first recorded birth of such an animal in over two thousand years.'

Knowing he had the cardinal's attention, Smith took the laptop and searched the folders until he found the series of images that he was looking for.

'These are the images Malachy sent before he was murdered.'

Brenard looked closely at the screen.

'This red heifer has been inspected by experts and rabbis from the Temple Institute, and they all agree that it is perfect. It has not one single blemish, it has no physical defects, it has never been touched by human hands and it has never been put to work. In fact once they find the Red Heifer they must sacrifice it three years to the day from its birth. Time is short.'

'Where is it now?'

'I believe under armed Israeli guard at a farm compound near Tel Megiddo.'

'Where Malachy was murdered?'

'The same place,' Smith replied. 'Or, as it's more commonly known in the West, Armageddon.'

As Brenard continued to look at the pictures, Smith wondered if he had succeeded in convincing him. With all the information he knew, he could have spent hours with the cardinal; going over the other prophesies, providing him with the proof, the evidence, arguments and counter arguments.

'I still can't accept this,' Brenard said with truthful conviction. 'I've been in Rome for little over twenty-four hours and a lot of what I've taken for granted has been questioned and challenged. Can you get me a copy of the encyclical?'

'No. The only person who can let you see it now is the Holy Father.'

'It's impossible to get an audience with him. They have access to him tightly controlled.' Brenard remarked. 'You said Malachy had a copy of the encyclical. Where's his copy?'

'They took it along with everything else after he was murdered.' Smith replied. 'But, there is someone I think you should meet.'

'Who?'

'I know for part of the research that Malachy sought the help from a fellow Irishman. His name's Fr. Donal O'Keefe. Malachy had no idea that I knew of Fr. O'Keefe's involvement.'

'Does this priest know about you?'

'I'm certain he doesn't,' Smith replied, as he returned to his laptop. 'I have a small confession to make. When Malachy asked me to source him a laptop, I deliberately synced it to my own so that everything, every scanned document, every email and photograph would be backed up on this device. Donal O'Keefe knows nothing about me, but from what I've read he is a man you need to talk to.'

'If we made contact with him, do you think he'd travel from Ireland to meet me while I'm in Rome?'

'He's not in Ireland,' Smith replied. 'He arrived here a few days ago for Malachy's funeral. He's staying at the Irish College.'

'Do you think we could arrange a meeting?'

'We could go back to the Irish College and speak to him,' Smith offered.

'No, give him this number', Brenard replied, as he handed over a card containing the details of Cardinal Boyer's private residence in Rome. 'Get him to ring me this evening.'

'I'll speak to him,' Smith said, as he took the card. 'I think you should take the laptop, prep yourself before you meet him. Hopefully, it will shed a lot more light on the many questions I'm sure you have.'

'Are you sure?'

'You have more need of it than I have,' Smith replied, with an ironic smile. 'If I'm right, and I believe that I am, I simply won't have enough time to complete a doctorate.'

20.

In his private study, Guarducci opened a thirty year old bottle of Mccallan and poured a large measure into three crystal tumblers, before handing a glass to each of his guests.

'To us!' He toasted, before sipping his scotch and taking a seat with the other two cardinals.

'To us!' Oliveri replied.

Boyer said nothing. He only sipped his scotch.

'We have done the difficult duty,' Guarducci said. 'True to our promise we have defended Mother Church.'

'Is that not a little premature?' Boyer spoke up.

'There is nothing to worry about, my old Friend,' Oliveri reassured.

'I only wish I had Your Eminences' optimism,' Boyer said.

'Everyone associated with the work of this encyclical has been removed from its association,' Guarducci replied, trying to settle the American cardinal's fear. 'It falls upon us now to govern the Church through the coming weeks and months. We have no choice but to stand united and firm.'

'Are you still anxious about what we have done?' Oliveri asked.

'Of course I am anxious,' Boyer replied. 'We have taken an unprecedented action in removing a Pope from office.'

'Warren, we never removed the Pope from his office,' Guarducci clarified. 'We removed the power of the papacy from an unpredictable Pope. The only issue that is unprecedented in all of this, is the fact we had on our hands a Pope who was psychologically unstable. We talked about this at length before we took our decision.'

'I know we did.'

'So, what is the issue?'

'I feel we should've consulted the entire College before going through with it.'

'That would never have worked!' Oliveri added, unsettled at Boyer's anxiety. 'There is no way we could have orchestrated this with the full knowledge of the College. It would have caused a schism right through the heart of the Church.'

'You should not worry Warren. What we did was for the future of the Church. Pope Clement would have destroyed its reputation overnight.'

'He was proposing some very questionable statements that were not founded on sound doctrine,' Oliveri said, backing up Cardinal Guarducci's point. 'I have silenced lesser men for writing, or even speaking about lesser things.'

'I accept all that you're saying,' Cardinal Boyer defended his position, before he reached over to the coffee table and tapped Guarducci's copy of the Encyclical. 'But, what if he was right?'

'What if he was wrong?' Oliveri rebuked. 'That encyclical is nothing more than the delusions of a mad man. There is no way we could have taken the chance in letting this become public. You were there the night we spoke to him in person and asked him not to proceed with his work.'

'I begged him Warren, but he would not agree to it. He was determined to make his encyclical available to everyone in the world.' Guarducci added.

Cardinal Boyer knew all the arguments. The three of them had decided the plan weeks ago, but stirring inside him were the questions that continued to trouble his conscience.

'We had no choice but to do what we did.' Oliveri said.

'I just pray that the faithful will never come to know of our conspiracy.' Boyer replied.

'That is all it will ever be,' Guarducci reminded him. 'A conspiracy. The history of the church is littered with conspiracies. Pope Joan, popes being murdered, popes fathering children, popes sleeping with women and some with men. You did have the choice to silence him for good!'

'We could not have done that!'

'Why not?' Guarducci asked.

'Murder the Pope?'

'It has been done before!' Oliveri added.

'When?' Boyer asked, shocked that such a thing had happened.

'Nineteen seventy-eight,' Guarducci admitted.

'Not?'

'Yes,' Oliveri replied, knowing that Boyer knew who they were talking about. 'He was about to overstep his position. So, a senior council was formed, just like us, and they did the one thing that would stop the truth from coming out.'

'Lethal dose of poison,' Guarducci added, somewhat enjoying the look of shock on Boyer's face. 'Slipped into his heart medication. One night, when he retired for bed he never woke up. With an autopsy never performed on the body of a Pope it was fool proof.'

'We did discuss that possibility, but you vetoed the idea.'

'I couldn't have had that on my conscience. What we have done is grave enough, and it will be enough to answer for when we face our eternal judgements.'

'My conscience is clear,' Guarducci spoke up. 'I only performed my duty. We cannot undo what we have done.'

'The Pope is safe. He's no longer a threat to us or the world anymore.'

Until the night Pope Clement called Guarducci to the Papal Apartment, the thought of having him removed from office was unthinkable. But, when the Pope revealed to him that he had received a vision and had written an encyclical, Guarducci's heart sank with fear.

He realised right away that Pope Clement was bringing the Church and the world to the brink. He had no choice but to do what he did. In showing Cardinal Oliveri the encyclical, Oliveri's response only confirmed his own fears. The Holy Father was not only going against established doctrine, he was in effect abusing the power of his office and presenting to the world a document that was flawed, not only in Church teaching, but verging on the heretical.

Something had to be done. Together they both consulted Boyer, who until his retirement was one of the most prominent Cardinals within the world. And having served as the archbishop of Washington, they knew his contacts with The White House would prove indispensable.

Together the three of them agreed to bury the encyclical, but when Pope Clement refused to do so, they felt they had no choice but to use the help of the American Government and set about silencing him. Now, it was only a matter of time before nature would take its course.

'I hear he is coming back to the Vatican tomorrow,' Boyer said, breaking the silence in the room.

'Yes.' Guarducci confirmed. 'He will be moved from the Gemelli in the morning. I think it is wise not to release that information until he is safely back in the Vatican.'

'Will he be making an appearance in public?'

'Absolutely not. Some photographs will be taken of his return and released to the media. With the gravity of his illness, he will be spending the rest of his days being looked after by specialist nurses within the apartment.'

'All we need to do for the next few weeks is manage him,' Oliveri added. 'Soon enough we will be holding a conclave to elect his successor.'

'I suppose both of you have already decided who that will be!' Boyer remarked, as he looked at Guarducci.

'I do not appreciate that, Warren!' Guarducci said. 'It will be up to the College to elect the one they see fit to take Pope Clement's place. We only have one vote each.'

'He is right,' Oliveri spoke up. 'The only thing we have ever discussed between ourselves is the fact that we need to destroy all evidence of what we have done before a new pontiff takes power.'

'And that includes the fourth copy of encyclical.' Guarducci said, to reassure Boyer.

'If we find it!' Boyer quickly replied.

'Trust us, Warren. Father Devine would never have misplaced that encyclical. He has hidden it for the right person to find it. Once we know who that person is, we will continue with our plan.'

'Which is?'

'To stop at nothing until we have retrieved it.'

'Does that include spilling more blood?'

'Like I have already said,' Guarducci replied, 'we will stop at nothing. We simply cannot take the chance.'

21.

Sitting alone in the apartment, Brenard waited for his host to return. In his right hand he clutched his rosary; threading through each bead in prayer. It had been a day beyond comprehension. He was exhausted with thought and worry, and although he tried to pray he could not ease the tension in his body nor the troubles of his mind.

He did not know what to believe. Either, Smith was telling him the truth or else he was being played for the fool. It was a truth too traumatising to accept especially now having spent several hours reading through the research notes on Smith's laptop.

Closing his eyes he tried to bury himself deeper in prayer, but his concentration lasted only a fraction before he heard the main door of the apartment opening. Cardinal Boyer had returned. Giving up, he put the rosary into his pocket and got to his feet to greet his host.

'Paul, how are you?' Boyer asked, as he walked over and embraced him. 'It's good to see you again.'

'And you too, old friend,' he replied, glad to have his company after the day's events. 'I'm sorry I didn't wait up last night, but the jet lag finally won the battle.'

'Perfectly understandable,' Boyer said, as he sat beside him. 'How did the funeral go today?'

'I got through it, that's the main thing. I never thought burying Malachy would've been such a difficult ordeal.'

'Friendships can sometimes be closer than our family bonds. It's the curse of old age, because the older we get the quicker our friends leave us alone in this world.'

'Except, very few of us ever have to bury a friend who was murdered.'

Murdered! The word hit Boyer hard.

'What time have you booked the table for?'

Boyer had to think for a moment, snapping his thoughts away from his guilt.

'Eight-thirty. Would you like a drink before we go?'

'That would be nice.'

'Gin and Tonic?'

'Just the thing!'

Getting up from the chair, Boyer walked into the kitchen to fetch two drinks. His conscience was troubled by the murder, and he fought to rid it from his mind. No one was meant to be murdered, silenced yes, but not through the grave. That weighed heavily upon him, but he felt powerless to control Guarducci and Oliveri, who he knew were determined to stop at nothing.

Lost in his own thoughts, Brenard did not hear Boyer return.

'You look as if you were miles away,' Boyer said, handing him his drink. 'Are you thinking about Malachy?'

'No,' he replied, smiling to reassure Boyer that he was fine.

'Is there something troubling you Paul?' Boyer asked, as he sat back down, sensing that Brenard had something on his mind. 'I had a phone call from the Irish College this afternoon. They were concerned that you left without your security detail. Did something happen?'

'I just went to lunch with an old friend,' he answered, hoping that Boyer would not sense that he was lying.

He did not.

Sitting, looking at the old cardinal, Brenard did not know what to say. He questioned Boyer's trust and loyalty, but then again he was a fellow brother of the College.

'I was told something today that has troubled me deeply,' he eventually spoke, immediately gaining the undivided ear of Boyer. 'Have you heard anything about an encyclical that the Pope's been working on?'

Steadying his hand, Boyer lifted the glass to his mouth and took a large mouthful. He could not believe that he had been asked the question. Afraid to speak he simply shook his head.

'Before he was murdered, Malachy sent a letter to his research assistant at the Irish College,' Brenard began, before he was interrupted.

'Malachy Devine had a research assistant?' Boyer asked, while quietly cursing everything that was good.

'A young Englishman, Stuart Smith,' Brenard confided, not realising the danger he was now placing Smith in. 'In the letter, Malachy told Stuart to tell me about an encyclical they'd been working on with the Holy Father.'

'Did he say what the encyclical was about?'

'Apparently, the Holy Father had a vision about the end of the world, and he's written about it in an encyclical. Malachy was his devil's advocate.'

As Cardinal Boyer listened, he knew the inner council had failed to silence the truth. They had been too quick to toast their own success. From beyond the grave Devine had the advantage over their plans. God only knew how many were aware of the encyclical's existence.

'Have you seen this encyclical?' Boyer asked, in the hope that the fourth copy had turned up.

'No, Malachy's only copy was taken while he was in Israel.'

If only it was, Boyer thought.

'Have you heard anything about it yourself, Warren?'

Taking another sip of his gin, Boyer had to think quickly on his feet. His very silence in itself was enough to give away the fact that he knew something.

'What is it Warren?' Brenard asked, sensing that Boyer was not forthcoming with what he knew.

'I don't know how to tell you this Paul,' Boyer spoke after a few long seconds, 'but there's something about his life that you don't know about.'

'What?'

'Malachy was fighting extradition proceedings filed by the High Court in Ireland. He'd been accused of sexual molestation.'

'Paedophilia?'

'I'm afraid so.'

The news was like a kick to the stomach for Brenard. The shock brought tears to his eyes. Never in a million years, would he have thought Malachy capable of such depravity.

'I had hoped that his death would've seen the accusations buried with him.'

'Why are you telling me this, Warren?'

Boyer had to see through his lie. There was no going back, even though he could feel the web of deceit getting bigger and bigger.

'When the proceedings began, he was suspended from his position within the Gregorian.'

'I never knew about this?'

'He withdrew from public life altogether.'

'Stuart Smith told me that for the last twelve months he had been working with the Holy Father on an encyclical.'

'That's not true!' Boyer reassured. 'He spent most of his time wandering around Rome, hiding from the truth of his own past.'

'Then why was he killed out in Israel?'

'I don't know,' Boyer lied. 'Israel can be a very dangerous country.'

This doesn't make sense, Brenard thought to himself. *Nothing makes sense.*

'I know this has come as a shock,' Boyer continued, hoping he had put a convincing doubt into Brenard's mind over the encyclical's existence. 'But you've dealt with this sort of thing before in your role as an archbishop. It always comes as a shock when it's someone we know and love, but there's very little we can do but accept it and move on.'

'Answer me this Warren,' Brenard spoke up. 'Why do you think Stuart Smith is trying to convince me that Malachy was working on an encyclical? Furthermore, why did the Holy Father allow him to be buried with full priestly dignity if he knew he was a potential paedophile?'

Boyer did not have to think long. He was becoming an expert in covering up the truth.

'He was never convicted,' Boyer replied. 'With his service to the Church in educating thousands of priests and hundreds of bishops, he was rewarded in a dignified manner. Any price he had to pay was paid on the night he was murdered.'

'What about the encyclical?'

'This is Rome we're in, Paul. Things happen all the time. Rumours spread like wildfire. This man Smith, has played on your emotions and there's nothing more despicable than that. My advice to you is never to meet or even speak with this man again. He has quite clearly lost his way, and would love nothing more than a prince of the Church to believe in his preposterous conspiracy.'

The day's emotional rollercoaster had left Brenard visibly wrecked. The pain was clearly etched on his face for Boyer to see. His lie had done the trick. Even if proof were needed, he could get it conjured up within a matter of hours.

'This is a tough time for you my friend.' Boyer replied, as he got up from his chair. 'I think it might be best if I cancel our reservation for this evening. I'll just order in some food for us both. We can talk more privately here.'

Brenard did not reply. He just stared into his drink, completely lost in his thoughts.

'I'm sorry, but the truth is never easy to hear and believe me, it's often harder to speak. I will leave you alone for a little while.'

Walking into his bedroom, Boyer closed the door gently behind him. He could feel the stress as his chest tightened. Taking off his jacket, he undid his collar and without thinking he lifted the phone and dialled the number. It rang three times before it was answered.

'This is Cardinal Boyer, I would like to speak with His Eminence.'

Sitting down on the edge of his bed, he waited for Guarducci to come to the phone.

'Hello?'

'Jean, we haven't contained it!'

'What do you mean?' Guarducci asked.

'Paul Brenard knows about the encyclical's existence?'

'How?'

'We over looked the fact that Devine had a researcher working with him. Before he was murdered he posted a letter to him, instructing him to tell Paul Brenard everything.'

'What did you say?'

'I had to make up some excuse that Devine was under investigation for sexual abuse.'

'Good! Did he believe you?'

'I think he did,' Boyer replied, praying that his instinct was true.

'Who else knows about it?'

'I'm not sure. I'll see what more I can find out.'

'This researcher, what is his name?'

'Smith. Stuart Smith. He's a resident at the Irish College.'

'Leave it with me Warren,' Guarducci replied. 'Whatever happens tonight, you must convince Paul that everything he has been told is simply not true.'

'Nothing's going to happen to Paul, is it?'

'Let us not talk about this over the phone. We will speak later. Just make sure you convince him!'

22.

'You had no business telling him!'

'Meet with the cardinal, you've nothing to fear. He's a man Malachy trusted. He's now the only hope we have of releasing the encyclical for the public to read. They deserve the chance to prepare themselves for what's about to come.'

'The encyclical is as good as dead!' Fr. Donal O'Keefe replied. 'Without the Pope it's not even worth the paper it's written on.'

'You know that's not true,' Smith insisted, as he spoke to O'Keefe in the Irish College's library. 'It's being silenced for the wrong reasons. You owe it to Malachy.'

'I owe him nothing! He's dead. The Pope's on his deathbed, and his secretary has been removed from Rome. There's nothing more any of us can do.'

'Malachy didn't think so!' Smith replied, holding up the letter he had just shown to O'Keefe. 'Give Cardinal Brenard a chance.'

O'Keefe was afraid to get involved. Until Smith approached him in the library he had no idea that someone else knew of his involvement with the encyclical. So far he had remained hidden in the background, working with Devine. He was too smart not to see the reality of what was taking place around him. Having listened to Smith, he now regretted coming to Rome for the funeral. He feared being dragged into something that he would never be able to control.

'It's up to you Donal,' Smith said, putting the letter back into his pocket. 'I told the cardinal everything I knew because I owed it to Malachy. I've given you the contact number. If you want to speak to him you can arrange it yourself.'

Getting up from the table, Smith left O'Keefe alone. There was nothing more he could do, except pray that O'Keefe would do the right thing and talk to Paul Brenard.

Leaving the Library, he walked towards the refectory for his evening meal. It had been a long day. Surreal in many ways.

He knew the turmoil and the fear that were undoubtedly going through O'Keefe's head; he had felt the same yesterday. But, having told the cardinal everything, he now felt as though a great weight had been lifted from his shoulders.

'Stuart!' A voice called out.

He turned to see Monsignor Magee walking towards him.

'Evening, Monsignor.'

'I'm glad I caught you,' Magee said. 'I'm just off the phone with Cardinal Paul Brenard.'

'He rang here?' Smith asked, wondering what he wanted.

'I tried to put the call through to your room but you weren't there.'

'I was in the Library.'

'He asked me to pass on a message. He'd like to meet with you tonight. He wants to discuss something with you about a conversation you had with him today.'

Smith could tell from the look on Magee's face that he was looking for some insight into what he had been talking to the cardinal about.

'He's arranged dinner for you both,' Magee explained, realising that Smith was not going to enlighten his curiosity.

'Where?'

'He wants you to meet him outside the Vatican Post Office at eight o'clock.'

Smith looked at his watch. It was already seven-thirty.

'He hasn't given you much time!' Magee replied, knowing that Smith would have to cross the city to the Vatican.

'I'd better get going,' Smith said, as he turned to walk to his room to freshen up and to change his shirt. 'Thanks for letting me know!'

'Pass on my regards,' Magee called after him, before heading off to the refectory to join the other priests and students.

The tourists were still thronging around the Vatican as Smith arrived in the taxi. He was already five minutes late. From the top of the Via della Conciliazione, he walked quickly towards the Vatican, turning right at the Piazza Pio XII. Walking by

Monsignor Hasler's old apartment he looked up, but the place was in complete darkness.

The Piazza Cittá Leonina lies to the east of the Vatican, right behind the right wing of Bernini's Colonnade; the famous arms of St. Peter's Basilica that enclose the Square, embracing the pilgrims of Rome. Yet, for Smith he did not pay too much attention to the splendour of Bernini's architecture, unlike the tourists who were being photographed in front of the Vatican's majestic backdrop.

Standing against one of the pillars of the colonnade, where he knew he could be seen, Smith looked around for the cardinal. He checked his watch. It was nearly ten minutes past eight.

'You're late!'

Smith turned his head to the left where the American accent came from.

'I'm afraid you've mistaken me for someone else.' Smith said, when he saw the stranger.

'Are you waiting for Cardinal Brenard?'

Smith sensed that something was wrong.

'He's not coming,' Mode said, as he pulled a gun from his pocket. 'Move around to the back so we can have a private chat.'

With no choice, Smith walked around the pillar until he was under the colonnade and away from the sight of the tourists.

'Who all knows about the encyclical?' Mode asked, as he pushed Smith up against the stone pillar.

'I've no idea what you're talking about,' Smith pleaded.

'We can make this difficult if you like,' Mode replied, as he pressed the barrel of the gun into Smith's abdomen and angled it towards his chest. 'If I shoot you at this angle, you'll have a painful death. Firstly, the bullet would enter your stomach, then through your liver, your left lung and exit out your back. The acids of your stomach would corrode your flesh, the damage to your liver would be inoperable, and as well as having a deflated lung you'd slowly drown in your own blood. By the time they'd get you to a hospital it would be too late.'

Overcome with fear, Smith could not speak. Looking around him he could see some tourists, but he knew he was helpless in his situation.

'Don't even think about shouting out!' Mode said, as he pressed the gun deeper into Smith's flesh. 'So, for the last time, who else knows about the encyclical?'

Smith knew that to tell him about O'Keefe would be the ultimate betrayal. Either way, he knew he was a dead man and handing over O'Keefe would not save him from his fate.

'You're a brave man,' Mode said, as he removed the gun from Smith's stomach. 'Foolish, but brave.'

Smith, frozen to the spot did not know what was happening as the man stepped back from him and smiled. Watching his last moment in this world unfold, Smith saw the man raise his gun and aim it directly at his head. He closed his eyes and took one last breath.

The crack of the handgun sent every pigeon in St. Peter's Square flying into the evening sunset in disarray. Tourists, in confused silence stopped as the echo of the gunfire ricocheted throughout the pillars of the colonnade. Suddenly, a few tourists screamed as they watched Smith's lifeless body fall forward, hitting the ground.

Mode was nowhere to be seen. Having slipped behind the pillar, he made himself invisible as he mingled in the confusion of the tourists.

23.

Wednesday, 9th April.

At six in the morning, Cardinal Guarducci stood in his bedroom drying himself with a white cotton towel after his morning bath. Following a long established routine, the housekeeper had left his clothing for the day neatly laid out on the dresser. Slipping on his underwear, he took a white linen grandfather shirt that hung from the dresser and put it on. The arthritis in his body had lessened after his morning soak, but his fingers still felt stiff as he buttoned the shirt, folded the double cuffs and fastened his gold cufflinks. After putting on his black trousers and placing the braces over his shoulders, he slipped his feet into a pair of black, tailor made Stefanelli shoes. Having a good hour before he was expected in his office, he left the rest of his attire hanging beside the wardrobe until he was ready to leave his quarters.

'Good morning,' Guarducci said, as he walked into his sitting room and greeted Cardinal Oliveri and the head of the CIA bureau in Rome, Jane Lincoln.

After pouring himself a cup of coffee, Guarducci sat opposite them. He could clearly see that Lincoln was nervous, having been summoned in the early hours of the morning to attend the meeting.

'Why was Mr. Smith murdered within the Vatican State?' Guarducci asked, making it quite clear that he was not happy.

'We thought it best not to get the Roman police involved in this murder.' Lincoln replied. 'With a different jurisdiction they can't investigate the crime. With their current investigation into the murder at the Irish College, we couldn't have taken the risk of them investigating this murder as well. There would've been too many connections.'

'Well, it did not work!' Guarducci replied, before he sipped on his coffee, 'It is now world news that a man was killed in St. Peter's Square. Furthermore, the media have already made the connection that he lived in the Irish College. And on a related issue, you should not have used Cardinal Brenard as your excuse to arrange the meeting. We cannot have his name involved.'

'That wasn't my idea.' Lincoln insisted. 'I simply gave my operative the instruction to deal with Stuart Smith. He planned and arranged the meeting.'

'For a woman who is known as The Handler, you do not seem to have a handle on those under your authority.' Oliveri said. 'It is shambolic.'

Jane Lincoln shifted uncomfortably in her chair.

'When the Commander of the Swiss Guard's informed me of Smith's death, I rang the Irish College as a matter of courtesy,' Guarducci explained. 'It was Monsignor Magee who informed me of the alleged meeting Cardinal Brenard had arranged with Stuart Smith. Thankfully, he has agreed to keep that information to himself. I told him I did not want Cardinal Brenard harassed by the police so soon after burying his closest friend.'

'We both discussed this at length last night. We are not happy.' Oliveri spoke up.

Lincoln knew why. Three deaths within ten days of each other, all associated with the Irish College. It was a case of two, too many.

'Your Eminences, we had no choice but to kill Mr. Smith!' Lincoln said.

'I understand that,' Oliveri replied. 'But, there is no excuse for how amateur the hit on Stuart Smith was.'

Guarducci got up and walked over to his desk.

'This was found on his person.' Guarducci said.

Lincoln watched as Guarducci lifted a letter.

'When the Gendarmerie investigated the murder scene, they found this in one of Mr. Smith's pockets. I think you should read it.'

Taking the letter, Lincoln started to read the warning Malachy Devine had posted from Israel.

'I do not need to remind you Miss Lincoln, we have taken a great risk in seeing this through. We cannot let it fail now. I have persuaded the commander of the Gendarmerie not to mention this letter in his report.'

'I understand, but what about Cardinal Brenard?'

'No more killing!' Guarducci insisted. 'We agreed to have Devine silenced because of what he knew. Yesterday's murder was not thought through properly. Now we have to contain it.'

'Is there anything more the CIA can do to help you?'

'Keep searching for Devine's copy of the encyclical. My gut tells me that it will somehow make its way to Cardinal Brenard. According to Cardinal Boyer, Cardinal Brenard has never seen a copy of the encyclical, but I simply cannot afford it coming into his possession, especially not after last night's events here in the Vatican.'

'Do you want us to deal with Cardinal Brenard?'

'No, leave him to me. I will make him see that everything he has been told is nothing other than lies.' Guarducci replied.

'How will you explain Stuart Smith's murder?'

'It would have been a lot easier if you had not killed him in the Vatican,' Guarducci said. 'Cardinal Oliveri has suggested, and I agree with him, that we should allow the Italian police access to our investigation. That way, we look as if we have nothing to hide, but we can control the investigation and play it out for a few weeks until it is no longer news worthy. Hopefully, with the Pope coming back from the hospital today and his impending death, the media will have enough to talk about.'

'Will it work?'

'Miss Lincoln, this is the Vatican. With the Pope in a terminal condition, I will be completely in charge and the Gendarmerie's investigation will focus on where I tell it too.'

'Should the CIA have anything to fear from Cardinal Brenard?'

'He will not be a threat once I speak to him.'

'What will you tell him?'

'We are working on him already. We now have him convinced that Malachy Devine was being investigated on charges of sexual abuse.'

'And if that plan fails?' she asked.

'Then, he will not leave the Vatican alive!'

'I thought you wanted no more murder.' Lincoln pointed out.

'Who said anything about murder?' Guarducci replied, with a menacing smile.

24.

The previous evening, after night prayer, Monsignor Magee stood forward in the chapel of the Irish College to address his students and fellow priests. When he informed them of the murder of Stuart Smith, they struggled to come to terms with the unimaginable, yet frighteningly dangerous reality, that someone was targeting members of their community.

When Fr. Donal O'Keefe heard the rector deliver the news, he immediately left the chapel. Outside, in the rear courtyard, he vomited with knowing trepidation that he could be next.

The following morning, as the college community gathered for morning mass, O'Keefe stood in the foyer, waiting for his taxi to arrive. In the early hours of the morning, he had managed to book himself onto one of the last seats on the eleven-thirty shuttle flight to Dublin. Despite his respect for Devine and Smith, he was not prepared to join their fate. He knew getting away from Rome was the only way to avoid being entangled in the growing danger.

From the foyer door he saw a car drive into the grounds of the college. Lifting his hand-luggage, he made his way down the main steps as the car pulled up alongside the entrance.

As the car stopped in front of him, O'Keefe realised it was not a taxi. Looking closely to see who was sitting in the back seat of the car, he noticed Cardinal Paul Brenard looking back at him through the window.

Not wanting to speak to him, he turned and headed back into the college. He heard the car door opening behind him.

'Excuse me, are you Fr. O'Keefe?' he heard the cardinal call after him, but he refused to answer.

Telling his driver to park the car, Brenard climbed the steps and entered the Irish College.

Amid the stillness of the morning, Brenard saw the young priest sitting on the green carpet of the main stairwell, resting his head in his hands. Believing that it was O'Keefe, he walked over and stood in front of him.

'What do you want?' O'Keefe finally asked, staring at the ground.

'If you are Father O'Keefe, I really need to know,' Brenard said, looking around the main hallway to make sure they were alone. 'If you're not, could you bring me to him?'

At a stroke, the frustrating horror of his predicament painfully swamped him. He was reluctant to admit to the cardinal who he was, and loathing the fact that he had no choice but to accept that he could not avoid his responsibility as easily as he had thought. 'I am O'Keefe, but I've nothing to say.'

'Please,' Brenard urged, as he took hold of O'Keefe's arm as he went to walk past him. 'You must tell me what you know.'

'Forget it!' O'Keefe snapped, looking Brenard right in the eye, his face white with fear. 'Don't you get it? They are targeting everyone who knows. Malachy and Stuart have paid with their lives, but I have no intention in following their lead.'

There was complete silence. Brenard let go of O'Keefe's arm and took a step back.

'You haven't heard!' O'Keefe said, seeing the shock on Brenard's face. 'Stuart Smith is dead. He was murdered last night in Saint Peter's Square.'

Brenard gasped and shook his head in disbelief. 'That was Stuart?'

'They murdered him in the very heart of the Catholic Church.' O'Keefe continued through gritted teeth. 'No one is safe, especially neither of us because we both know the truth. Now, if you'll excuse me I simply want to get back home. You'd be best doing the same. They'll stop at nothing. And I mean nothing!'

'Who?' Brenard managed to ask.

'Darker forces than you could ever imagine. Stuart made the mistake of lifting his head above the crowd and being noticed. I won't be making the same mistake.'

'You can trust me,' Brenard appealed. 'Please, I need to know.'

'Stuart trusted you, now he's dead!' O'Keefe replied, cutting Brenard to the core. 'You were the only man who knew of his work with Malachy. And, just like Malachy, Stuart was killed because of what he knew.'

Until that moment, Brenard never saw it with such clarity. The only other person he told was Cardinal Boyer.

Surely not! He thought. *It couldn't be possible. Someone else must've known?*

'I have no doubt that you are a good and holy man,' O'Keefe said, as he watched his taxi drive through the main gate, 'it's just that I can no longer trust anyone.'

'I have read the documents on Smith's laptop.' Brenard said in a panic, knowing that he had once last chance to persuade O'Keefe to confide in him. 'Is it true that you were advising Malachy on biblical prophesies that relate to the dangers surrounding the building of a third temple in Jerusalem on the Temple Mount?'

His question stopped O'Keefe in his tracks. Turning to face the cardinal he walked back up the steps and faced him.

'Don't ever repeat what you've just said to anyone. Understand?' O'Keefe threatened in revealed frustration. 'What you have just said is enough to put a price on anyone's head.'

'Is it true?' Brenard demanded.

'All I can do is pray for you,' O'Keefe said. 'Trust no one. I've done my bit for the Church, there's nothing more for me to do.'

'Stay and help me get to the truth,' Brenard pleaded.

'I think you know everything you need to know for now. The only one I ever trusted was Malachy Devine and he never let me down.'

With that, O'Keefe stretched out his hand and offered it to Brenard.

'I can't do this on my own,' Brenard replied, as he took O'Keefe's hand. 'I beg you, stay here in Rome with me.'

'You must speak to the only one who knows the truth!' O'Keefe said, as he let go of Brenard's hand.

'Who?'

'Speak to the Holy Father.'

'I can't get near him,' Brenard replied, in frustration. 'Senior cardinals are preventing that from happening.'

'Then what's the point of wearing that?' O'Keefe asked, as he pointed to Brenard's ring.

Brenard knew that whatever answer he gave would have been inadequate to the point O'Keefe was going to make. Looking at his ring he knew it represented his office as a cardinal, a sign of his loyalty to the Church and the great authority it gave him over many.

'You are a Prince of the Church. You have the right to speak to the Holy Father in private. No one in the Vatican can stop you, they might try too, but stand your ground and demand your entitlement. You have to do this, trust me when I say that time is not on your side. When Father Devine wrote that the Pope was in grave peril, he was referring to a conversation he had with him before he left for Israel.'

'What was said?'

'The Pope believed that senior cardinals within the Vatican were planning to kill him.'

'That's impossible,' Brenard replied in shock.

'Three weeks ago the Pope was fit and healthy,' O'Keefe went on. 'Now we're being told that he only has weeks to live? That doesn't add up in my books. I'm convinced that those who've tried to silence the truth have already silenced the Pope in the hope that the truth will never come out. That's why they won't let anyone near him. You must insist. Remember, if the Pope dies the truth will be lost.'

'What will I say to him?'

'When he sees you he'll tell you everything you need to know. He's being brought back to the Vatican today.'

'How do you know that?'

'Like everyone else I have my sources.'

'Then I'll go today.'

'Be prepared to fight, it won't be easy.' O'Keefe advised. 'I trust that you'll do the right thing, after all you're the only hope now.'

Having said all that he was prepared to reveal, he left Brenard and got into the taxi.

After watching O'Keefe get into his car, Brenard looked behind him and into the Irish College. Through the main door he could see the rear doors that led onto the quad, and through them the students making their way back from morning mass. Not wanting to be seen, he descended the steps and made his way across the gravelled path, waved goodbye to O'Keefe as his taxi pulled away, and got into the back of his own car.

'Where too, Your Eminence?' His protection officer asked.

'The Vatican.' Brenard replied. He had never felt so alone.

25.

The queue to enter the Vatican Museums was an estimated two to three hours long. Tourists snaked their way from the museums' entrance, along the east wall and into Saint Peter's Square; each one prepared to wait to see the treasures of the Sistine Chapel, the Gallery of the Candelabra, Egyptian antiquities, the priceless collection of Etruscan gold jewellery, tapestries, maps, the Stanze of Raphael, the Borgia Apartment of Pope Alexander VI, the Vatican Library and much more.

Suddenly, the line of tourists along the road and footpaths surrounding the Gate of Saint Anne was cleared. Outside the Vatican boundary, the Roman police began to line the curbs with barricades to keep the route clear, while the Swiss Guards within the Vatican stopped all traffic from leaving.

Amid the confusion of the tourists, a wail of police sirens filled the air; growing in strength as they approached closer to the Vatican. Unexpectedly, the people lining along the east wall of the Swiss Guards' barracks, exploded into a frenzy of shouting, cheering and clapping. Bags, coats, hats and anything the tourists had on their possession were waved in the air, and on their phones they recorded the Pope as he returned to the Vatican.

As the popemobile passed through the Gate of Saint Anne and into the Courtyard of the Belvedere, Pope Clement looked behind him to see the streets of Rome for one last time. For he knew, he would never leave the Vatican again as he was being brought back to die with apostolic dignity.

In the courtyard, the Swiss Guards stood in formation as the cavalcade made its way towards the entrance of the Apostolic Palace. The majority of cardinals, archbishops, bishops, monsignors, priests, brothers and nuns who worked within the Vatican had gathered, and when the popemobile came to a stop they too started to applaud, knowing that this would be the last time they would welcome Clement back home.

'Just wait until they open the door,' Cardinal Guarducci, replied from the seat behind the Pope. 'Give them your blessing.'

The Pope did as Guarducci requested, but despite their warm welcome he wanted nothing more than to retire to the privacy of the Papal Apartment. The move from the Gemelli had been more exhausting than he had anticipated.

With military precision, the papal ushers stepped forward and opened the door. When they saw the Pope, each one of them had to look twice at his wretched appearance. Gone was the healthy man they once knew, replaced by a dying man whose illness now engulfed him.

Releasing the latches on the bottom of his seat they turned it around, making it easier to assist him out.

'Gentlemen where is the wheelchair?' Guarducci asked, before they lifted the Pope out.

'Inside, Your Eminence,' one of the ushers replied. 'We thought it would be more discrete.'

'Bring it to the Holy Father,' Guarducci demanded, knowing the walk up the steps and into the palace would be too much for his frail condition.

Walking the short distance to the door of the palace, the ushers returned with the papal wheelchair. Unlike a normal wheelchair, the Pope's wheelchair was disguised as a cream suede throne; an attempt by the Vatican to hide the fact that they were pushing a fragile and dying Pope.

With the wheelchair alongside the popemobile, they reached in and supported the Pope under his arms as he climbed down the three steps, while the Vatican photographer took his pictures; evidence for the world to see that Pope Clement was now a terminally ill man.

With the Pope safely seated in his wheelchair, they turned him around so he faced those gathered in the courtyard. Then returning to the popemobile, an usher pushed forward the papal chair and assisted Cardinal Guarducci as he stepped out. Fixing his clerical attire, he waited for the vehicle to pull away before he walked over to Pope Clement.

As a single drum beat echoed around the courtyard, a unit of four guards marched forward in rhythmic motion to the beat. Making their way across the courtyard, they stopped a few feet short from the Pope; each one carrying the rolled up standard across their arms.

'Given them your apostolic blessing,' Guarducci spoke gently into his ear.

Lifting his right hand, Pope Clement struggled to give an apostolic blessing as he painfully moved his hand from the left, then to the middle and then to his right.

With his blessing received, the guards reverently backed away from him until they reached the centre of the courtyard, where they turned and attached the papal standard to the flag pole.

Once the band of the Swiss Guard struck up the national anthem of the Vatican State, two guards raised the papal standard; a sign to let the world know that the Bishop of Rome, the Servant of the Servants of God, the Vicar of Christ, the Sovereign of the Vatican and the Supreme Pontiff had returned to his official residence.

For the duration of the ceremony, everyone who had come to see the Holy Father observed a dignified silence throughout. Even Cardinal Oliveri, stood with his hands joined as he watched the standard being raised; resisting the temptation to look a Guarducci with an approving smile.

'Take him in,' Guarducci instructed the ushers, once the anthem drew to a close.

Reaching the bottom of the steps, the four ushers gripped the handles around the wheelchair, and with as much dignity as they could display, they lifted the Pope up the five steps to the main door.

'Turn the Holy Father around. Let them see him one last time,' Guarducci requested, as he joined them.

Following his request they turned Pope Clement around, giving those who had gathered their last glimpse of their beloved Holy Father. To show them his appreciation, Clement ignored the pain and raised both his hands in a dignified salute to their warmth, as they cried out in unison: 'Viva il Papa! Viva il Papa!'

Even Guarducci applauded as a daughter of one of the Vatican's employees was led by her mother to meet the Pope. In her hand the girl carried a single red rose, and when she approached the Pope she handed it over to him. Leaning forward, Clement placed his hand on her head and smiled warmly.

With a nod from Guarducci, the ushers turned the wheelchair and started to push the Holy Father through the main reception of the Apostolic Palace, while Pope Clement waved his final goodbye.

Once inside, they took the Pope to his private elevator that would take him straight to the Papal Apartment. Waiting at the bottom of the lift, under the small dome that concealed the lift shaft, the operator stood holding open the wrought iron gates. With the lift designed to transport popes to and from the Papal Apartment for mass in the basilica, it wasn't designed to accommodate wheelchairs. So, the ushers had to assist the Pope into the mahogany lift, placing him onto a seat. Then they respectfully withdrew, allowing Cardinal Guarducci to enter the lift with him.

Closing the doors from the outside, and locking the wrought iron gate, the lift operator stood back, signalling to the cardinal that he was free to use the lift. As Guarducci placed a key into the fifth barrel and turned it, the lift started to slowly ascend, going through the opening in the dome as it headed up the apartment. As they watched the lift disappear from their sight, the ushers knew that the next time they would be of assistance to their Holy Father would be the day they would carry his body from the Papal Apartment to lie in state in St. Peter's Basilica.

'You did well today,' Guarducci said, as he placed a reassuring hand on Clement's shoulder. 'Once we get you settled, you will be able to rest.'

As the doors opened, the Pope was met by his new nurses who had been appointed by Guarducci. Smiling warmly, they waited for the cardinal to step out of the lift before they entered to assist the Pope. Without wanting to cause him too much discomfort, they quickly lifted him and sat him into a cushioned wheelchair, making sure that he was comfortable before they moved him.

After reassuring them that he was fine, one of the nurses turned the wheelchair towards the main entrance to the Papal Apartment. When Guarducci turned to follow, he could not believe what he was seeing when he saw Cardinal Brenard waiting for the Pope to return.

Unaware of Vatican protocol, a nurse stopped pushing the wheelchair as Cardinal Brenard approached.

When Paul Brenard looked at the Holy Father, he was so taken aback by the illness that was ravaging his body that he shot a look of disgust at Guarducci. Brenard had no doubt that the Pope was now dying. His body was withered and grey. Even his eyes looked as though his soul had given up all hope. Gone was the charismatic Pope that the world loved from the first moment he appeared on the balcony of St. Peter's, now he was a man who was clearly approaching the end.

'Holy Father,' Brenard replied, as he knelt beside him, took his hand and reverently kissed his ring. 'It is so good to see you.'

Clement feebly gripped his hand and smiled.

'Cardinal Brenard,' Guarducci spoke up, fearing the purpose behind his visit, 'we need to get the Holy Father inside the apartment.'

'I understand,' Brenard replied, as he stood aside allowing the nurses to push the Pope through. Then, much to the frustration of Guarducci, Brenard followed.

26.

As Pope Clement was taken into his study, Guarducci had to act quickly. He did not want Brenard walking into the room. Knowing that the nurses had to make the Pope comfortable and give him some medication, Guarducci closed the door to give them privacy, leaving Brenard and himself alone in the hallway.

'It is good that you could come,' Guarducci said, as he turned and faced Cardinal Brenard, smiling warmly.

'I want to speak to the Holy Father,' Brenard replied, unable to get past Guarducci as he blocked the door.

'Today is not the best time to see His Holiness. He needs rest. Let us arrange a meeting for another day.'

'No!' Brenard insisted, standing his ground. 'I want to speak with him, today!'

Facing a confrontation he knew he could not win, unless he ordered the Gendarmerie to physically remove a fellow cardinal, Guarducci had to think quickly and take control of the situation.

'Okay, you can see him,' Guarducci replied. 'Just, let the nurses get him settled and then you can have a private audience. Let us get something to drink while we wait.'

Having been granted access and not wanting to prolong an unnecessary confrontation, Brenard followed him across the hallway and into the kitchen.

'Could you please give us some time alone,' Guarducci instructed the nurse, who was making soup for the Pope's lunch.

Obliging his request, she turned off the gas stove and left them alone.

'Would you like some water?' Guarducci asked, lifting two glasses from the cupboard.

Nodding his head, Brenard accepted Guarducci's offer as he took a seat at the kitchen table.

'Can I ask, what it is that you wish to discuss with the Holy Father?' Guarducci asked, as he opened the fridge and lifted out two bottles of sparkling mineral water.

'I'd prefer not too,' Brenard replied, unable to trust Guarducci.

Not wanting to push Brenard, Guarducci handed him his water and a glass, before opening his own bottle and pouring his much needed refreshment.

'His Holiness has not been told about the murder that took place here last night,' Guarducci said, before he took a sip of his water.

'Why not?'

'I thought it best to get him back to the Vatican before I broke the news. Terrible affair altogether. Did you know the victim?'

'Why would I know him?' Brenard asked, letting Guarducci know that he was not happy with his probing questions.

'In a telephone conversation with the rector of the Irish College, he informed me that the victim was working under a doctrinal scholarship with Malachy Devine. I just thought that you might have made his acquaintance, that is all.'

'I didn't know that,' Brenard lied, taking a mouthful of his water.

'The Irish College has gone through a lot recently,' Guarducci continued, all the while looking at Brenard to see if he would give anything away. 'How are you coping after the funeral?'

'As well as could be expected given the circumstances.'

'I know Malachy meant a lot to you,' Guarducci said, as he leaned against the worktop. 'Despite the accusations against him, he was a good man and I am sure a loyal friend.'

Brenard did not reply. Although he was angered that the subject had been brought up, he did not want to get into a conversation about Malachy, especially not with Guarducci.

When they both heard the nurses leave the Pope's study they set their glasses down, knowing that Pope Clement was now free.

'I think they're finished,' Brenard said, as he got up from his seat.

'Just give me a few moments with the Holy Father before you go in,' Guarducci insisted. 'Then you can have as much time with him as you need.'

Knowing he had no other option but to agree, Brenard stood aside and let Guarducci leave the kitchen. With his audience granted he had nothing to lose.

Walking into the Pope's study, Guarducci closed the door behind him. Beside the window, sitting in an armchair, Clement admired the view of the dome of Saint Peter's Basilica.

'Are you comfortable?' Guarducci asked, as he walked over and took a seat beside him.

Clement nodded as he adjusted the oxygen tube around his nose.

'We have a problem,' he confided. 'Cardinal Paul Brenard knows about our operation.'

Clement looked concerned as he sat back into his chair.

'I have a feeling he is here to ask you if you penned the encyclical.' Guarducci surmised. 'I know that you find it difficult to speak, but you must find the energy to answer his questions. You must deny that you penned that encyclical. He will believe it when he hears it coming from your lips. We cannot risk him leaving here today with any doubt.'

Closing his eyes to find an inner strength, Clement wished he could just be left alone. He was exhausted and wanted to do nothing but sleep. But, he knew the importance of what Guarducci wanted him to do. For their plan to succeed, they could not have people like Brenard asking questions that could uncover the truth. So, no matter how much it took out of him, Clement was determined to make sure that Cardinal Brenard was left in no doubt whatsoever that he had never written an end of times encyclical.

'I will not let you down!' Clement said, in a grasping voice.

Walking over to the window, Guarducci looked down at the pilgrims and tourists as they walked across Saint Peter's Square. Clement had sacrificed much in going along with his plan, and for that Guarducci would be forever grateful. Not once, even during his time at the Gemelli Hospital, did Clement complain or let the truth of their agreement slip. For Guarducci, he thought it would be easier to have the Pope back in the Vatican where he could be tightly controlled. Never did he envisage such circumstances as he was now facing. Everything now rested on Clement playing his part in fooling the one man who had been dragged into the truth of their conspiracy.

'I am going to send him in,' Guarducci said, as he walked toward the door. 'Listen mostly to what he has to say, say as little as possible and remember, you are the Pope and every word you speak carries with it an authority that will be accepted by the likes of Paul Brenard. Towards the end of the meeting call me in, and I will provide the linchpin to your argument.'

With an understanding nod from Clement, Guarducci opened the door.

'He is ready to see you now?' Guarducci said, as he walked back into the hallway.

'Thank you!' Brenard replied, as he walked into the room, ready to hear the truth from the mouth of the Holy Father himself.

Closing the door to the study, Guarducci took a deep breath hoping that the matter would be settled once and for all.

Walking down the corridor, Guarducci stood at the entrance to the Pope's private chapel. He was not in the need, nor in the mood for prayer, but closing his eyes he hoped that the meeting between Paul Brenard and Clement would not hinder his greater plans.

27.

Alone, Brenard knelt before Pope Clement, took hold of his right hand and kissed his Fisherman's Ring, while Clement placed his other hand upon Brenard's head to give him his blessing.

'Holy Father,' Brenard said, as he lifted his head to look into the Pope's dying eyes. 'Thank you for granting me this private audience.'

As the Pope looked at him, he smiled and motioned with the hand Brenard was holding for him to stand up, before urging him to take a seat in the chair beside him.

Accepting the invitation, Brenard sat down and turned so he was facing the Pope.

'You've been foremost in my prayers, and in the prayers of the people of Chicago,' Brenard said, with a sympathetic smile as he looked upon the Pope and his body that was ravaged with the illness that would, in a short matter of time, take him from this world.

Pope Clement waited for Brenard to begin. Words were hard to speak, and he knew this conversation would take a great toll on the little physical strength he had left.

'Holy Father,' Brenard began, his nervousness clear to hear in his voice. 'Before I return to America, there is an important matter that I need to bring to your attention. Two days ago, after celebrating the requiem mass for Malachy Devine, I was handed a letter written by Malachy days before he was murdered in Israel. In his letter, Malachy had instructed one of his students to speak to me as a matter of urgency, regarding an encyclical he claims you have written.'

Hoping that the Pope would give some reaction, Brenard was left a little disappointed as the Pope closed his eyes and listened with intense concentration to what he had to say.

'Malachy's student, a man named Stuart Smith, took me to Malachy's office at the Gregorian. While we were at the university he showed me an official letterhead from your office, onto which he claims you wrote the references to twenty biblical prophesies that you wanted Malachy to research. Prophesies relating to an alleged vision witnessed while on retreat in Castel Gandolfo. In this vision you were apparently instructed to write an encyclical to prepare the world for the Second Coming of Jesus Christ. I've come here to see if it's true, because in his letter Malachy warned that you were in danger from evil forces at work within the Vatican. Your Holiness, I don't know what to believe, that's why I need to hear it from you in person. Did you write such an encyclical?'

Placing his joined hands onto his lap, the Pope opened his eyes and slowly opened his mouth to utter the one word he hoped would give Brenard the closure he needed. 'No!'

Disbelief. Shock. Surprise. Anger. Every emotion that he could experience at that moment ran through Brenard's mind. From the mouth of the Holy Father he had received the absolute truth. But, it was not the truth he was expecting.

Having heard the Pope's adamant denial, Brenard felt ashamed that he had believed all that he had been told. The Holy Father had no reason to lie to him, and as he struggled with his speech and his breathing, Brenard felt that he was putting him through too much.

'Forgive me, Holy Father,' Brenard said, bowing his head so the Pope couldn't see the tears of shame in his eyes.

'What is there to forgive?' Clement asked, his voice hoarse and wheezing. 'Do not let your heart be troubled.'

As tears rolled down his face, Brenard resigned not to ask the rest of the questions that had troubled his mind. With no encyclical every other question or concern now seemed irrelevant. He had put the Pope through enough, there was no need for any more.

Lifting a small bell from the table beside him, Pope Clement rang it. As Brenard wiped the tears from his eyes, the door leading into the study opened moments later and Guarducci entered.

Walking into the study, Guarducci was glad to see the positive signs from Cardinal Brenard's eyes. When he looked at him he smiled, hoping that he now believed the denials of the Holy Father.

'Jean, Paul is aware of the rumours about the encyclical,' Clement struggled to say, as Guarducci took a seat opposite them. 'I would like you to tell him the truth.'

With Guarducci in the room, Clement finally breathed a heavy sigh of relief. Although his mind was fully alert, his body felt exhausted and he knew he would struggle to explain everything that Brenard needed to hear before he left. Furthermore, he knew that Guarducci could explain it with better insight.

'Paul, several weeks ago I received information from the Israeli Government that a priest within Rome, namely Father Devine, had been in contact regarding end of time's prophecies that he was allegedly working on with the Holy Father. Upon hearing this I summonsed Malachy to the Vatican to talk with him as a matter of urgency.'

'Why didn't you tell me this before now?' Brenard asked, as he leaned forward in his chair. 'These past few days have seen me literally shaken to the core of my belief.'

'I could not tell you until I had the authority from the Holy Father to do so.' Guarducci said. 'This is such a sensitive issue.'

'I can understand that,' Brenard replied, 'but I hope you can see why I have so many unanswered questions.'

'For the past several months, we tried to persuade Malachy to return to Ireland to face the charges brought against him for the sexual abuse of minors. Yet, despite our requests he refused to go back to Ireland on his own accord. Instead, he has used his acquired Vatican citizenship as the way and means to fight his deportation request as it was filed with the Italian Republic. As a sovereign state we have no extradition treaties with any other country, therefore his application for extradition back to Ireland could not be enforced, and if we were to force his return it would have quashed any subsequent trial back in Ireland. So, we took it upon ourselves to convene a commission and to put him on trial here in the Vatican. Now, I do not know if it was the shame, denial or even madness, but we believe that Malachy conjectured the idea of a papal encyclical to blackmail us. Knowing that the Holy Father was ill, we now believe that he had planned to go public in the event of the Holy Father's death, to make it look like he personally had penned the encyclical.'

'Did this involve Monsignor Hasler?'

'No!' Guarducci said categorically, as the Pope lowered his head with the shame of what had happened. 'Unfortunately for us, Monsignor Hasler's growing scandal is true. But, he had no involvement or contact whatsoever with Malachy Devine.'

'Your Holiness, is that true?' Brenard asked.

'It is the truth,' Clement replied, before taking an uncomfortable breath. 'Gustave Hasler had nothing to do with this.'

'I accept your word, Holy Father, but why involve him if they knew he would deny their lies?'

Clement shrugged as he fought to regain his breath.

'We do not know!' Guarducci added.

'What about Stuart Smith?' Brenard asked, knowing that Guarducci had not briefed the Pope on his murder. 'The coincidence is too obvious to ignore. First he alleges he was working with Devine and then he too is murdered!'

'I wish I knew.' Guarducci said. 'I simply do not know. Perhaps there is a link between both murders, perhaps it is simply a coincidence. It is being investigated and I assure you that once we find out the truth you will be personally informed.'

'You must forgive my directness,' Brenard said, as he tried to make sense of his own clarity of thought. 'I am prepared, no, I am fully accepting of all that I am being told here today, but it still doesn't explain as to why Malachy would go to such lengths.'

'To hide the truth about himself?' Guarducci suggested. 'My sources from within the Gendarmerie have discovered that Malachy was being paid by influential Americans who were members of a Christian Zionist movement. Whether or not they were aware of the legal battle facing Malachy remains unclear, but with his reputation as one of the world's most influential biblical scholars, his name alone was enough to give their cause credibility?'

'Christian Zionism?' Brenard asked, somewhat disbelievingly. 'The Malachy I knew often scoffed at the ideas of such movements. He was too well versed to side with them.'

'With no offence,' Guarducci said. 'You clearly did not know Malachy as well as you thought. He was in a difficult place. These people somehow reached out to him, aided him, affirmed him and ultimately used him. Faith, unless we control it has a way of corrupting us with misled truths. The storms of dangerous religious ideologies have darkened the world for decades. Look at what has happened in recent years, with the establishment of an Islamic Caliphate in Baghdad and the perilous situation Israel finds itself in defending its borders. While here, in the so called liberal west, multitudes have turned to embrace the philosophy of atheism. By choosing the path he chose, Malachy made more than enough enemies. Do you really think the Israelis were happy with him? Could you imagine the train of events that would unfold if the Islamic States sensed for one moment there was the slightest possibility that a Third Temple could be built on the Dome of the Rock? I do not have the answers to all the questions that you have. But, I must be direct with you. I fear that you have been dragged into the fringes of a conspiracy that was conceived to damage the credibility of the Holy See, to cause division and great scandal. There is no encyclical, only a web of deceit and lies. Why would we lie to you? We are ministers of the truth! Surely, you must see that you have been used, misled and conned by a friend you thought you knew?'

Brenard was stunned into silence. He wished for the wisdom to say something in response to Guarducci. But, he felt like the fool. Sitting before the Pope and the most senior cardinal of the Sacred College, he could not believe that he had brazenly walked into the inner sanctum of the Holy See and laid his unfounded allegations at the feet of his dying Pope, only to discover that he had indeed been used.

'With all due respect, my brother,' Guarducci said, as he clasped the gold pectoral cross that hung around his neck. 'We are mere workers in the vineyard of the Lord, not the orchestrators of skullduggery in the pits of earthly deceit.'

As Brenard lowered his head, Guarducci glanced towards Clement. Without doubt they both knew they had won the argument and had now silenced the truth.

Amid the embarrassing silence, Clement reached over and took hold of Brenard's hand. While Guarducci, the master of coercion, sat and watched, happy for the silence to linger.

'May I have your blessing to leave?' Brenard finally asked, as he gripped the Pope's hand. 'I have caused enough upset by bringing this to your attention. I simply beg both of you for your forgiveness, especially for causing such distress in these difficult days.'

'I consider you a friend,' Guarducci said. 'You did the right thing in coming here today. At least in seeking out the truth you have found your peace.'

Brenard humbly, and with considerable embarrassment, nodded his acceptance of Guarducci's words. Never in his life had he felt so humiliated and so blinded by betrayal. He wanted nothing more than to leave, and without hearing a response from the Pope he stood up.

'I would like you to have this,' Clement said, as he lifted a rosary from the table beside him.

'I couldn't possibly accept such a gift,' Brenard replied, when he realised that each bead was finely engraved with the papal coat of arms.

'I want you to have it,' Clement insisted, as he held it out for him to take it. 'I have no need for personal belongings now.'

'I'll treasure it Holy Father,' Brenard said as he held the beads tightly in his hands.

'Pray for me, Paul,' Clement uttered.

'I always have and I always will,' Brenard replied, struggling to hold back his tears as he bent down to embrace the Pope for what he knew would be the last time.

'May the Lord go with you,' Clement replied as he blessed him, before gently touching his cheek.

28.

'How are you feeling?' Guarducci asked, the moment Brenard left the room.

'I feel fine!' Clement replied, as he breathed deeply on his oxygen feed. 'Did I do well?'

'Better than expected,' Guarducci replied, as he moved over and sat beside him. 'To be honest, I thought he would have refused to accept our argument. I did not even have to send for the papers I had arranged regarding Malachy Devine's extradition proceedings. I think he will go back to Chicago convinced he has been entrusted with the truth.'

Pouring the Pope a glass of iced water, Guarducci handed it to him to drink.

'Is everything alright?' Guarducci asked, sensing a questionable sadness from the old man.

'It feels so final.' Clement confided, after taking a much needed sip of the water.

'You still afraid of facing death?'

The look in his eyes said it all. He was. Even more so than he did before.

'Are you still afraid that your death will be the end?'

As Clement wiped his mouth with a linen napkin he nodded in agreement. For deep inside, despite the reassurances, he could not see beyond the darkness that was coming his way. The looming end that would see no hope, only the eternity of nothingness. But, it was the cruelty of leaving behind the untruth that he had lived, knowing that he would never be able to put right the life he had betrayed.

'You are not the only one to face this struggle,' Guarducci replied, placing a comforting hand on the old man's shoulder. 'I have seen great men, one of whom was a Pope, fight their last breath, afraid to let go and enter the reality of the unknown. I have no doubt that you should have nothing to fear, for I am convinced that you will be greatly rewarded for saving the Church. The mystery of God is not an illusion and death is not like falling into a deep sleep from which you will never awake. Our very souls are greater than the bodies that possess them. By doing what you have done, you have given the world future hope and meaning. And although they will never know it, you are the one who has given them a future of promise within the world. Had you not agreed to help us silence the encyclical, the world would have become even more unstable and dangerous. By accepting to follow our plan, you have prevented unimaginable consequences from taking place.'

'And look at why I did it!' Clement said with a painful sigh, revealing the depth of truth he felt.

'Has the payment unsettled you?' Guarducci asked, knowing that his actions where based, not on faith, love or God or the Church, but on reasons far more sinister.

Clement shook his head, but found it hard to look at Guarducci.

'Is it your daughter?'

Guarducci had no doubt that this was the thorn in Clement's flesh. The agreement they had made was very simple when put on paper. His denial over the encyclical's existence and an agreement to allow Guarducci to run the affairs of the Church in the last few weeks of his life, all in exchange for ten million dollars to be paid into his daughter's bank account on the moment of his death. The hard reality being, he would never get to see his child again. He had to die alone in the Vatican, like a true pontiff who would be exalted in his death while the truth of his life would remain hidden from the world.

'My life has been one huge lie,' Clement said, as tears ran down his face.

'You do know that your mission calls for this to happen,' Guarducci replied, trying to console his grief. 'We cannot go back on our agreement now. It just would not be possible.'

'I know!' Clement insisted, as he wiped away his tears. 'I just wish I could see her before I die. To explain it all to her.'

'That is out of the question,' Guarducci forcefully insisted, hardly believing that he had even mentioned it. 'What impact do you think that would have on her? The moment you accepted this office you left your private world behind you, we cannot have it known that you have fathered a child. When you made me aware of your past you told me that you last saw your daughter when she was six years old. What age is she now?'

'Forty-one,' Clement replied, as he looked beyond his tears and out through the window into the world that held a love he would never see again.

'By your very calling you had to leave her behind. She could never have been involved in knowing the truth. It would have been too dangerous for both you and her. It is best to leave it. You are only thinking of yourself, not her. She could never cope with the truth that her father had intentionally lived a double life and deliberately abandoned her and her mother to pursue his own ambitions.'

Clement knew that Guarducci was right. He walked away from all his rights the moment he walked out of her life when she was a child. Even her own mother took the secret to her grave, making sure that her daughter never knew the truth about her father. Still, as his death approached it was his past that came back to haunt him and he desired only the opportunity to heal the harm he had caused. But, his current circumstances, his call and mission in life, had put a stop to it from happening.

No matter where his earthly mission took him throughout the world, he never stopped thinking about her. Wondering what she looked like, dreaming of her smile and her childish laugh. It was not the life he wanted to lead, but it was the life he had no choice but to live. He had sworn an oath and he had to follow it through. Still, he could not stop himself from desiring that one last meeting before his time on this earth came to an end.

'I will promise you one thing,' Guarducci said, knowing that he could not fully comprehend his pain having never fathered a child himself. 'Write her a letter about how you feel and how much you have loved her over these years. As long as you do not reveal to her the truth about who you are, I will make sure she receives it once you have passed away. You can explain to her that the money will be your legacy to her for all the wrong you feel you might have caused.'

'Will you do that for me?' Clement asked, as he turned to look at him.

'I will,' Guarducci truthfully promised. 'When I consider all that you have done for me, it is the least I can do.'

29.

'In this abbey you will be known as Brother Gustave, and you will serve as a novitiate brother. You are not allowed to celebrate mass in public or in private. You will not hear the confession of any fellow monk or member of the public. Few people outside this abbey know that you are here, and that is the way I wish it to remain. Therefore, you are not permitted to leave the grounds of the abbey nor speak to members of the public. You will be permitted to write and receive letters, but these I will personally approve and read before they are posted or delivered to you. You will be expected to follow a strict observance of the Rule of Saint Benedict. You will pray, eat, work and rest with the other members of the community. You will be allocated a cell in the novitiate wing. My brother monks know who you are and what you have done, but I have instructed them not to discuss these matters with you. Until your archbishop summons you back to Munich, you will remain subject to my authority. You will address me as, Abbot Father. Is that understood?'

'Yes, Abbot Father.' Hasler replied, as he stood before the abbot's desk.

'You have been sent here for a period of penance and reparation for your soul,' Abbot Karl continued. 'You are not the first public sinner, who has shamed the Church, to be sent our way and you most certainly will not be the last. We will talk in the weeks to come. But, for the time being, I recommend that you immerse yourself into the timetable of prayer, work, contemplation and community. I have appointed Fr. Rahner as your spiritual director. He will meet with you tomorrow morning and begin a program of spiritual renewal. Do you have any questions?'

Hasler shook his head.

'We have a saying in the Cistercian community that humility comes through small humiliations, and you my brother are in great need of humility.' Abbot Karl said, as he got up from behind his desk and walked around to Hasler. 'Tradition informs us that a reformer of our order, Saint Bernard of Clairvaux taught his followers that the first step on the way to humility is to obey an order without delaying it for a moment. You are far from Rome now. Unless you wish to be transferred to a Carthusian cell in the middle of France, then I advise you to follow every instruction I give you.'

Hasler was confused. He sensed that the abbot was unhappy with him, but he couldn't understand why.

'What was the first directive I gave you less than an hour ago?' Abbot Karl asked, as he looked Hasler up and down. 'I told you to do it immediately the moment you arrived?'

'You told me to go to my cell, remove my clothing and put on this grey novitiate habit,' Hasler replied, while his mind wondered if he had mistaken the abbot or was being tricked into a humiliation.

'Then what is this?' Abbot Karl asked, as he took hold of the thin gold chain around Hasler's neck and pulled it up over his habit, to reveal a small, but ornate golden crucifix.

'It was a personal present from Pope Clement,' Hasler replied, as he turned to look at the abbot. 'I have worn it for years!'

'When I told you to strip away the visual signs of your past I did not just mean your Roman tailored suit and immaculately starched collar. I meant everything, including this!' Abbot Karl said, as he let go of the chain. 'Vanity of vanities my young man. Take it off. You have no need for it now.'

Lifting both his hands, Hasler placed them around his neck and fumbled to undo the fastener on the chain. Inside he felt his humiliation complete, as nothing physical in his world belonged to his past. Everything had now changed, and although he yearned for his truth to be heard, he knew that no one was ready to listen. Removing the crucifix from his neck, he fastened the chain before placing it into the outstretched hand of the abbot.

'I will keep this until you are sent for,' the abbot said, as he returned to his desk and placed the crucifix and chain into the top draw, before calling out, 'Brother Angelo!'

'There is still time for work detail.' The abbot said, as a young novice opened the door and walked into the room. 'Brother Angelo, take Brother Gustave to the latrines, he can work there for the time being.'

Bowing his head, Angelo turned and motioned for Hasler to follow him.

As they walked, Angelo remained silent as he led him along the cloister. Every monk they passed along the way deliberately lowered their heads and refused to acknowledge Hasler. Their very demeanour alone was enough to let him know that Hauterive Abbey was not a place flowing with peace, joy and love. Instead he could feel the real repression that filled not only the abbey, but the very community that lived within its walls.

When they arrived at the latrines, Angelo pointed to a bucket of water and scrubbing brush that sat beside the main door. Then pointing towards the eight cubicles he turned to leave.

'Do you want me to clean them?' Hasler asked, not out of protest but simply to keep himself right. Yet, the moment the words left his mouth, Angelo turned on his heel to face him, and raising his right index finger to his lips he instructed Hasler to be silent. Not wanting either of them to be disciplined for breaking the grand silence of the abbey, Angelo simply nodded his head before he turned and left Hasler alone in the latrines.

There to scrub the toilets, Hasler got on his hands and knees, entered the first cubical and started to scrub away the encrusted urine and rust from the screws that fastened the seat to the ceramic bowl. Then around the white floor tiles he started to scrub the stains embedded in the grout. He was not going to be told to redo the job. So, for all the strength he could manage, he scrubbed backwards and forwards, making sure that the stains were being removed.

As he felt his pulse race and his face redden, he thought of Guarducci and the way he had been treated by him back in Rome. Then he thought of the abbot who without doubt believed his guilt. He scrubbed even harder to get rid of his anger towards them.

Quiet tears started to flow. Everything had been taken from him and now his life had been reduced to this. The sound of the water and the force of his scrubbing echoed around the cubical and around the latrines. In a bid to kill his emotion he scrubbed even harder, but the harder he pushed and pulled the scrubbing brush, his tears eventually turned into a cry of help.

'Jesus, help me!' He cried, as he threw the brush into the bucket, before collapsing onto the floor in inner turmoil. Then drawing breath, he yelled in the agony of his torment.

Minutes later, as he lay collapsed in a heap, he felt a gentle touch on his shoulder. Ashamed that he had been discovered in his emotional rawness, he pulled himself together before he turned to see who was with him.

'God has not forsaken you.' The old monk kneeling beside him said. 'I have dreamt about you. Soon everything will be made right, and the light of truth will shine on the darkness that has attacked you. Remain strong and never lose the faith. The Lord is sending someone to take you from this place. But, you must be ready, for he will come like a thief in the night.'

30.

Thursday, 10th April.

The following morning, Brenard was packed and ready to return to Chicago. His flight was scheduled to leave Rome at twelve noon.

After kissing the altar, he walked to the front of the sanctuary and joined the other priests who had concelebrated the early morning mass with him. Genuflecting, he turned and waited for the rest of the clergy to form the procession before following them. Raising his right hand, he gave the American seminarians his episcopal blessing as he walked down the chapel aisle.

Following the custom of every American cardinal or bishop who came to visit Rome, he spent his last morning celebrating a mass at the Pontifical American College. Although he always declined to stay there while in Rome, he knew it would have been improper to leave the city without paying them a visit.

Walking into the sacristy, he bowed his head towards the large crucifix that hung above the vesting table; signifying the end of the celebration.

'Thank you gentlemen,' he said, as he turned and greeted his concelebrants with a smile. 'I hope I haven't kept you too long?'

'No doubt, the students will have heartburn after rushing their breakfast if they're to make the nine o'clock lectures at the Gregorian,' the rector of the college humoured, knowing that Cardinal Brenard had taken longer than usual to say the morning mass. 'Would you like to join us for breakfast?'

'You're very kind! But, unfortunately I'm going to have to head straight to the airport.'

'I totally understand. Hopefully, next time.'

Taking off his vestments, Brenard began handing them to Francis Roche, the only deacon from Chicago who was studying in Rome.

'How are the studies going?' Brenard asked.

'They're going well, Your Eminence,' Roche replied, as he placed the Cardinal's chasuble and stole onto a large wooden hanger. 'I've just submitted my dissertation yesterday.'

'What was it on?'

'Oscar Romero and the Liberation Theology Movement in Latin America.'

'How things have changed in Rome!' Brenard said, as he pulled his alb over his head. 'In my day, even to have suggested such a title, would've seen you suspended from your studies.'

'You don't approve?'

'Quite the opposite,' Brenard insisted, as he took a comb from his pocket and brushed back his greying hair. 'I'm delighted to see that young men like yourself are being allowed to broaden your minds, instead of reciting and being tested on the catechism and Church doctrine. When do you finish your studies?'

'Hopefully my dissertation will be approved next week,' Roche replied. 'I've just to get through my final defence before the Theology Faculty Committee on Thursday evening.'

'What do you plan to do come Friday?' Brenard asked, with his characteristic wry smile.

'That's entirely up to you, Your Eminence,' he replied, wondering if the cardinal was going to ask him the question. He looked nervously at the other priests who were watching on.

Still smiling, Paul Brenard lifted his jacket and put it on. Everyone in the room watched him as he followed the usual custom that all bishops went through with their deacons as they approached the end of their studies. Reaching into his inside jacket pocket, he lifted out his phone and opened his diary.

'Francis, I would like to ordain you into the sacred priesthood,' he finally said, turning to him with a glowing smile. 'How does the first Sunday in July sound?'

'I'd be honoured, Your Eminence!' Roche delightfully replied, knowing that after seven years of study he had achieved the dream of being ordained into the priesthood.

'And so would I,' Brenard replied, before he walked over and embraced him.

All the priests in the sacristy acknowledged Roche's rise into their ranks with welcoming applause.

'My secretary will be in contact with you over the next few days to arrange the final details,' Brenard said, as he typed the event into his phone. 'Now gentlemen, if you'll excuse me I'll need to get going. I don't want to be disrupting the Roman rush hour too much.'

Leaving the sacristy he was escorted to his car by the rector, Monsignor Richard Reagan.

'I'm sure you'll be glad to get back to a sense of normality?' Reagan asked, with his usual informality.

'I'll be glad to get back to a few day's rest,' Brenard replied. 'I've freed my schedule until Sunday. I'm in need of a little quality me time.'

'The most important time of all, especially with the weight of your responsibility.' Reagan said, as they neared the main door. 'There's something I must give you before you go. It would appear that a lot of your friends thought you'd be staying with us while you were in Rome. We've received a lot of post for you over the past week or so. I think it's mainly sympathy cards.'

Walking over to the glass hatch of the reception, Reagan asked the secretary for Cardinal Brenard's correspondence.

'I took the liberty of sealing them in this padded envelope for you,' Reagan said, as he handed the large brown envelope over to him. 'I was going to post it to you, but you've saved us a few Euros.'

'You're most kind,' Brenard replied. 'Goodbye, Richard.'

'Have a safe flight!'

After shaking Reagan's hand, Brenard descended the steps and thanked his chauffeur for opening the rear door as he climbed into the back of the car.

Setting the envelope down on the seat beside him he fastened his seatbelt, and waved back at Reagan who remained at the main door to see him off.

With him safely in his car, the police escorts started the engines on their motorbikes and led the car towards the main gate of the college, past the security and out into the morning rush hour traffic. Immediately, they started their sirens and stopped the oncoming vehicles to allow the cardinal's car to leave the grounds.

'I am afraid it will take a while to make it to the motorway, Your Eminence,' the chauffeur apologised, as his car merged into the morning rush hour. 'There is no way our escort will be able to clear this road.'

'We've plenty of time,' Brenard reassured.

'We Romans are always in a rush, apart from when we sit down to eat or have to listen to the wife complain.' He remarked, before winking at Brenard in his rear-view mirror.

The tongue-n-cheek banter brought a smile to Brenard's face as he lifted the envelope and opened it. Reagan was right, it was mostly sympathy cards expressing regret over the murder of his friend. The friend who had betrayed so many people. With Malachy foremost in his thoughts again, he went to seal the envelope only to notice another large envelope inside. Reaching in, he took it out.

Sweet Jesus! He thought, to himself as he recognised the writing and saw that the postal-mint was from Haifa, Israel. *It couldn't be!*

But, he knew that it was. There was no mistaking it.

He felt his throat starting to dry as nervous perspiration broke out on the palms of his hands. He looked at the driver to see if he was watching him, but he was too busy looking at his side mirrors as he navigated his way through the traffic. Unsure what he should do, he reached for his briefcase, opened it and placed the envelope inside not realising that he now had in his possession the key to unlocking the whole truth.

31.

'Good Morning, Your Eminence,' the purser said, as he escorted Brenard into United's First Class Lounge. 'Would you require a table for breakfast?'

'Somewhere discrete please,' Brenard replied.

Following the male purser across the lounge, he was taken to a small table that was set for two. Deliberately, and out of years of habit, he took the seat that afforded him the best view of his surroundings.

'Would you like some tea or coffee?'

'A pot of coffee would be nice and some fresh orange juice.'

'Would you like to see the menu?'

'I'll just have some Eggs Benedict,' Brenard replied, knowing that it would be enough to see him through until lunch was served onboard the flight.

'Yes, Your Eminence. I will fetch you your coffee and orange juice. Your breakfast will be with you in about ten minutes.'

Setting the briefcase down beside him, he quickly flicked through the morning papers that were neatly set on the side of his table. Each one carried the main story of the Pope's terminal diagnosis, and three of them carried the moving picture of the dying Pope receiving the red rose from the little girl upon his return to the Vatican.

'Here we are,' the purser said as he stood beside him, placing a silver tray with his coffee and orange juice onto his table. 'Is there anything else Your Eminence would like?' he asked, as he poured him some coffee.

'No, thank you.'

Leaving him alone, the purser went over to the kitchen to place his breakfast order.

Opening the briefcase, Brenard took out the envelope and sat it in front of him. There was no time like the present. As he broke the seal, he looked around the lounge to make sure no one was watching. Confident that no one was taking any interest in him, he took out the pages that were bound together.

On the front was a letter from Malachy. He glanced through it quickly before removing the paper clip that attached it to the bound document. Setting the letter onto the table, he felt sickened to the pit of his stomach when he realised what he was holding in his hands. The title said it all:

ENCYCLICAL LETTER

SOLA FIDE

OF THE SUPREME PONTIFF

CLEMENT XV

TO ALL CHRISTIAN AND NON-BELIEVERS

OF THE WORLD

ON

FAITH ALONE

THE GREAT TRIBULATION

Why are you doing this to me, Malachy? He questioned, before he lifted the letter and began to read it.

In flowing blue script, Malachy had penned his letter on a sheet of lined paper. From the mistakes and crossed out words, it was clear for Brenard to see that he had written it in a hurry.

Paul,

By now I'm sure you've already spoken to Stuart Smith, if not, I think he's a man you should contact. He's currently living at the Irish College.

I've just arrived in Israel, about to undertake a mission given to me by the Holy Father himself. It's complicated to explain everything in a letter, but I trust if you speak to Stuart Smith he'll explain everything to you.

I've enclosed a copy of a Papal Encyclical that I've been working on with His Holiness. The reason I am doing so is, I fear for my life and the truth that this encyclical contains. You must read it carefully, and come to accept the truth of its words for the sake of everyone in the world.

I've been unable to speak to you about the work that I've been doing, but I trust that you'll understand my loyalty to the Holy Father, for whose safety I greatly fear.

For eleven months, I've worked closely with His Holiness and his secretary Monsignor Hasler. Until recently, we've kept the content of our work strictly between ourselves. Several weeks ago, the Holy Father discussed our work with Cardinal Guarducci, and from that moment he's experienced nothing but opposition from him and a group of senior cardinals.

The day before his hospitalisation, His Holiness confided in me that there was a plot to silence him. He entrusted me with the responsibility that should anything happen to him, I should break my vow and publish the truth to the world, a truth Christ himself wants them to hear. In coming to Israel I know that I shall never return, for it is the Lord's will that my blood shall be shed for the truth of His word. They may silence me, and even the Holy Father, but they will never silence the truth.

Pray for me,
Malachy.

Having read the letter, he read it once again before placing it back into his briefcase. In his hand he held the encyclical, the very encyclical Pope Clement had personally told him that he had not written. Then again, despite his loyalty to the Pope he held the same encyclical that Malachy, Stuart Smith and Donal O'Keefe were convinced had been penned by the very man who denied it.

With nothing to lose, he turned to the first page and began to read it for himself.

32.

Three weeks previously.

'If I ask you a question, will you answer me truthfully?'

He said nothing, but waited for the question to be asked.

'Do you think people will believe that I have lost touch with reality?'

'Why do you ask?' he questioned, wondering if he was starting to have second thoughts.

'I have just had a meeting with the prefect cardinals from State and Congregation of Faith.'

'Cardinals Guarducci and Oliveri?'

'Yes. They have presented me with an ultimatum,' Pope Clement confided, as he handed Malachy Devine a written copy of their proposal.

Taking the letter from the Pope, Malachy sat and read it carefully. Like most memos and documents that went around the Vatican it was very legalistic, but one word jumped from the page -ABDICATION!

'Surely, they can't be serious.'

'Unfortunately, they are,' Clement replied, as he calmly walked over to the fire that burned in the corner of his study. 'They are not willing to support the publication of the encyclical. They believe that not only would it be unsettling for the world, but its impact on the Church would be irreversible.'

Lifting some coal with a set of tongs, the Pope placed the coal onto the fire where it cracked in the heat.

'Did you explain everything to them?'

'I did,' Pope Clement replied, as he walked back to his chair and sat back down. His face reflecting the despair and worry that sat heavily on his heart. 'Cardinal Guarducci made it quite clear that he did not accept that I had experienced such a vision. Furthermore, he made it quite clear that if I proceeded with the publication, he would convene the College of Cardinals and seek to have me removed from office.'

'He can't do that!' Devine reassured. 'Your office is for life. Surely, as a cardinal he has no choice but to accept your will and discernment.'

'Cardinal Guarducci has a lot of power,' Clement replied, as he looked deep into Malachy Devine's eyes, allowing him to glimpse his inner pain and frustration.

'Remove him from his office,' Devine advised.

'There would be no point. Even if I removed him from his post as Secretary of State, he would still keep his elected post as Dean of the College of Cardinals. Such a position gives him the authority to convene the College, and if he can persuade them that I am psychologically unfit for the papacy, then they can force my abdication with a two-thirds plus one majority.'

'Surely, that would be impossible!'

'Technically it would not be impossible, but I doubt if Cardinal Guarducci could manage to gather the number of votes he would need. After all, they would have to facilitate and listen to my defence.'

'So, what are you going to do?'

'To make sure that this truth is delivered to the world!' Clement insisted, as he lifted a copy of his encyclical from the coffee table in front of him. 'I have a duty to make this message known, even in the face of men who will stop at nothing to silence it. I do not fear the terror of night, nor the arrow that flies by day, but as a witness to the Lord I know that the price I will be asked to pay will be great.'

'How great?'

'Malachy, my very blood will be shed for the truth. The powers of darkness will stop at nothing to keep the people of this world in their subdued state of existence, where they will fail to question their meaning of life and the purpose behind their creation. You have played my devil's advocate well. Now I am in no doubt that the world is about to enter its final chapter, when everything and everyone will be handed over to the powers of darkness.'

'Surely, there must be a way to persuade Cardinal Guarducci? Perhaps, together we could persuade him to see the truth!'

'Cardinal Guarducci does not have the faith to see the truth,' Clement calmly said. 'Anyway it must be this way and no other.'

'Why?'

'The Lord has shown me everything that will come to pass, and I know that my own future will not be of my choosing. Like Peter himself, a belt will be placed around my waist and I will be taken to a place where I will not want to go. But, it is a place and a future to which I must surrender for the love of the Lord and the calling to which he has ordained me.'

Malachy Devine said nothing. He could only sit and look uncomfortably into the eyes of the Holy Father as he stared intensely at him.

'I have seen the future through the eyes of God himself. I have walked in His shoes and His words have been branded onto my very heart. In a matter of days it will all begin. The Lord will allow Cardinal Guarducci to prevent me from revealing the truth, for it must be so in order for His will to be carried out. Cardinal Guarducci is being used by powers greater than he understands to silence me, but it will only be for a short period of time.'

'How will you be silenced?' Malachy asked in a whisper.

Clement questioned as to whether he should tell him everything, but he knew that he could only reveal so much at any given time.

'The message of truth will be heard Malachy,' he finally said, 'and it will come from my very lips, but the moment I speak the truth I will be martyred for the faith.'

'Surely not, Your Holiness?' Devine defended, 'They'll accept the truth when they hear it.'

'They will accept it as the word of evil!'

'Who will?'

'I will be made to stand before the very Antichrist himself, and I will be forced to deny the vision. Yet, I will not be able to deny the Lord who did not deny me when he was nailed to the cross. I will proclaim the truth before the world,' he said. 'They will listen, but their hearts will have become so hardened and corrupted by the promises offered to them by the Antichrist that they will reject me.'

'Who will reject you?'

'Those who now call me their brother,' Clement confided. 'I will be stripped naked and raised up before them all, in the very same way they crucified our Lord. In the end they will see me as the one who has brought the discontent into the world, and that will be their excuse to silence me. But, the moment the truth is silenced the very gates of hell will be unleashed upon the world. Only those who will accept the truth of the message I have been sent to proclaim will see the face of God and live.'

'How long before all this comes to pass?' Devine asked, fearing that the end was coming sooner than he had expected.

'This time next month, the Lord will have allowed Cardinal Guarducci to move against me, weakening my pontificate to silence the truth, but he will not succeed. The truth will be circulated, and unrest will be felt within the world. Everything that I have seen in the vision will come to pass very quickly.'

'How long?' Devine asked.

'Do not let your heart be troubled with such thoughts,' Clement said, as he reached across and took Devine's hand. 'You must not be afraid. Stay on task with what you must do and go to Israel. You must get the proof for the one who will need it.'

'Who?'

'Your friend from Chicago, Cardinal Brenard.'

'Paul?'

'Last week, when I asked you to tell me of someone that you trusted with your very life, you told me that it was Cardinal Brenard. If they are willing to come after me, then you too must be prepared for them to come after you. If you feel that you can no longer bear the sole burden of keeping this truth alive, then tell Cardinal Brenard everything you know. But you must not do it in person, because it will be a journey that only he can make before coming to accept the very truth for himself.'

Lifting a pen from his desk, Clement turned to the last page of Devine's copy of the encyclical and penned an inscription. When he had finished, he walked over and handed it to Devine.

'Saint Augustine once wrote that the blood of the martyrs is the seed of the Church,' the Pope said, as he stood over him. 'I am willing to shed my blood in witness to the truth. Make sure your copy of the encyclical does not fall into the wrong hands, but makes its way to Cardinal Brenard when the time comes. When he reads it he will understand what he has to do.'

Sitting back into his chair Clement lifted his rosary, closed his eyes and started to pray, leaving Malachy Devine to contemplate a future that was no longer his own.

33.

Shortly before noon, Cardinals Guarducci, Oliveri and Boyer arrived at the communication suite, in the heart of the Apostolic Palace. Having established a secure line with The White House, the young priest who operated the suite left the room, leaving the three cardinals alone. The large screen in front of them remained blue, but the white wording on the top right hand corner, *communication established,* let them know that the American delegation was waiting to address them. Reaching across the table, Guarducci pressed the green button on the control panel, allowing them to see each other. The image of Debra Conway, the President's National Security Advisor appeared in front of them.

'Good Morning, Ms. Conway,' Guarducci said, as he sat back in his chair.

'Good Morning,' she replied. 'The news coverage of the Pope returning to the Vatican looked well. Are you happy with how it's going so far?'

'It went better than we had expected,' Guarducci replied. 'He is resting as we speak!'

'It's good to see that everything is going to plan.'

The three cardinals glanced at each other. It was Guarducci who told her about the meeting the previous day with Cardinal Brenard and the Pope.

'Do you think he believed our side of the story?'

'I think so,' Guarducci confirmed. 'He is already returning home to Chicago.'

'I doubt that,' she replied, as the mask slipped from her face, revealing the worry and the concern that troubled her. 'The President has asked me to discuss with you a matter that concerns us regarding the encyclical.'

As she flicked through her papers they waited.

'In the second half of his encyclical, Pope Clement has written that America would not be part of any future battle regarding the defence of Israel. Can you explain to me why this is so?'

Guarducci invited Oliveri to speak, for he knew that with his doctrinal and scriptural expertise, he was far better placed to answer her question.

'Forgive me, I do not have a copy of the encyclical in front of me,' Oliveri apologised, as he shifted in his chair. 'But, if we were to take the encyclical literally, within the context of scripture, then there is no prophecy to indicate that the United States will be around to defend Israel should it be attacked in some future war.'

She flicked further through her notes.

'The Holy Father mentions that in his vision, and I quote, "America will reap the torture of Satan's bite that will paralyse her for eternity, making her a shadow of her former self." In your meeting with the Holy Father did he elaborate on this aspect of the vision? I ask because our military command structure has just raised its level of operation readiness to DEFCON two, following reliable intelligence that a significant chemical attack on our country is believed to be imminent.'

Oliveri looked at Boyer in disbelief before they turned to look at Guarducci. They both knew what the Pope had told them, but neither of them had believed him. Now, it appeared that what the Pope had predicted was beginning to unfold right before their eyes.

'Can you tell me again what the Pope saw in his vision?' she asked.

Clearing his throat, Oliveri started to tell her the exact details. 'In the vision the Holy Father had, he was told that before an attack on Israel could take place, its great defender, namely the United States, would be weakened in a blink of an eye.'

'By what exactly?'

'A plague the likes of which the world has never seen, orchestrated by both terrorists and a foreign government on American soil, critically damaging its political, economic and military capabilities.'

'Did he say by whom?' she asked, as she penned notes.

'His Holiness believed that,' Oliveri continued, before pausing to carefully consider his words. 'According to the prophecies in the Book of Revelation, there will be a period of time, seven years exactly, in which the world will be ruled by forces of evil. It will be governed by the man referred to as the Antichrist. He will begin his rule by uniting the world into a false sense of peace, but that can only happen after nearly a third of the world is lost as a result of a conflict so great, that it will shake humanity to the very core. What we are talking about here are the infamous Four Horsemen of the Apocalypse. Each one will be released upon the world in the build up to this seven year period known as the Great Tribulation. The first Horseman is believed to be the Antichrist, the second is a powerful military leader, the third will be the destroyer of security and economy, and the fourth will bring instant death to many. Pope Clement believed that the first three Horsemen had already arrived. He believed that the Antichrist is here but has yet to reveal himself. He believed somewhere in the world that there is a ruler of great military might who would support the position of the Antichrist and his rule. As for the third Horseman, well His Holiness was convinced that the world economy is literally on the brink of collapse. All we need now is a trigger for the fourth Horseman who would ignite the war, which would see the deaths of at least one-third of the world's population. This would trigger the security of the world to collapse, especially the economy for those who survived, and it would pave the way for the Antichrist to reveal himself with the support of a great military power. Pope Clement was in no doubt, this initial conflict would centre on the United States, which would be attacked by the Islamic States and then by Russia.'

Conway paused for a moment to clearly consider her position before she replied.

'Several days ago, a senior member of the Caliph's Council in Baghdad defected to the United States. He has informed us of a plan, orchestrated by the Caliph himself to release the chemical agent VX in four major cities here in the United States,' Conway confided. 'We believe that these weapons were smuggled across our borders from Canada some weeks ago after being shipped from Europe. At this moment in time, we have no idea who has these weapons or where they even are. We are expecting attacks in New York, Los Angeles, Dallas and here in the heart of Washington DC.'

'Surely they can be stopped?' Boyer asked.

'All they need to do is place the chemical agent into the trunks of four cars, drive them into the middle of each city and release them. Our security analysts believe that the Islamic States have produced such a large quantity of VX that its release would dwarf a nuclear attack. Any such attack would result in an incalculable loss of life. We're talking about tens of millions.' She said, as she joined her hands and placed them under her chin. 'Plus, we have another major concern. Military satellites have also recorded large scale military movement in Russia as well.'

'What kind of military movement?'

'A large military buildup of Russian troops, in the tens of thousands, is being deployed just north of the borders of Georgia and Azerbaijan. High resolution photographs have also revealed that along these borders, they've stationed mobile long range BM-25 surface-to-surface missiles, capable of reaching Israel and capable of carrying nuclear warheads.'

Placing the palms of his hands over his face, Oliveri covered his look of concern as his heart sank into despair.

'Your Eminences, our military sources are convinced that a collaborative strike between the Islamic States and Russia is being orchestrated against our nation. I don't need to spell it out to you that the implications of such an attack, if it took place, would have a great effect on the future security of the world!'

Unable to speak, Guarducci stood up and walked over to pour himself a glass of water.

'What is your government's plan?' Oliveri asked.

'We are evacuating all branches of government from the capital.' She replied. 'We are considering every option that we have, but in the end the President has a moral obligation to protect and defend the people of the United States. She will have no choice but to retaliate if a chemical attack is made against the American people. Military calculations for this conflict could see an ultimate death toll of between one and two billion people.'

Sitting back down, Guarducci looked at the other two cardinals, and he could see that they were greatly unsettled. No doubt they now realised their mistake, and realised there was no turning back on the path they had taken.

'In a matter of hours the President will address the American people, informing them of the imminent threat we all face. She's also going to sign an executive order, imposing military curfew on all major cities, towns and ports taking immediate effect. She will also be suspending all trade on the stock exchange. All flights within, to and from the United States will be grounded. Our borders will be closed. The Military forces, the National Guard and the police will be given unrestricted warrants to search and locate the terrorist cells who have this deadly chemical agent. As we speak, the Secretary General of the United Nations is being instructed to convene an emergency meeting of the Security Council outside New York, which the President will address, in person, tonight. Our efforts to resolve this through a diplomatic solution will continue right to the end, but we need to be prepared. I'm sure you'll understand, as the President, she can't rule any military response off the table.'

'We respect you for consulting us,' Guarducci finally spoke up. 'For the next few days you will be very much in our prayers.'

Conway smiled. 'Prayer? It'll take a direct Divine intervention to see this one through safely. It looks like we were wrong to underestimate the warning that was given to us by Pope Clement.'

Her words summed up how Oliveri and Boyer were now feeling.

'Thank you for taking the time gentlemen,' she replied, as she gathered her papers in front of her. 'I now have to go and brief the President.'

'We wish you every success,' Guarducci said, before he reached over and switched off the secure line to The White House situation room.

'What have we done?' Oliveri said, as he looked at the other two Cardinals.

'Maybe we should release the encyclical after the President makes her address to the United Nations Security Council,' Boyer argued. 'What's happening in America is exactly what His Holiness predicted would happen!'

'It is too late!' Guarducci said. 'We need to remain calm.'

'But you heard her,' Oliveri insisted. 'An attack like we believed could never happen is about to take place!'

'And what good would releasing the encyclical do the world now? What good would it ever have done?' Guarducci asked, raising his voice to show the unrest he was now feeling. 'If this does happen it could take place a lot sooner than we could ever have anticipated.'

'And you know why that is?' Oliveri said, cutting him short. 'It is because we failed to take heed of the warning. Now that we have all but silenced the will of God, we are about to experience His wrath like it has never been experienced before.'

'We took our decision in the best interests of the Church,' Guarducci snapped, 'and we cannot go back now.'

'Why not?' Oliveri replied. 'We could bypass the College of Cardinals and release the encyclical to the world's media.'

'And how do we explain to them the truth of what we have done?' Guarducci asked.

'They will understand,' Oliveri said, knowing he sounded hollow.

'Are you being serious? They would never forgive our betrayal. We need to stay united and know that if this does happen, then we will do our sacred duty and guide the world through the aftermath and into a future that will need us all the more.'

Getting up from his seat Guarducci walked across the room, and stood below the portrait of Pope Clement that hung on the wall behind his empty chair. With his back to the cardinals he looked deep into the oil painted eyes of the Pope who appeared to be looking back at him and into his very soul. Guarducci smiled. He had set out to silence the truth, and so far he had succeeded. All he had to do was to let time take care of the imminent future, before he would be revealed for who he really was.

34.

With a nervous tremor in his hands he read one page of the encyclical after another; his mind flooded with trepidation with the power of each and every word.

True to all Stuart Smith had said, the first part of the encyclical dealt with the twenty biblical prophesies and an outline of the visions Pope Clement allegedly received at Castel Gandolfo.

Could this be true? He repeatedly questioned himself as he read, startled by the language and familiar style attributed to Pope Clement in the encyclical's structure.

Half-way through the encyclical, he began to read an outline of predicted future events that would take place within the world before the second coming of Jesus Christ. The language was indeed apocalyptic. The visions graphically depicted Pope Clement being shown the downfall of America; an event that would spark a world nuclear war and an attack on Israel. The encyclical gave a detailed account surrounding the rise of the unnamed Antichrist, his formation of a one world government right through to his dividing the people of the world with his mark. While images of earthquakes, famines, diseases, plagues, meteors, contamination, pollution, worldwide wars, sporadic murders and the final great persecution of all Christians were written with haunting clarity. He could now see how powerful, and potentially dangerous, the document was to read.

Coming to the end he read the plea, allegedly from Pope Clement himself, for the world to repent and to turn back to Christ before it became too late for their souls to be saved.

Turning to the last page, he skipped the last few typed lines when he noticed a handwritten message at the bottom of the page.

These things are being fulfilled today, even as you read them. Listen to Him!

Clemente PP XV

A quote from Luke's Gospel? Brenard questioned, finding the penned words similar to those spoken by Christ himself when he first preached at the synagogue in Nazareth. *Who is Him?* He wondered, before questioning the very authenticity of the encyclical once again.

Suddenly, his attention was drawn to a growing commotion of noise within the lounge. As he looked up from the encyclical to see what was going on, he noticed other passengers walking towards the bar as the purser turned up the volume on the television. The closer he looked at the screen, it soon dawned on him that something major was happening back home. Placing the encyclical back into his briefcase, he got up from his seat to see what was being reported.

On CNN, a reporter was speaking live from the dawn lit lawn of The White House, while on the second half of the screen, live pictures of grounded planes at JFK were being streamed. The reporter kept using words and phrases like, *shutdown, emergency security measures, restricted airspace, heightened security level* and *terrorist plots.* Brenard looked on in horror as he read the words printed in bold on the bottom of the screen – US AIRSPACE SHUTDOWN - SUSPECTED TERRORIST PLOT. PRESIDENT TO ADDRESS NATION.

'That's the first time they've grounded all aircraft since nine-eleven,' one of the passengers said, when he saw Brenard join him. 'Doesn't look like we're going to be leaving Rome for a while!'

'What's happened?' Brenard asked, still not too clear with the details behind the story.

'The President has ordered the entire airspace across the States to be shutdown,' the purser replied, giving Brenard the little information he had. 'She has grounded all domestic flights and all international planes crossing the Atlantic and the Pacific are being instructed to either return to their country of departure or are being diverted.'

'Has there been a terrorist attack?'

'No! But, they're reporting that the President, her Cabinet and most of the Government have been moved overnight to secure locations.'

'Why?'

'I don't know!' The purser said, as he watched the television in disbelief. 'It looks bad!'

Returning to his table, Brenard reached into his briefcase and lifted out his cellphone. Through his contacts, he searched for the Papal Nuncio in Washington.

He selected the number. It took a few seconds, but eventually it rang.

'The Papal Nunciature,' the softly spoken voice at the other end answered.

'This is Cardinal Paul Brenard, I'm calling from Rome. Would you please put me onto His Excellency.'

'Your Eminence, I am afraid he is in a meeting with some government officials and does not want to be disturbed.'

'Father, I want you to listen to me. As a cardinal I want you to get me the archbishop, right away!' Brenard demanded in frustration.

'Yes, Your Eminence,' he promptly obliged.

Brenard could hear the young priest as he ran from his office and opened the doors to fetch the Nuncio.

Why is he having a meeting with government officials at six in the morning? Brenard wondered, as he calculated that the East Coast was six hours behind Rome time.

'Hello?'

'Francisco, it's Paul Brenard, can you speak?'

'I will ring you back!' The nuncio replied, before he hung up.

What's he at? Brenard questioned, as the call was terminated.

Less than a minute later his cellphone started ringing.

'Francisco?'

'Yes,' the nuncio replied. 'Forgive me, I had to return the call to make sure it was you.'

'I'm in Rome at the moment, what's happening back home? I've just been informed that the airspace has been shut down.'

'It is not something we should discuss over the phone, Paul,' he insisted, knowing that the line was not secure.

'I'm in a meeting with the Vatican's Secretary of State,' Brenard lied. 'He asked me to ring you to see if you know what is going on.'

'It is very grave, Paul,' the nuncio confided. 'There is a great chance that there could be a serious chemical attack on the States within a matter of days if not hours. The President is about to address the nation. Although it has not been reported, she is also closing the borders and an operation is underway to locate chemical weapons that have been smuggled into the country. Apparently, they are in the hands of terrorists loyal to the Islamic States. The President has already left Washington this morning on Air Force One. As far as I am aware, the Vice-President, and other members of the government are being transferred to military bunkers.'

'Sweet, Mother of God!' Brenard uttered, in stunned disbelief.

'That is really all I know,' the nuncio insisted. 'I should get back to this meeting, they are wanting the Church to use its influence in whatever way it can.'

'Thanks. Take care and God bless, Francisco,' Brenard replied, as he switched off his cellphone.

Sitting back into his seat he lifted his briefcase, took out the encyclical and began to flick through the pages until he found the passage he wanted to read again.

The Great Nation of the West will be destroyed by a hand which will strike with famine and pestilence. From the East and the West, from both the sky and ground they will attack. A holocaust unseen in human history will be waged unto the nation, removing the strength of its power.

Like a scorpion she will strike down those who have wounded her, an act of revenge that will bring the world to its knees. With her strength she will smite them, but never from her wounds will she heal.

The Gates of Hell will be opened, and the world will shake with fear as the power of evil will torment every land. While fire spills into the sky and blood runs into the sea, the people will cry out, Lord why have you forsaken us? Still, they will only have touched the beginning of their Great Tribulation, because the fall of such a great nation will bring forth evil's darkest abomination.

With nowhere to go and with his mind in turmoil, he knew he had only one real choice open to him. Taking his cellphone from his pocket, he searched the internet for the offices of the archbishop of Munich. Finding a contact he selected the number. After a few seconds he heard the ringing tone.

'Guten tag, das buro des erzbischofs,' the man who answered the phone said.

'Sprechen Sie Englisch?'

'Of course!' The voice replied. 'How may I help you?'

'This is His Eminence, Cardinal Paul Brenard calling, I would like to speak to His Excellency, Archbishop Küng please.'

'I will contact him for you now,' the man replied. 'Just a few moments.'

Brenard quickly realised it was highly likely that the archbishop would not disclose Hasler's whereabouts if Guarducci had already instructed him not too. He had to think quickly.

'Hallo?'

'Hello, this is Cardinal Paul Brenard, am I speaking to Archbishop Küng?' he asked, hoping that the archbishop was as good at speaking English as his secretary.

'This is Archbishop Küng, how may I help you, Your Eminence?'

'Archbishop, I've been assigned by His Holiness to investigate Father Gustave Hasler's recent scandals.' Brenard said, hoping his excuse would work.

'This is quick. I never thought it would be possible for the Vatican to investigate him so soon.' Küng replied. 'But, I should prepare you that Gustave is still protesting his innocence over the whole affair, even his criminal conviction.'

'That is often the way in a case such as this, but over time when the shock of being caught wears off and the reality of their wrong settles into their conscience, these men often talk quite openly.'

'I hope so. I would hate to see his life ruined by the denial.'

'Do you have a contact address for Father Hasler?' Brenard said, as he took a pen from his jacket pocket and lifted a napkin from the table. 'I need to draw up a report file before I fully begin the investigation.'

'Ja, sollte ich... I am sorry,' the archbishop said. 'Just give me one moment.'

As he waited, Brenard could hear Küng flick through the pages of his directory, looking for the address.

'Here it is,' he finally said. 'He is under the care of the Abbot of Hauterive Abbey, Fribourg, Switzerland.'

'Great,' Brenard replied, as he wrote the address onto the napkin, not quite believing that it had been so freely given by the Archbishop.

'Would you like the telephone number for the abbey?' Küng asked, knowing that it would be useful for the file.

'Yes, please,' Brenard replied, as he folded the napkin and slipped it into his pocket, not having any real use for the number. 'You've been most kind, thank you. Auf Wiedersehen.'

'Auf Wiedersehen.'

He hung up. He had what he needed. Even though he had no idea where the abbey was, he knew he had to get there before the end of the day. So, lifting his briefcase, he made his way over to the bar.

'I need your help!' Brenard said, to the purser. 'Would you be able to rent me a car?'

'That should be no problem.'

35.

Every bone in his body ached, but still he waited for them all to leave. Even in his ninetieth year, nothing could deter him from serving his community and the Lord he had served all his life.

'Good night, Hans,' the last monk said, as he went to leave the choir stalls. 'Do you need any help?'

'You are most kind Brother Basil, but I will be fine to serve the Lord this night.'

Understanding his desire, Basil smiled and walked on. Blessing himself with the holy water, he genuflected and left Hans sitting alone in the choir stalls.

Gripping the elbow rest of the stall in front of him, he pulled himself up; gritting his teeth to dull the pain in his hips that rubbed like burning embers as he moved. There was nothing he could do but offer it up for the Lord.

Hopefully, it will shorten my time in purgatory, he humoured with his Lord.

As he walked up the aisle, he began the same routine he had carried out for over sixty-five years. Sickness nor old age, had never hindered him. Walking up to the altar, he bowed before the Blessed Sacrament, before walking over and locking the tabernacle in which it was contained. Then blowing out the four candles that had been lit for night prayer, he took a red velvet cloth and covered the surface of the altar. The day in the abbey had now ended.

Walking away from the sanctuary, he shuffled down the aisle until he reached the main door. Placing his arthritic fingers onto the light switches, he started to push them; turning off one light after another until the chapel was engulfed in darkness. In the silence of the moment he paused, just like he did every night, alone with his thoughts and with his faith. Then stirring into the silence of the night, he uttered the words he truly felt in his heart. 'I love you.'

Lastly, he flicked the final switch. High in the rafters, a spotlight shone straight down unto the altar, making it the focal point for any of the monks who happened to visit the chapel during the night.

Closing the chapel door behind him, he slipped into the dark cloister. Ignoring the agonising pain of his hips as he walked, he kept his eyes focussed on the eerie red lantern that hung from the ceiling at the turn in the cloister.

It had been an unsettling two days in the abbey since the arrival of the new priest. Instead of maintaining an air of secrecy and respectability surrounding the priest's arrival, the abbot had gone out of his way to make sure everyone in the community knew exactly what he had done in Rome. Yet, the moment the young priest arrived at the abbey, Hans knew that he was the one he had been shown in his dreams; the one close to God's own heart. He was special. A chosen one. One who was destined to be persecuted for the truth.

Arriving at the main archway doors, he undid the bolts and opened them. The rain fell heavily and the wind rushed through the courtyard. Still, it did not deter him. Gripping his rosary, he walked through the pelting rain and headed straight for the main gate of the abbey. The thunder cracked in the sky, and the lightning lit up the ivy covered buildings and walls of the inner courtyard.

Reaching the main door, he opened the spy box and looked through it and onto the street. There he was. In that split instant the lightning illuminated everything around him. Just like he had seen in his dreams, the man had arrived like a thief in the night.

Lifting his keys, he unlocked the main abbey door and opened it.

When he looked into the traveller's eyes, every detail of his dreams became alive in that very moment. Reaching out, he took hold of the traveller's hand and kissed it with deep respect.

'I have been expecting you!' Hans said, as he brought the stranger into the shelter of the abbey. 'This very night, I knew that you would come.'

Soaked through to the skin, it was not the reception that Cardinal Brenard had been expecting.

'I'm Cardinal Paul Brenard, I would like to speak with the abbot.'

'I know who you are.' Brother Hans smiled. 'Come, follow me.'

36.

'What happened to you?' Abbot Karl inquired, when he opened his study door to see the old monk standing before him, his habit soaked from the rain.

'Look, he is coming on the clouds, and everyone will see him, even those who killed him; and all the earth will mourn because of him. So shall it be! Amen. "I am the Alpha and the Omega," says the Lord God, "who is, and who was, and who is to come, the Almighty." He is coming!'

In the dark of the night, the abbot felt an unholy fear creep through his body as he listened to Hans. It was not like him. As the old monk spoke, the abbot sensed he was looking right through him and into a different realm of certitude.

Suddenly, the lightning flashed, and through the large stain glass windows of the cloister the abbot could see the figure of the man standing behind Hans. He was startled to see his dishevelled appearance.

'And then the lawless one will be revealed, whom the Lord Jesus will overthrow with the breath of his mouth and destroy by the splendour of his coming.' Hans said, before he walked over and gripped the abbot's arms tightly. 'Do not be afraid, Karl. In our very midst we shelter the one who will reveal the truth to the nations.'

'Hans, who is this man?'

'The one who will set the truth free!'

As he stood behind the old monk, Cardinal Paul Brenard was startled to hear the words that were coming from his mouth. With no doubt, he knew that the old man knew everything about him and what was to come.

'Stranger, do you have a name?' the abbot asked.

'I am His Eminence, Cardinal Paul Brenard from Chicago.'

'Pardon me?' the abbot asked, as he peered out from the warmth and light of his room into the darkened cloister.

'I need to speak with you.' Brenard replied. 'May I come in?'

The abbot stood to one side.

'Hold fast to the truth,' Brother Hans said, grabbing Brenard's elbow as he passed him. 'Doubt no more, but believe. For the hour is close at hand.'

'How do you know this?' Brenard asked.

'The Spirit that sent you, revealed it to me,' Hans replied. 'Whatever happens to you, you must not be afraid!'

Having said what he needed to say, Hans turned and walked away.

'Please excuse Brother Hans,' the abbot apologised, as Brenard walked into his study. 'He is a very old man and the curse of an ageing mind is taking hold of him.'

For a few moments, silence lingered in the room as Brenard walked over to the open fire to warm himself.

'I have come to speak with Monsignor Gustave Hasler.' Brenard finally spoke.

'I have been given strict orders from both the Vatican and the archbishop of Munich that no one from outside this abbey is to have contact with Brother Hasler.'

'I take it you have heard what is happening in the United States?'

'I have watched the news.'

'Then trust me when I say that this relates to work Monsignor Hasler was closely involved with,' Brenard said, as he walked closer to the desk. 'I have been sent here as a Papal Envoy to question Monsignor Hasler, and if necessary bring him back to Rome. Now, please go and get Monsignor Hasler.'

Abbot Karl knew he had no choice, as he deliberately hesitated and looked at Brenard. For a man who had ruled his abbey without question or accountability, he was infuriated that he was being ordered by an outsider, who had the rank and the authority to demand from him whatever he wanted.

'I will go and get him for you,' he finally agreed.

'I've been driving for close to twelve hours,' Brenard said, as he turned to follow the abbot. 'I'd appreciate it if you could give me a guest room for the night where I can freshen up before talking to Monsignor Hasler.'

'Follow me,' the abbot replied, as he lifted a bunch of keys from the hook beside his door.

They did not have far to walk. Two doors from the abbot's study, there was a guest room. Taking his keys, he opened the door and allowed the cardinal to enter.

The room felt warm and it looked comfortable, and for those small mercies Brenard was thankful. Yet, after his journey that day, he would have willingly slept on the stone floor of a monk's cell if that was all the abbot had to offer.

'In the wardrobe you will find all that you will need for the night; towels, night gowns and toiletries. There is also a shower room and a lavatory through that far door.'

'Thank you,' Brenard replied, as he moved a wooden chair close to the radiator. 'If you wouldn't mind giving me a few minutes to shower and dry before sending for Monsignor Hasler, that would be greatly appreciated.'

'I will do that,' the abbot replied. 'If there is anything else you need, you know where to find me.'

Exhausted, Brenard removed his clothes and placed them over the back of the chair to dry. Then stepping into the shower, he relaxed as the hot water sprayed onto his body; killing his tiredness and the ache in his muscles.

Reaching out for the tap, he turned it to increase the water pressure. Suddenly, he saw a bright white light and he felt himself being forced down onto the shower tray. His head thumping with such a pain that he thought it was going to explode. Grabbing his head with both hands he cried out.

He woke up.

Someone was knocking on the door.

'Your Eminence, are you alright?' The abbot shouted, as he knocked on the door. 'Do you need help?'

'Just give me a minute!' Brenard called out in reply, as he struggled to pull himself back up onto his feet.

Lifting a towel, he wrapped it around his body before walking over to the sink. His heart was pounding in his chest with the fright of what had just happened. With his right hand he wiped away the condensation on the mirror.

He remembered. He had seen it with his own eyes. Standing before the masses of the world, he saw the silhouette of a bishop. The masses of the world called out to him; *Man of Peace, Man of Love, Prince of the Earth* and *Ruler of Kings.* He grew in strength with their praise, before he turned on them with fire that came from his eyes and the sword of death he carried in his right hand. No one was safe from the might of his wrath, for in his hands he controlled the very power of evil itself.

37.

'Your Eminence, Brother Hasler is here!' The abbot said, from the other side of the shower room door.

'I'll be out in a few minutes,' Brenard replied, as he unwrapped the towel from his waist and began to dry himself.

The vision repeated itself over and over again in his head, as the image of the unknown man tormented his very soul. Nothing like that moment had ever happened before in his life. Yet, in that moment he knew he had been shown something important, something that he was meant to see, even though he did not understand the significance of what it meant. Convinced there was a conspiracy within the Vatican to stop the encyclical, but unsure why the Pope had denied writing it, he knew he had to remain calm, focused and open minded as he sought the answers from Gustave Hasler.

Having dried himself he lifted a night gown and slipped it on, before putting on a dressing robe to make himself feel more modest. Then opening the shower room door, he walked into his room. When he saw Hasler he was shocked at how wretched he looked. The grey habit looked about as comfortable as a hair shirt. His hair was tousled and his eyes were bloodshot like those of a tortured soul. Brenard gave the abbot a look of disgust.

'I would like to be alone with Fr. Hasler,' Brenard said, as he closed the bathroom door behind him.

The tears which had never left Hasler's eyes began to flow once more.

Despite his hesitation to leave Hasler alone with the cardinal, the abbot knew he had no control of the situation. So, he quietly took his leave from them both, hoping that he would be spared the humiliation of the cardinal discovering the truth that he had treated Hasler with the utmost contempt.

'Gustave!' Brenard said, as he walked over and embraced him.

Hasler held Brenard tight. From his embrace, he felt the humanity and acceptance he had longed for since his dismissal.

Brenard could feel the coarseness of the habit, and not wanting Hasler to suffer the indignity any longer, he went over and opened the wardrobe. There were several sets of linen night gowns and cotton dressing robes. Lifting a pair, he told Hasler to go into the shower room and change into them.

While Hasler changed out of his habit, Brenard lifted two cups from beside the kettle and placed them on the reading table beside his bed. Sitting on the edge of his bed he lifted up his briefcase and took out the encyclical and a bottle of Rioja he had purchased from a service station on the Italian-Swiss border. He filled the cups, one for Hasler and one for himself, and then set the remainder of the wine onto the reading table for later. Sitting back he opened the encyclical and started to read through it again.

'Where did you get that?' Hasler asked, surprising Brenard as he walked back into the room.

'Father Malachy Devine sent it to me from Israel,' he replied, as he handed Hasler a cup of wine. 'Please, sit down. I've come here to talk to you about this very thing.'

Hasler sipped the wine and calmly took up Brenard's offer as he sat beside him on the bed.

'Did you know Stuart Smith?' Brenard asked.

Hasler swallowed a mouthful of wine. 'I knew him.'

'He was murdered two days ago.'

Hasler was not surprised by the news, for he knew that those behind the conspiracy would stop at nothing in seeing those who knew the truth from being silenced. Taking another sip of wine he looked at Brenard, 'Why are you here?'

'To find the truth.'

'For Cardinal Guarducci?'

Brenard shook his head.

'I was travelling home to Chicago this morning when I received this encyclical in the post.'

'So, why come here?' Hasler questioned, not fully convinced of Brenard's motives. 'After all, I am now the official black sheep of the fold.'

'Until this morning I was convinced you were too, especially after the Holy Father himself dismissed you as part of a conspiracy to write a fraudulent encyclical in his name.'

'He did what?' Hasler asked in shook. 'Why would he say that?'

'I'm convinced he's being very tightly controlled by Cardinal Guarducci and several other Cardinals.' Brenard confessed.

'Oliveri and Boyer?' Hasler asked.

Brenard nodded, as the feeling of betrayal upon hearing Boyer's name swelled once again inside him.

Placing his cup of wine onto the floor, Hasler lowered his head and closed his eyes, hoping for some sign, no matter how small, to show him that he could trust Brenard.

'What's the problem?' Brenard asked.

'I do not know who to trust!' Hasler honestly replied.

'Do you think I'm here to get information for Guarducci?'

Hasler's silence spoke volumes.

'I understand. I feel the same,' Brenard reassured. 'I still don't know who to fully believe and who to doubt. But, something is happening that's leading me to believe that this encyclical was authentically written by the Holy Father himself.'

Getting up from his chair, Brenard walked over to the small television that was mounted on the wall opposite his bed. He turned it on. He did not have to search for the news channels, because every station he flicked through was covering the story live.

'This is what I mean.'

Stepping back from the screen, he allowed Gustave Hasler to see the rolling news of the terrorist hunt in the United States, President Cleary's address to the nation and the emergency convening of the UN Security Council onboard the USS Gerald R. Ford Aircraft Carrier, which was currently stationed somewhere off the East Coast of the United States.

'That's why I'm here,' Brenard said, as he walked back and lifted his copy of the encyclical. 'This has got to be more than just a coincidence.'

'Where do you want me to start?' Hasler asked, as he turned away from the television, knowing the time had come.

'The beginning.'

38.

The wheels of Air Force One screeched as they touched down on the runway of Rawlins' Air Force Base.

Safe on the ground, the Colonel engaged the four CF6 thrusters to slow her down, before allowing her to gracefully run the full length of the runway. Then with military precision, he turned the aircraft and travelled along the designated taxiway towards the hangar that would hide her in mountainous Wyoming.

'Are you sure you still want to do this?' Tom Donahue asked. 'It's not as if he's going to tell you something we don't already know.'

'I need to see him face to face,' The President replied, as she placed her briefing papers into the top drawer of her desk. 'Maybe then, he'll be willing to tell us a little more.'

'I still think this is a bad idea.' He said, still not understanding why she was so adamant to visit Rawlins and to meet with the one man they should have killed when they had the opportunity. In less than four hours she had to address the United Nations Security Council, and Donahue knew that this was a distraction she did not need.

'This might well prove to be a waste of a trip, but it's better giving it a try than flying around in circles waiting for something to happen.'

Donahue had lost the argument with her not to land Air Force One until they were in Virginia, and ready to be transported on Marine One to the USS Gerald R. Ford for the meeting of the Security Council. Having been given a direct order, he had no choice but to obey her as the Commander In Chief on the eve of potential war.

'Who knows that he's here?'

'Very few people know that we've brought him into the country; yourself, the Director of the CIA and two of her operatives, Debra Conway, the Joint Chiefs, the General in charge of this base and myself.'

'How can the General keep this a secret from the rest of his men?' the President questioned, still not believing that they had managed to keep his very presence in the base a secret.

'He's being held in solitary confinement deep within the bunker. He's being treated like any other terrorist suspect. No one has direct contact with him except the General.'

'Well, shall we get this over and done with?' The President asked, noticing that her aircraft had come to a stop inside the hangar.

Leaving the presidential suite, they descended the stairs to the lower level of Air Force One, and made their way to the fixed access door on the undercarriage of the plane. By the time they arrived, a young military officer was lowering the steps. Then standing aside, the officer saluted the President as she passed.

There was no customary reception party waiting to greet her as her personal security was at code red. Looking around the hangar as she descended the steps, President Cleary noticed the marksmen who had their guns trained on everyone who was within close proximity to her. After being greeted by General Durkin, she walked alongside him as they crossed the tarmac and made their way towards an opened elevator door on the far side of the hanger.

The sheer vastness of the military base became apparent to the President once the elevator brought her below ground.

'Madam President, if you'd like to follow me,' the General invited, once they stepped out of the lift.

Replacing her regular fleet of armoured black cars, the General had lined up a convoy of military styled gulf buggies. Climbing into the back of one of buggies with her Chief of Staff, the President was driven by the General himself, while the rest of the secret service detail followed in the other buggies that were provided for them.

Driving through the underworld of streets and military warehouses, they travelled along a road so long that the lights on the ceiling tapered off into the distance.

'General, how big is this place?' the President asked.

'It's the biggest bunker we currently have in operation,' the General explained. 'Where we're heading to is about a further three hundred feet below ground. There's enough room down there to keep yourself, your Cabinet and members of the Senate, along with their families for up to six months.'

'Are any members of the Cabinet or the Senate here now?'

'No. They are currently in different military bases across the country,' The General answered. 'Although it looks empty now, we can have this facility fully operational within twenty-four hours. At full operational capacity, we can also house up to ten thousand military personnel to protect the base and the government, should the need arise.'

'That's good to know,' The President replied. 'We might be needing this facility sooner than any of us could have predicted.'

Moments later, the General steered their buggy off the main road and drove towards a heavily guarded entrance to what looked like a tunnel. But the closer they got, the President and Donahue realised that it was a fortified entrance to one of many similar government bunkers. Stopping alongside the entrance they followed the General's instructions, got out of the buggy and followed him through the open blast doors and towards an opened elevator door.

Once they were inside, the doors to the elevator closed as the General placed his key into the security lock and turned it; releasing the number pad from behind the glass screen. He typed in his code. Immediately the descent of the lift could be felt as it made its way into the bowels of the bunker.

'The lift's the worst part,' the General reassured her. 'The bunker is so well equipped it's like being inside a purpose built office block.'

With a sudden change in air pressure, their ears popped as the lift gradually slowed as it reached the base of the shaft. When the doors opened, the bright neon-lights forced them to squint their eyes for a few moments while they adjusted to their new surroundings.

Stepping out from the lift, the secret service detail approached another manned door, but only the General,

Donahue and the President were allowed beyond that point, while the secret service detail had to remain behind.

Once inside, the final blast door began to close behind them; sealing them into one of the most secure environments on earth.

Walking a short distance, the General stopped beside a solid metal door.

'This is where he is being held,' the General said. 'Would you like us to accompany you?'

'That won't be necessary,' the President replied. 'He won't cause me any harm.'

'The wheels are going up in thirty minutes,' Donahue reminded her, knowing that she could easily lose track of time once in the room.

Entering yet another code, the General pushed the door open once the light above it turned green.

Stepping into the room the President looked at the man who stood in front of her wearing an orange jumpsuit. Their eyes locked.

'Why are you here?' The man asked.

'I've come to see if there is a way we can stop this country from being wiped off the face of this earth.'

'It is too late for that.' The man replied, as he walked towards her. 'Do the right thing and let me go!'

39.

The news of an imminent attack on the United States awakened in Hasler an urgent sense of duty and responsibility to the promise he had made. 'I am convinced there are dark forces beyond the Vatican at work, governments, people, establishments who have greater power.'

'Who?'

'I do not know for sure, but a few rogue Cardinals from the Vatican's Curia simply would not have the ability to silence this on their own.'

'Is it true what they are saying about you in the press?'

Hasler lifted his cup of wine and took another sip. He shook his head. 'Of course it is not true. I was set up by your good friend Cardinal Boyer.'

Brenard sighed his discontent upon hearing the name again. 'What did he do?'

'While on administrative leave during Pope Clement's hospitalisation, I was invited by Cardinal Boyer to join him for lunch. Knowing that I had little to do with my time, except wait for the Pope to return to the Vatican, Cardinal Boyer asked me to meet with a student from the American College who was questioning his calling and was about to leave. Boyer wanted me to talk to him and reassure him that every student for the priesthood experiences doubt at some point in their training.'

'Did that not sound like an unusual request?'

'It did.' Hasler agreed. 'But, what was I meant to do when asked by a senior cardinal?'

'Do you remember his name?'

'I think he was called James.'

'Did you meet up with him?'

'Cardinal Boyer gave him my cell number. It was less than an hour after our lunch before the student rang me. We arranged to have dinner later that night as no other date suited him.'

'What happened?'

'All I can remember about that night is travelling to the restaurant, sharing a bottle of white wine and briefly waking up in the back of a car as I was being driven through Rome.'

'Were you drugged?'

'More than likely,' Hasler admitted, sitting further back on the bed as he tried to recall other details. 'The next thing I remember for sure, is waking up in my apartment the following morning and discovering that someone had sold a story to the Italian press.'

Brenard did not doubt him for a moment, but some things still did not add up.

'What about the pictures?'

'Whatever happened that night, I know for certain that someone brought me back to my apartment, there they stripped me of my clothes and staged the pictures. There is no other time those pictures could have been taken.'

'Do you remember what this student looked like?'

'I cannot remember.' Hasler said in frustration. 'He is just a blur in my memory. Anyway, I doubt he was ever a student in the first place. He knew exactly what he was doing and what he was looking for.' Hasler explained, as he poured himself and Brenard some more wine. 'He was sent by someone to find my copy of the encyclical and he found it. I am convinced, that whoever instructed him wanted me silenced too. I knew too much, and for the likes of Guarducci and Boyer I was too much of a walking liability to their plans.'

'What do you think their plans are?'

'To silence the Holy Father and discredit the vision he had received.' Hasler replied. 'They thought he had gone insane. But, I was there, I saw him experience that vision and I know that his experience was genuine and real.'

'Is this the vision the Holy Father experienced during his retreat in Castel Gandolfo?'

'I take it Stuart Smith has told you about them?'

'Not at any great length. What exactly happened?'

'Last year, after celebrating Easter Sunday Mass in St. Peter's Square, the Holy Father was taken by helicopter to his retreat in Castel Gandolfo. Upon arrival we had lunch together, and to celebrate the solemnity of the day we had a glass of wine with our meal. Afterwards the Holy Father retired for his daily riposo. We had planned to take a walk together in the evening as the weather was quite pleasant, but when I went to wake him he was not in his room. He had gone to his private chapel. Not wanting to disturb him in his time of prayer, I sat a few rows behind him and waited for him to finish. I ended up sitting there for over three hours, and throughout that whole time he knelt upright and looked up into the crucifix that hung above the altar. He never moved or flinched once. It was as if a momentary gaze had been stretched over several hours, and nothing could have snapped him out of it.'

'What happened when it finished?'

'He sat back in his chair and started to cry. I went over to see if he was alright, but he appeared confused and shocked. Then he told me under strict orders not to mention the incident to anyone.'

'You didn't feel like probing him a little further into what had happened to him that afternoon?'

'He is the Holy Father and I serve him as his secretary. I am not his confessor, so I was not in a position to question him.'

'When did he tell you about what he saw in the vision?'

'The first night we arrived back from Castel Gandolfo. As usual, I always kept his diary clear for the first night of his return, to allow him to settle back into the Vatican and to collect his thoughts for future engagements. Except that night he was too unsettled to work. So, I made him some tea and brought it into his study, that is when he first told me.'

'Can you remember what he said?'

'He told me everything that he had witnessed, as he was led by the hand of Christ himself and shown everything that would come to pass within a short matter of time. Nothing was held back from him, including the fact that he would be the last Pope before the end of times. No wonder he was in shock after each vision, he even saw his own future martyrdom on the very steps of Saint Peter's Basilica.'

Brenard could see from the look on Hasler's face, and the way he recalled his meeting with the Holy Father, that he truly believed in what he had been told.

'He was shown how the end of times would happen, in which the gates of hell would be unlocked and the power of Satan would rape the world with an evil we could never imagine. He saw nations fight against nations before turning in on themselves. He saw bombs of fire crossing the globe, extinguishing a multitude of innocent lives. He saw the nations of the East and the North make their move against Israel, but he also saw the right hand of God Himself protect his chosen people from those who wished them harm.'

Hasler had triggered a question in Brenard's mind that he'd been wanting to ask. Flicking through the encyclical, he found the page he was looking for.

'*"Then the Lord showed me the beast rising from the ashes of a smouldering world. In his hands he held the sceptre of evil and an orb of deceitfulness. He spoke peace to the nations, and they hailed him as the saviour of mankind before anointing his peace treaty onto their hearts. For forty-two months he will rule with unquestioned authority, secure in the peace he will have delivered to the world. Then under his wings he will gather in the nations, and lead them to even darker days where those who perished by pestilence and fire in the Great War will be seen by the many as fortunate, as they will have been spared the lingering wrath of the beast."* Gustave, who is the Antichrist the vision speaks of?'

Hasler paused for a moment, staring into his cup of wine as he contemplated telling Brenard his own suspicions as to who he believed the Antichrist to be. Having thought of nothing else since he was forced to leave Rome, he believed he had worked out the truth for himself. Yet, he knew that in mentioning the name to Brenard he would be destroying the essence of everything that ever was. There would be no going back.

'Gustave?'

'Your Eminence, you are a smart man. Have you not already worked it out for yourself?'

40.

Father Donal O'Keefe had been sober for over fifteen years, but now more than ever he needed a drink.

After watching the American President's address to her nation, he went into Maynooth town and bought himself a litre bottle of Black Bush and twenty Marlboro Reds; having given in to his inner temptations that there was no point in trying anymore.

Even being back in Ireland he still did not feel safe. So once back in the relative safety of his room in the college, he locked the door and pushed a filing cabinet across it to stop anyone from getting in without a struggle.

Sitting beside the open window he nursed a tumbler of whiskey, and started to smoke his way through the packet of cigarettes. As he watched the news, he became aware that Pope Clement's vision was starting to unfold. Despite not knowing everything that was written in the encyclical, he was conscious that the world now stood on the brink.

Looking around him, he realised he had made a huge mistake in not following Devine's explicit instructions not to leave a paper trail. Every piece of research and thought he had penned, now littered his room. If they came to get him he could not take the risk of the evidence and correspondence he had, falling into the wrong hands.

Throwing back the whiskey that remained in his glass, he took one last smoke on his cigarette and flicked it out the window. Aware he had to hide the evidence, he dragged a plastic box into the middle of the room and emptied out his students' exam papers onto the floor, before he started to fill the box with his own papers.

Once the box was filled, he went to his desk to find the keys he needed for the one place no one would think of looking. Searching through his drawers, he finally found the keys and slipped them into his pocket, before putting on his coat and pushing the filing cabinet away from the door. Looking through the spy hole, he checked to make sure no one was in the corridor. Then opening it as quietly as he could, so as not to disturb the other priests, he lifted the box and walked out.

Through a labyrinth of corridors and small staircases, he carried the box to the ground floor of the college. As the box was too heavy to carry all the way, he searched the caretaker's store for the pull trolley and for a flashlight to help him find his way in the dark.

Ready to bury the evidence once and for all, he loaded the box onto the trolley and pulled it outside. Sneaking into the dark of the night, he took the long way around the gable wall of the college chapel and headed for the sport's fields and the parkland at the rear of the college. Stopping to catch his bearings, he stared into the darkness until he could vaguely see the white glare of the Calvary shrine. With his sight fixed on where he wanted to go, he pulled the trolley across the lawns. The further he walked the more into focus the statues on the shrine became, and behind them the dark entrance to the graveyard.

Reaching the shrine, O'Keefe sat the trolley upright and took the flashlight from his pocket. Shining it through the long canopy of the deep arching yew trees, he could see the graveyard gate at the other end; about sixty or seventy feet away. Grabbing the trolley he headed into the darkness of the canopy and quickly walked towards the gates of the walled graveyard.

Satisfied he was alone, he turned right and walked over to the old brick mausoleum. There he searched through the keys until he found the one he was looking for. With his torchlight, he was able to find the lock and push his key through the keyhole with little difficulty. At first the lock resisted, but with just enough force he was able to turn it open.

Pulling the door open towards him, he shone the torchlight inside, directly onto the casket of Monsignor O'Growney that rested on a bricked plinth. A little nervous he walked into the chamber, his hand slightly shaking as it held the torch. He was in no doubt that the plain casket, covered in the dust of decades past, was the perfect place to bury the secret. Undoing the screws of the casket, O'Keefe hoped there would be enough room inside to store the papers.

With the four screws loose, he pulled the lid towards him. But, years of damp had warped the joints making it nearly impossible to remove. So walking around to the head of the casket, he gripped the edges and with all his strength pushed as hard as he could to prise it open. With the lid free from the casket he slid it off, seeing for the first time the decayed remains of the Monsignor who had been dead for over a hundred years.Dressed in priestly vestments, the withered skeleton was just a few years from turning completely into dust.

Blessing himself for what he was about to do, O'Keefe placed his hand onto O'Growney's skull, and gently pushed. The whole skeleton crumbled with the pressure, as he forced the dusty remains into the bottom half of the casket.

He now had enough room. Going outside to fetch the box, his heart missed a beat when he heard something rustle in the bushes on the other side of the graveyard wall. He stopped dead in his tracks and listened; his heart pounding with the fear rising in his chest.

In the stillness of the night he stood and waited. But, with no other sound disturbing the silence he decided to move quickly, lifted the box into the mausoleum and placed it inside the casket.

With a bit of a struggle, he managed to fit the lid back on, before leaving the mausoleum and locking the door behind him. Then, lifting the trolley, he walked back under the arched trees and hurried as fast as he could. Reaching the Calvary shrine, he stopped the moment he heard a noise behind him.

Looking back towards the graveyard, he was horrified to see the silhouette of a man standing at the gate. He watched for a few seconds before the man started to walk towards him.

Stumbling over the trolley as he backed away, O'Keefe fell to the ground. He could hear the footsteps approach closer by the second, as he struggled to get back onto his feet. An unimaginable fear swept through his mind that this was the moment when he would have to pay the price for what he knew. Then, just as he was about to run, he heard the man call his name. He stopped the moment he recognised the voice.

'It's me Donal,' the man said. 'You've nothing to fear!'

41.

'Is it someone that we know?' Brenard hesitantly asked.

Hasler nodded, before finishing the wine in his cup.

'One evening, in early March this year,' Hasler began, as he drew a deep nervous breath, 'the Holy Father asked for Cardinal Guarducci to come to the Papal Apartment as he wanted to speak to him. That is when he first told him about the encyclical.'

'Were you there?'

'The Holy Father wanted me to be present, for he knew he would have great difficulty persuading Cardinal Guarducci to accept the encyclical. As the Holy Father told him everything, Cardinal Guarducci listened intently. He spoke very little, and to be honest we both felt that the meeting had gone well when the cardinal left us and took a copy of the encyclical to read. But, the following evening we both realised that he was far from happy, when he arrived back to Papal Apartment with Cardinals Boyer and Oliveri and demanded an audience with the Holy Father. The three Cardinals wanted me to leave the room, but the Holy Father insisted that I stayed.'

'Was the meeting heated?'

'Not at the beginning. Having read the encyclical, the three of them listened as the Holy Father recounted his experiences at Castel Gandolfo. It was only when he finished speaking that they started questioning him.'

'What kind of questions did they ask?'

'How could he know the visions were true and not some delusional episode? Did he accept that the world would be thrown into turmoil if he went ahead and published the encyclical? What would happen to the future of the Church if it all turned out to be untrue? The Holy Father answered each one of their questions in great length, leaving them in no doubt of his conviction over what he had witnessed in the visions. It was only when Cardinal Oliveri put it to him that the College of Cardinals could see his encyclical as being heretical, that the mood in the room changed.'

'Cardinal Oliveri accused the Holy Father of committing heresy right to his face?' Brenard asked, stunned with Oliveri's irreverence.

'Yes, and the other two Cardinals nodded in agreement when he suggested as much.'

'How did His Holiness react?'

'I remember looking at him once it was suggested, but he just sat in his chair with both his hands gripping the armrests, trying to keep control of his own dignity and serenity.'

'But what did he say?'

'He did not say anything. His silence was a clear answer to them all. Then Cardinal Guarducci started to press upon him the reality that the College would stand by their perception that he was guilty of heresy, and they would force his abdication.'

'By getting the necessary two-thirds plus one!' Brenard said, as he recalled the governing rules of the Church. 'Can't that rule only be enforced if the Pope is mentally or physically incapacitated to carry out his duties?'

'They left the Holy Father in no doubt, that an act of heresy would be seen by the College as a mental incapacity, hindering him in effect from continuing on with his Papacy.'

'They'd have had a hard time getting it through the College. There's no way we would've gone public and forced the Pope's hand to abdicate.'

'It was only a threat. His Holiness knew that if Guarducci convened the College of Cardinals, he would have nothing to fear. He told me so himself. For he was convinced that if the visions contained in the encyclical were genuine, then nothing would stand in the way of God and their publication. For nearly three hours, His Holiness engaged in a frank discussion with them in an attempt to persuade them to follow him and to trust that the encyclical contained truthful revelations. When he realised he was getting nowhere, he eventually raised his hand for them to fall silent. Then, before they left, he gave them a very strict warning to go away and pray about what they had discussed, because he wanted them to either pledge their full support for his encyclical or to tender their resignations as prefects to their respective congregations.'

'I take it they didn't tender their resignations?'

'No!' Hasler replied. 'That very night I believe they tried to kill him.'

Brenard did not know what to say. He felt numb. His very vocation to which he had dedicated his life was now nothing more than a tattered illusion. His trust in the government of his Church, which he once held so dear to his heart, was literally evaporating from his soul.

'After the cardinals left him that evening, the Holy Father had a private meeting with Malachy. I was not in the room to hear what was said between the two, but after an hour Malachy left the Papal Apartment in quite a hurry. I went into the Pope's study to see how he was, but he was exhausted and simply wanted to go to bed. As it was well past midnight, his valet had already left and the nuns had retired for the night, so I walked him to his bedroom. After I turned down his bedsheets, he asked me to bring him some warm milk as his stomach was upset. Not wanting to disturb the nuns, I went into the kitchen to heat the milk myself. Just as the milk in the saucepan was beginning to simmer, I heard voices coming from further down the corridor. So taking the pan off the stove I went outside to see what was going on.'

As Hasler retold the story, his voice became emotional.

'It's okay Gustave,' Brenard reassured. 'Take your time.'

'When I looked up the corridor I saw Cardinal Guarducci standing outside the Pope's bedroom while several men ran into the room. When he saw me he turned and give me a look of utter distain, before he started to shout at me for not responding to the panic alarm. Walking closer I could see the red light flashing above the bedroom door but there was no sound. Someone must have silenced the alarm.'

'Who would have triggered the alarm?'

'Beside his bed, the Pope has a panic button that he must press if he feels ill or feels his security threatened. Once he presses it, an alarm goes off throughout the Papal Apartment and certain parts of the Apostolic Palace. The moment the alarm is triggered, the Swiss Guards have to shut down the Palace, the Pope's security detail must secure the Apartment and a team trained in first aid must make their way to the residence.'

'What happened in the room?'

'I do not know. Cardinal Guarducci told me to wait in the hallway as medics were working with him. It all sounded very chaotic, as if there was a struggle taking place. I must have looked alarmed, because Cardinal Guarducci told me that the Holy Father had collapsed and that they were working with him before taking him to the Gemelli. Eventually things quietened down, and Cardinal Guarducci entered the bedroom. That was when I took my chance to see what was happening. His Holiness was lying on the floor, his soutane unbuttoned at his chest. At first I thought he was dead, but when one of the medics saw me he reassured me that he was going to be fine.'

'How many medics did you see in the room?'

'Three, but I did not recognise a single one of them. Within seconds they were lifting the Holy Father onto a stretcher, and that is when I saw the empty syringe lying on the floor. When Cardinal Guarducci realised I was there he ordered me to go back down to the kitchen.'

'Did you?'

'I felt like I had no choice. Everything was happening too quickly to stop and think. The nuns who had heard the commotion were standing in the corridor crying, and I felt I had to attend to them. Seconds later, they were carrying the Holy Father out of the Papal Apartment.'

'Did they take His Holiness straight to the Gemelli?'

'Yes.' Hasler replied, with a heavy heart. 'And that was the last time I saw him.'

Immediately, all of Brenard's remaining uncertainty dissolved. In his mind he had taken the decision to accept without doubt that Hasler was telling him the complete truth. Despite having many questions left unanswered, he felt a deep sense of peace, because he knew that Hasler wasn't the source of a conspiracy but the victim of one. He knew in that moment that this was the calling of his life.

'Gustave, do you believe,' Brenard began to ask, 'that Cardinal Guarducci is the Antichrist?'

Hasler looked at him intently.

'Like you I have similar suspicions, but that is all they are, suspicions!' Hasler replied. 'Several days after they took the Holy Father to the Gemelli, I met with Malachy in my apartment before he went to Israel. When I told him about what had happened that night in the Papal Apartment, he confided in me that Donal O'Keefe had his suspicions as to the identity of the Antichrist. If you really want an answer to your question, then you are going to have to ask Donal O'Keefe.'

'Then that's what we'll do,' Brenard said, as he got up from his seat and walked towards the door. 'Let's get your things and we'll go visit Donal O'Keefe.'

'I cannot leave,' Hasler replied, as he watched Brenard open the door. 'I have been instructed to stay here until my archbishop decides to send for me.'

'You're leaving with me tonight,' Brenard answered, as he turned and looked at him. 'You are under my authority and protection from now on.'

42.

Friday, 11th April.

Cardinal Guarducci gently rapped the door before opening it.

'Are you awake?' he asked, as he looked into the darkened room.

He heard a slight stirring.

'It is only me, Cardinal Guarducci,' he replied, as he walked in.

Rubbing the sleep from his eyes, Clement reached out his hand and turned on the lamp that stood on top of his bedside cabinet.

'Did you sleep well last night?'

Clement shook his head, as he struggled to find the strength to lift himself up in the bed.

'Let me help you,' Guarducci insisted, as he linked his arms under Clement's frail frame and helped him to sit up.

With Clement sitting upright against his pillows, one of his nurses came in carrying a tray with a glass of water and his medication.

Taking the tablets and water from her, Clement did not question what she was giving him, but like an obedient child he swallowed the tablets before washing them down with the water.

'We need to talk.' Guarducci said, once the nurse left the room. 'I think things are going to unravel a lot more quickly than we had planned. President Cleary has just finished addressing the UN Security Council. It has been leaked to the media that the entire military and security infrastructure of the United States is looking for chemical warheads, which are in the hands of extremists from the Islamic States. Things do not look good.'

'What happens now?' Clement managed to say.

'Apart from a full scale search for these weapons, President Cleary is trying to use the UN to place pressure on countries who have influence with the Islamic States to encourage them to stand down. She has made it quite clear, that if America is attacked then the consequences for the Islamic States and those who side with them will be severe.'

Clement sat still in his bed, pondering the argument Guarducci had once made that such an attack on America was simply inconceivable. How wrong he was.

'What is it?' Guarducci asked.

'Have we made a mistake?'

Guarducci looked at him, not quite believing that he had asked the question, the very same question that tortured the souls of both Oliveri and Boyer.

'You are going to have to make a public appearance today,' Guarducci said, changing the subject as he poured him some more water.

'No!' Clement murmured in frustration.

'The Americans need your help,' Guarducci said, as he placed the glass of water against Clement's lips. 'The American Secretary of State is flying into Moscow this afternoon, to try and gather their support. He is making a short stop here along the way. With the eyes of the world on him this morning, he wants to meet with you, to be seen with you in public and ask you to call for world peace.'

Clement shook his head, daunted by the prospect.

'You will not have to speak. At ten this morning you will receive him in the State Rooms. A single camera crew from Vatican Television will broadcast it live. All you will have to do is sit in your chair and greet him, give a blessing and exchange a gift of some sort. We will organise a bible. I will speak on your behalf, and call out for the children of the three Abrahamic faiths to find a peaceful resolution where we can all live under the one God we all profess.'

Clement knew that it would prove to be a pointless exercise.

'Now, one of the nurses will be in shortly to wash and dress you,' Guarducci said, as he went to leave the room. 'Do not worry, I have everything under control.'

'Cardinal!' Clement struggled to call out, as Guarducci opened the door.

'What is it?' Guarducci asked, as he walked back over to the bed.

'Maybe there is still time,' Clement said in a whisper, as Guarducci sat on the edge of the bed, 'to give the world a...'

'Listen to me,' Guarducci interrupted, looking him right in the eye. 'This is not a matter for you to discuss.'

'Why are you doing this?' Clement asked, struggling for breath.

'I am doing it for the betterment of the world.' Guarducci replied, as he took a firm hold of Clement's frail wrist. 'You have no say in these matters. Do you understand?'

In that moment Clement had never felt so far from God.

43.

'Shall we proceed?'

Fixing his tie and then adjusting his cufflinks, Bannon nodded that he was ready.

With a signal from Cardinal Guarducci, two Swiss Guards opened the doors.

Stepping into the Papal Library, Guarducci bowed.

'Your Holiness, the American Secretary of State, Christopher Bannon.'

As Cardinal Guarducci stood to one side, Bannon could see Pope Clement sitting right in front of him; aged and very frail. Nervously, he made his way towards him as a cameraman covered the live proceedings for the television networks who were streaming the pictures across the world.

'Holy Father,' Bannon said, as he shook Clement's hand. 'How are you keeping?'

Heeding Guarducci's warning not to speak, Clement gave a warm smile and nodded.

'I've brought you a small present from my wife's home state of Nevada,' Bannon said, as one of his aids handed him a box. He opened it and held out it for Clement to see. 'It's a small stone cross, carved from a rock in the Grand Canyon by Native Americans.'

Clement smiled, the cross looked beautiful. Then reaching out, he instructed his newly appointed private secretary to hand over to Bannon a leather bound Douay Rheims bible.

The black bible was his standard present to all dignitaries who visited him. It was a beautiful gift to receive, and it adorned many presidential, prime ministerial and royal offices around the world.

Taking the bible in his hands, Bannon was quite impressed with the fine detail of the carvings made across the leather binding and the small golden papal crest on the bottom left of the front cover.

As all this took place, Cardinal Guarducci stood alongside Clement, watching, smiling and playing the role of the attentive papal servant. Yet, he did not want it to linger for too long. Informing one of the ushers to bring over the microphone, he politely asked Bannon to make his address.

Following the formal protocol of a Papal Audience, everyone in the Library took their seats as Bannon walked over to the microphone. When his aid handed him his folder he opened it, and began to read his statement.

'Holy Father, your distinguished Eminences and Excellencies, I bring with me the warm greetings of my President and our nation, and our prayers are with you at this time as you continue with your recovery.

'Our relationship with the Vatican has been long and distinguished, and despite the Christian bonds between our two states, we have been two nations not only united under God but under human friendship and respect.

'As you will have been made aware, Your Holiness, our nation and the freedom of the world is facing a threat like it has never faced before. That is why I am about to engage on a diplomatic tour to seek the necessary support my government and the world needs to prevent an unprecedented war from taking place.

'When President Cleary was inaugurated on the steps of the Capitol, she made it clear that war between world nations should be avoided at all costs, and that peace should always be sought to seek democratic ways forward for the security of all our children's futures; no matter what their colour, nationality or creed.

'As I begin to embark on this diplomatic tour I would like to thank you, Your Holiness, for all the work your nuncios have undertaken throughout the world in working with governments to seek a peaceful resolution to the current crisis we now face. Furthermore, I would like to ask you for your continued support and prayers, that the God of Abraham whom we all worship whether Muslim, Jew or Christian will give us the guidance we need, to share the future of this world together in peaceful harmony.'

Closing his folder, he handed it back to his aid before taking a seat beside Clement.

With the American speech concluded, Guarducci bowed towards Clement before he walked over to the microphone to deliver his reply on behalf of the Pope.

'Mr. Secretary of State, I extend to you my Apostolic Blessing as you begin to engage on this diplomatic tour, and remind you of the Gospel message; Blessed are the Peacemakers, for they will be known as the sons of God.

'As you begin your mission of peace, I hope that you will seek to bring with you the Christian message of love and tolerance in your heart, knowing that where you go, so too will go the message and love of the Gospel.

'I would like to take this opportunity to address my Muslim brothers and sisters of the Islamic States, and in particular the Caliph of Baghdad. Your faith, like the Christian faith, is rooted deep in the message of love; a love for God and a love for one's neighbour. Your faith is one of purity and self-obedience to the message of the Great Prophet, but like those who profess Christ, there are those who will take this message and use it to justify the shedding of blood in the name of the peaceful faiths we treasure so dearly.

'On my knees I beg you, use whatever influence you have over any extremists to encourage them to come back to the core certainties of their faith, and to build a world of peace and love together for the future of all our children.

'Finally, I would encourage restraint from all world leaders. Do not use your weapons against fellow nations. Show true leadership within the world, knowing that through dialogue and peace greater things can be achieved for the future security of the nations of this precious world.'

Having delivered the short address, Guarducci stood aside, allowing Clement to bless Christopher Bannon and his entourage who were with him.

With the formalities concluded, the director of Vatican Television terminated the main feed from the Papal Library. Immediately, the television crew took their equipment, and along with the American entourage and papal staff left the

Library; leaving Clement, Guarducci and Bannon alone to continue their discussions.

'How long do you have?' Guarducci asked.

'I need to be leaving here within ten minutes,' he replied. 'Your Holiness, I would like to thank you on behalf of the President for taking the advice of both her government and your senior counsel not to proceed with the publication of your encyclical. The fear that's raging through the States at present, would only have been exacerbated if that encyclical had been published.'

Clement lowered his head.

'How is the effort going in the States to locate the chemical weapons?' Guarducci asked, taking the focus of conversation back off the Holy Father.

'The odds are stacked up against us,' Bannon replied, sounding rather deflated. 'Personally, I think we'd have an easier job finding a needle in the middle of the Grand Canyon. Our only real hope is that those with influence within the Islamic States will realise that our retaliatory strike would see them wiped off the face of the earth. At the moment, and despite our differences, Moscow has arranged a face to face meeting between ourselves and a senior advisor to the Caliph. I just hope that they will listen to us and back down. If they don't, then the political vacuum will pull us all to the brink.'

'If they succeed in detonating these chemical weapons, what would the impact be on the human level?' Guarducci asked.

'The death toll could reach somewhere between thirty and fifty million within the first 24 hours, that's even before we take into consideration the fallout of such an event; the disposal of dead bodies, treating survivors and maintaining food and water supplies.'

Clement shook his head in disgust.

'That figure is from the terrorist threat alone. If we go to retaliate, we could be looking at a situation where Israel will feel the need to protect herself against the Islamic States that surround her, and that could drag Russia into the conflict as well. Everything is so uncertain. We have contemplated every scenario from strategic retaliatory nuclear strikes, to a conflict that could see the world engaged in an all-out nuclear war. One thing that is for certain is this, if we are attacked we will not sit back and do nothing. We will hit back hard. Our military strength must now be used to back our diplomatic efforts. America doesn't go begging cap in hand.'

Guarducci, knowing that Bannon was limited in his time, drew the meeting to a close. After bidding the Holy Father a gracious farewell, Bannon took his leave and followed Guarducci out of the Papal Library.

'Could we have a minute alone?' Bannon asked Guarducci.

'Sure,' Guarducci replied, as he opened a door and led Bannon into an anteroom.

'Before I landed, the President's National Security Advisor contacted me on the plane with some information she wants you to be made aware of.'

Reaching into his inner jacket pocket, Bannon took out a folded piece of paper. Unfolding it, he handed it over to Guarducci.

'This is a copy of a flight register from an airfield near Dublin,' Bannon pointed out. 'At eight-fifteen this morning, a privately chartered jet touched down carrying two Vatican diplomats.'

'What?' Guarducci said, as he scanned the page, noticing that Brenard and Hasler had registered with Irish Passport Control. 'This is the first I have heard about this.'

'Jean, you reassured the administration that you'd taken care of Monsignor Hasler and Cardinal Paul Brenard.'

'I believed I had.' Guarducci insisted.

'We are not happy that these two have established contact with one another.'

'I totally understand.'

'Their plane flew out of Bern shortly after five o'clock this morning,' Bannon informed him. 'It appears to be obvious that Brenard went out of his way to meet up with Hasler. The Cardinal was booked onto a flight to Chicago yesterday morning, but when the airspace over the United States was shut down, he travelled to Switzerland by car. He knows that you're hiding the truth.'

'How?'

'Surveillance cameras in the departure lounge recorded him opening an envelope posted from Israel. When we enhanced the images, we were able to take a closer look at what was sent to him. He has the fourth copy of the encyclical.'

Guarducci could not believe what he was hearing.

'As we speak my President is flying somewhere God only knows, while our security and intelligence bodies are searching for these chemical weapons that are literally time bombs waiting to go off. Meanwhile, while we're struggling to find a Security Council resolution and a diplomatic way out of this, the last thing we need to be worrying about is two priests on some religious crusade, threatening to expose what we've gone to great lengths to hide.'

'I understand.'

'Jean, you need to prepare yourself. Something big is going to be asked from you.'

'Like what?' Guarducci replied, noticing that Bannon looked extremely uncomfortable as he moved closer to him.

'The President has asked me to tell you to expect a phone call today and to trust her in whatever decision she makes.' Bannon answered, as he placed a reassuring hand on Guarducci's right shoulder. 'No matter what happens, nothing between us will change. In fact, the President wants you to know that her decision is going to bring us even closer together.'

44.

As a sense of crisis grew in America, more commercial flights were grounded worldwide. To get to Ireland, Brenard had to secure a private jet to travel from Bern to Dublin; the cost covered by the vast wealth of his archdiocese. Having left the abbey at four in the morning, it took them less than an hour to get to Bern Airport. With their private Gulf Stream fully fuelled and ready, they were airborne in less than ten minutes. Unable to travel through closed French and German airspace, their jet had to fly south towards the Mediterranean before flying over North Africa and out into the Atlantic before heading for Ireland. Onboard Hasler slept for the whole flight while Brenard, unsettled by the future, prayed for the strength to get through the day. Three hours later they touched down at Casement Aerodrome southwest of Dublin.

Thirty minutes later, when their taxi swept into Maynooth Pontifical Seminary, past memories of visits to the college swept over Brenard. They were happy memories spent in the company of Malachy, but they were memories that belonged to decades past.

After paying the driver, they both walked into the inner quad. Brenard stopped and looked around him. It still looked beautiful, with the ivy covered dormitory buildings overlooking them and the dominant grey stone gothic chapel, with its piercing spire reaching high into the clear blue morning sky. Ahead of him he recognised the President's Arch, so called because the college president's rooms were above the arched entrance to the cloister and the lecture rooms. Beckoning Hasler to follow him, he made his way over to the main entrance of the seminary.

Opening the door of the archway, he walked into the cloister. Unsure of his bearings, Brenard was glad when he saw a young man walk towards him.

'Could you take me to Father O'Keefe's room please?'

'Father O'Keefe has just started his morning lecture,' the young man replied, recognising him as one of the leaders of the Catholic Church in America. 'Are you Cardinal Brenard?'

'Yes.' Brenard answered, as he shook the young man's hand. 'Then, could you bring me to Fr. O'Keefe's lecture room?'

'Yes, Your Eminence, please follow me,' the young man said, before leading Brenard and Hasler along the main cloister, passing the yearly class photographs of all the ordinations that had taken place in the college; each previous year having more and more ordinations, a sign of the times and the crisis that had taken hold within the Church.

Towards the end of the cloister, the young man turned left into the only adjoining corridor, entering the main theological wing of the seminary. It was very quiet, but the closer they came to the lecture rooms, the clearer the voices of the lecturers teaching theology to the young, influential trainee priests became.

'This is where Fr. O'Keefe is lecturing,' the young man said. 'Would you like me to tell him that you're here?'

'You've been most helpful,' Brenard replied, 'but I'll just slip into the back of the room and wait until he's finished.'

Opening the door ever so quietly, Brenard and Hasler walked into the room.

'As priests you will have the task of representing Christ,' O'Keefe said, with his back turned to the students, as he wrote onto the white board *In Persona Christi.*

Brenard's presence did not go unnoticed, because as O'Keefe wrote the words onto the board the students started to whisper amongst themselves, asking each other if the two men who had just walked into the lecture hall were the archbishop of Chicago and the Pope's secretary who had been all over the news. Slipping into the back row of the lecture hall, Brenard and Hasler sat and waited for events to take their course.

O'Keefe turned around when he heard them talking, infuriated with the noise his students were making. Immediately, he realised the source of the commotion when he saw Brenard sitting at the back of the hall. Very quickly, he felt a cold sweat breaking out. He tried to remain calm.

'In persona Christi,' O'Keefe said, as he fumbled through his notes stacked up on his lecture podium. 'In persona Christi is one thing that...'

He was thrown. He glanced back up. The cardinal was still there, and then he noticed Hasler sitting beside him.

'As priests, by the virtue of the sacrament of Holy Orders you will act in the person of Jesus Christ when celebrating the Eucharist,' O'Keefe tried to continue undeterred. 'Your sacrament of Holy Orders will communicate a sacred power which is none other than that of Christ himself.'

O'Keefe sat down his pen and looked at his watch. There was no point in continuing.

'Gentlemen, we'll call it time for today thank you.'

As the student priests got up and left, none of them could have imagined the real significance behind the visit of the two men.

Glad that he had stopped his lecture, Brenard got out of his seat and started to make his way down the steps to meet with O'Keefe.

The last student closed the door behind him.

'You seem to have been busy,' O'Keefe said to Brenard, as he nodded in Hasler's direction.

'Where can we talk?'

45.

With his hands shaking with nerves, Donal O'Keefe fumbled through his set of keys. Finding the one he was looking for, he opened the door of his sitting room, stood back and allowed Cardinal Brenard and Monsignor Hasler to enter first.

It was clear from walking into the room that O'Keefe was a man who was well read. Shelves of books lined the four walls, and Brenard knew that O'Keefe, an academic like Devine had read and studied his way through every one of them over the years.

'Can I offer you a drink?' O'Keefe asked, as he walked over and sat his keys and lecture notes down on his desk.

'Coffee please,' Brenard answered, as he sat down on the leather settee.

'The same for me,' Hasler replied.

'I meant alcohol.' O'Keefe said, as he poured himself a rather large measure of Black Bush into the same tumbler he had used the night before. 'It's whiskey or nothing.'

'Then we will do without,' Brenard replied, as he watched O'Keefe take a mouthful of the whiskey, not even flinching as he swallowed it.

'So, I trust you're not here for a holiday then?' O'Keefe smiled, as he sat beside Brenard.

Brenard ignored his flippancy, turned in his seat and looked him straight in the eye. 'I want to know about your work with Malachy.'

O'Keefe now looked uncomfortable, and Brenard noticed his eyes glance to the bookcase on his right.

'Your Eminence, you should not have come here.' O'Keefe finally said. 'Somethings are best left buried.'

Lifting his briefcase onto his lap, Brenard opened it, lifted out the encyclical and handed it over. O'Keefe knew exactly what it was, and it came to him as no surprise that the cardinal had it in his possession.

'I need to know the whole truth surrounding this encyclical. With all the developments taking place around the world, time is not on my side.'

'In the end of times there will be great distress. The sun will be darkened, the moon will lose its brightness, the stars will come falling from the sky and the very power of heaven will be shaken.' O'Keefe began to quote, as he swirled the whiskey in its tumbler. 'I tell you solemnly, before this generation has passed away all these things will have taken place. Heaven and earth will pass away, but my word will not pass.'

As he listened, Brenard once again felt the hairs stand up on the back of his neck. He could now sense that the words spoken by Christ and quoted by O'Keefe, were now about to be fulfilled.

'You've read the truth,' O'Keefe said, as he lifted the encyclical. 'So what are you going to do about it?'

'I honestly don't know!' Brenard replied. 'I'm trusting the Lord to guide me. But for now, I need you to tell us about your meeting with Malachy in which you told him you had established the identity of the Antichrist.'

'I've no idea what you're talking about.'

'Yes, you do.' Hasler insisted, as he walked from the fireplace and took a seat in the armchair across from them. 'I know for certain that you were studying the potential emergence of the Antichrist. You could start by telling us who you think he is.'

'You think it's that easy?' O'Keefe said, before he finished off the whiskey in his glass. 'Look at what they've done to silence the truth. They've murdered and they'll continue to murder, and they're still denying the truth even though the world is literally about to go up in flames. The truth now belongs in the hands of darkness. Give up and go home. There's nothing either of you can do to rectify the betrayal that's been shown to the truth.'

'We're not leaving,' Brenard replied. 'I need to know the truth.'

O'Keefe sat for a moment, looking into his empty glass.

'The truth you seek is behind that bookcase.' O'Keefe said calmly. 'If you really want to see it then I'll show you.'

Glimpsing the mystery in O'Keefe's eyes, Brenard turned and looked at the bookcase with intrigue.

'Shall I open it?'

Brenard nodded.

Walking over to the bookcase, O'Keefe removed the planted palm that sat alongside the end of it, then he undid the two latches that the palm kept hidden. Very carefully he swung the bookcase open to reveal a hidden door.

Rising to his feet, Brenard cautiously walked across the room to O'Keefe

'When Pope John Paul II came to visit Maynooth during his papal visit to Ireland in 1979, they needed a secure room in case there was a breach of security within the campus.' O'Keefe said, as he lifted a key from the top of the bookcase. 'Thankfully it was never used.'

Unlocking the door, O'Keefe flung it open and stood aside.

Brenard looked deep into the darkness. At first he could not see anything beyond the open door, but then he saw someone emerging from the darkness.

O'Keefe walked over to his desk to pour another drink.

'Impossible!' Brenard cried out, as Malachy Devine emerged like Lazarus from his tomb.

46.

In the shock of the moment, Brenard went over and poured himself a large whiskey. With a trembling hand he tried to drink it. It was too hard to believe. It simply was not possible.

'Hello, Paul!' was all Devine could manage to say.

Brenard felt like throwing the drink around him, as his disbelief gave way to a swelling anger.

'I see you got the encyclical!' Devine said, noticing it sitting on the settee.

'Why did you not make contact?' Brenard replied, his anger clear to see. 'You could've gotten word to me that you were still alive. For crying out loud, I mourned at your funeral.'

Devine always knew it would be tough to explain.

'Come to think of it,' Brenard snapped, 'who did I end up burying?'

'I don't know his name. It was a body of a homeless man that Kevin managed to get from a morgue in Tel Aviv.'

'Who's Kevin?'

'He was the American agent who was sent to Israel to make sure I didn't leave alive,' Devine explained. 'Except he had a major conversion of heart and ended up saving my life.'

'What? A road to Damascus conversion?'

'Something like that. He managed to intercept the encyclical after I'd posted it to you. In the days we travelled around Northern Israel he read it cover to cover, and knew his government were asking him to hide something big.'

'Where's Kevin now?'

'He's back in America, no doubt fearing that he'll be exposed as a traitor for not following his orders to assassinate me.'

'You're very lucky that you met one of the good guys,' Brenard said, 'because whoever's running the operation in Rome is sparing no prisoners.'

'I've heard!' Devine said, all too aware that Stuart Smith and Father McAuley had been murdered. 'But Kevin did struggle with the decision. After I saw the red heifer and wired the pictures to Stuart, he took me from the car and pulled his gun on me.'

'What stopped him from pulling the trigger?'

'The encyclical,' Devine replied, as he sat down beside Brenard. 'Knowing that he'd intercepted the encyclical, I realised that unless I convinced him, the truth would be lost forever.'

For a moment Brenard sat in silence. The surreality of the moment flood his mind with so many questions.

'Kevin took me back to his hotel room and told me everything about his operation,' Devine said, knowing he had to give more to Brenard. 'He told me that a senior Vatican source had asked his government to make absolutely sure that I didn't leave Israel alive.'

'Guarducci?' Hasler asked.

'Yes.' Devine confirmed. 'When I found out that I was being set up, I knew I'd no choice but to tell Kevin everything. I showed him all the information I had on my computer and the different files about each of the twenty prophecies. In the end, he believed in what I was doing.'

'How did you fake your own death?' Brenard asked.

'Kevin took care of that. He knew a Mossad agent who owed him a favour. Kevin asked him to supply him with an unclaimed body of someone who'd died of natural causes. The Mossad agent set up the whole thing, from the murder scene to the very publicity that I had been murdered.'

'So how did you get back to Dublin?'

'It wasn't too difficult,' Devine replied. 'Kevin managed to get me an American passport. Then together, we flew from Tel Aviv to Sydney and onto Los Angeles. I stayed in the States until the funeral was over, travelling by train to Philadelphia before I took a flight into Shannon yesterday morning.'

'Are you facing charges back here in Ireland?' Brenard asked.

'Absolutely not!' Devine replied. 'Donal told me about that last night. It's a lie without a shred of truth or evidence.'

'Why didn't you just come straight back to Rome?' Hasler asked. 'Appearing at your own funeral would've revealed the truth and would have spared us the pain we've all had to suffer.'

'I had to protect Kevin for sparing my life. I simply couldn't just turn up at my own funeral. There would have been consequences.'

'You could have witnessed to the truth and forced the release of the encyclical!' Hasler quickly answered back.

'That would never have happened,' Devine explained. 'The encyclical was never written to prevent these events that are about to unfold. It was written to give the people of the world the chance to put right their lives and souls with God before these events take place. We tried but we failed. The encyclical is entirely useless now.'

'What do you mean?' Brenard asked.

'Dark forces have silenced it good and proper.' Devine replied. 'They don't want the world to see the blue print that the Antichrist will follow once these events take place in America. By silencing it, the Antichrist is still able to hide from the world and continue his rise to the top of political, economic, military and spiritual domination.'

'Do you know who the Antichrist is?' Brenard asked.

'There is no doubt in my mind,' Devine replied, before looking them all one by one in the eye. 'It has to be Cardinal Jean Guarducci!'

47.

'If the visions are true, America will soon be at war with the Islamic States and Russia. It will be a brief war, but it will see hundreds of millions killed. In the immediate aftermath, with the Holy Father close to death, Jean Guarducci as the Dean of the College of Cardinals will be highly tipped to replace him.'

'No one can be sure of that,' Brenard insisted. 'Each member of the College casts one free vote.'

'Come off it, Paul!' Devine argued. 'You know as well as I do that the right influences can swing it, and if the Pope dies following a world war of such magnitude that we are expecting, then the Vatican will be looking for someone who'll fill the shoes of Clement's Papacy.'

'But that's not possible,' Brenard interrupted. 'Gustave told me that Pope Clement confided in him that, during his vision, he was told quite clearly that he would be the last Pope of the Church.'

'Think about it Paul,' Devine said. 'Pope Clement is going to die within the next few weeks, so someone will have to succeed him. Except the person who'll succeed him will not be a true Pope, but will use the papacy as the new Roman Empire to take a political lead within the world. The leaders of the world will be in disarray, and they will seek someone to lead them into a future that will look uncertain. The Roman Church has the infrastructure across the world to make this happen, from its nuncios to parish halls, from its schools to local charities. They will see Guarducci as a man of peace, but he knows that he will lead them away from the truth and into an eternal darkness.'

'How can you be so certain?' Brenard asked, as he recalled his own vision in which he saw a bishop lead the world into the fires of hell.

'In the coming days and weeks the world will literally be torn apart, and the people of the world will be looking for someone to bring them together, to end the conflict, to literally feed them, keep them warm and reassure them that everything will be alright. The person they will be looking for simply cannot be an existing political figure, because with the world in disarray, and fear growing among the people, no nation will be able to trust any other nation. Such political events will see a massive spiritual crisis take place and people will be looking for answers. Once Clement dies, Jean Guarducci will be in the best position to put himself forward for the papacy. He's already in a strong position and influence, but as the Dean of the College of Cardinals he has the right to celebrate the requiem mass for Pope Clement, set a date for the conclave and preach one of only two sermons to the candidates before they start casting their votes.'

Paul Brenard found himself looking to Gustave Hasler, who seemed to be understanding Devine's argument a lot better as he nodded his head in agreement.

'It makes sense,' Hasler said. 'A conclave held during such times will be small. Once the Dean sets the fifteen day deadline following the Pope's death, they have to be in Rome, and those who cannot get there will lose their right to participate in the conclave.' Hasler said, looking to Devine for some reassurance that he was right. 'Cardinals far from Rome would find it nearly impossible to make their way there. We are talking about the European cardinals mainly, and they know and trust Cardinal Guarducci.'

'It's not only my suspicions that I base these claims upon, but Cardinal Guarducci fulfils every scriptural reference to the Antichrist,' Devine said. 'The fifth Psalm calls him a Man of Bloodshed and Deceit. Isaiah spoke of the one who was born from the Branch of the Terrible One, the Son of the Final Evil and the Destroyer of Nations. Jeremiah talked about the Cruel One. Daniel called him the Vile and Despicable One of The Little Horn. Think about all Cardinal Jean Guarducci has done in the last few weeks. He's silenced a Pope and has imprisoned him in the Vatican. He tried to have me murdered and succeeded in making sure that Stuart Smith paid with his life for what he knew. He created deceitful lies regarding Monsignor Hasler, removing him from Rome so he could leverage his influence and power over the Pope and prepare for his own ascent to the papacy. Yet, the greatest of them all, while he sits back like Nero himself, the world is about to burn.'

Brenard listened, but he did not speak. He knew that Guarducci had acted with such dishonour over the last few days, but he still struggled to accept that the man he knew and worked with, was the possible Antichrist. After all, by the virtue of his priesthood he was a man of God.

'Paul, I have researched this intensely and so has Donal,' Devine continued. 'We are two of the most highly rated scripture scholars of our time. We have gone through every single reference in scripture that referred to the Antichrist and we honestly could not find one that did not apply to Cardinal Guarducci. There is no doubt, not one shred of doubt in my mind that Pope Clement witnessed that vision. I believe that everything he has written in his encyclical will come to pass, and I am in no doubt that in the wings the Antichrist is waiting to emerge. We are not talking about some average man emerging from nowhere, we are talking about a man who has the power, the opportunity, the desire and the support to seize control. No one else in the world fulfils the criteria that is needed more than Cardinal Guarducci. Everything is now weighted in his favour, and he is fulfilling every scriptural prophesy ever written about him.'

Walking over to O'Keefe's desk, Devine lifted a bible before returning and sitting beside Brenard. He flicked through the pages until he found the book of Daniel.

'*And a people with their leader that shall come, shall destroy the city and the sanctuary: and the end thereof shall be waste, and after the end of the war the appointed desolation*. Daniel 9:26,' Devine began. 'The book of Daniel clearly states that the Antichrist will come from the people who destroyed the Temple. The Romans destroyed the temple of Jerusalem in 70AD. Daniel was clearly stating that the Antichrist will emerge from Rome.'

Devine flicked back a page.

'*And after their reign, when iniquities shall be grown up, there shall arise a king of a shameless face, and understanding dark sentences. And his power shall be strengthened, but not by his own force: and he shall lay all things waste, and shall prosper, and do more than can be believed. And he shall destroy the mighty, and the people of the saints.* Daniel 8:23,' Devine read out, showing Brenard the passage. 'The Antichrist can only come to power once all other power is destroyed. He will fool multitudes with his words and will lead those who trust in the saints into an evil annihilation. Does that not sound a bit Catholic to you?'

Devine flicked back another page.

'*I considered the horns, and behold another little horn sprung out of the midst of them: and three of the first horns were plucked up at the presence thereof: and behold eyes like the eyes of a man were in this horn, and a mouth speaking great things.* Daniel 7:8.'

Devine flicked forward several pages.

'*And the king shall do according to his will, and he shall be lifted up, and shall magnify himself against every god: and he shall speak great things against the God of gods, and shall prosper, till the wrath be accomplished.* Daniel 11:36,' Devine said. 'The Antichrist will stop at nothing to seek his power. He will willingly see major civilisations destroyed for his own gain. He will also be living in a place and a time where he will convince the people that he is God, and he will continue to grow in strength in his own belief. But, he needs to be a king. What is the papacy if not an absolute monarchy? Don't forget that until recent decades all Popes were crowned with a triple tiara and anointed as the Sovereign of Sovereigns.'

Devine flicked towards the end of the bible.

'*Whose coming is according to the working of Satan, in all power, and signs, and lying wonders. And in all seduction of iniquity to them that perish; because they receive not the love of the truth, that they might be saved.* 2 Thessalonians 2:9.' Devine read aloud. 'The world will see the Antichrist as something good. He won't appear like a devil, but he will deceive the world because the power of evil, the power of deception will be in him. What better way to show the world that you are good and virtuous, than assuming control of the largest religion in the world?'

Devine flicked back to the book of Daniel.

'And he shall make no account of the God of his fathers: and he shall follow not the lust of women, and he shall not regard any gods: for he shall rise up against all things. Daniel 11:37.' Devine read, before he turned to Brenard. 'Two things are important here. Firstly, he will appear to come from a deeply held faith, he will use it to rise up and gain authority and control, but in his heart he will not believe. Secondly, he will be celibate and will never have known the touch of a sexual encounter.'

Devine closed his bible and looked at Brenard.

'I could sit here for hours flicking through this book and finding prophesy after prophesy to prove my point.' Devine said, hoping that his words were not causing division. 'Everything we need to know about the Antichrist is in this book. We know that he will sign a seven year peace treaty with the world. We know that he will defeat those who will stand against him. We know that his rise to power will be meteoric. We know that he will rule the whole world politically, spiritually, militarily and economically. We know that no one will escape his wrath. We know he will control the armies, the banks, food, water and life itself. We know that he will accumulate so much power that he will be able to force every single person in the world to be branded with his mark. We know that he will arise from unprecedented destruction. We know that his aim is to destroy everything and everyone. We know that he will form a one world government. We know that he will rebuild the third Temple in Jerusalem, before entering it and proclaiming himself to be God. We know that only those who worship him will live to see the final battle of Armageddon. The only thing that isn't mentioned in this book or in the encyclical is his name. But I ask you, who else could it be?'

For a few moments they sat in silence, looking from one to another before fixing their eyes on Brenard, waiting to see what he would say or do.

'I believe you.' Brenard said, as he placed his right hand on top of Devine's as they clutched the bible. 'Last night I had a vision.'

In that moment not one of them doubted him.

'I believe I saw the Antichrist for myself,' Brenard explained, as he cried silent tears. 'I didn't see his face, but I could see that he was a bishop. Before him the world fell at his feet, they trusted him and loved him, but in the end he set about destroying them.'

'So, what are you going to do now?' Devine asked. 'You came here seeking the truth. It was no coincidence that you met me here today. I've told you everything there is to know. It's now up to you. You must do what you believe God is telling you in your heart.'

Brenard sat back in his chair and took a moment for himself. He dried his eyes, then closed them and prayed into the silence of his soul for a sign.

'I feel I should return to Rome,' he finally spoke. 'I don't know what I'll do when I get there, but it's the one place where I feel I am being called to go.'

48.

With everything she was facing, the situation with the Vatican was the one thing she could do without. Resentment and anxiety were not emotions she expected to feel in light of all that was happening. The prospect of the conspiracy being exposed was no longer a remote possibility. She could not stomach the thoughts of her involvement in silencing Pope Clement from leaking into the press. How their plan had not unraveled was beginning to look like an act of sheer luck. As the President, she knew she had breached every protocol of her office and the personal principles upon which she had based her presidency. When she first agreed to assist Guarducci, she believed she was doing it to protect the world from a mad Pope who was determined to see nations engage in a conflict too terrible to imagine. Now, she could see that the Pope was right, but she could not undo what she had done. Instead, she had to contain and control the truth, so it would never become known to the world.

Lifting the phone on her desk, she asked for a secure line to the director of the CIA

Following an earlier briefing, the Director had warned her that Brenard and Hasler were going to expose the truth about the encyclical. She did not know the full extent of what they knew, but the risk that they knew the full truth, especially with Hasler now involved, was a risk she could no longer afford to take.

'Good morning, Madam President.' Virginia Moore answered.

'Are you alone?'

'I am, Ma'am.'

'Where are we in relation to Cardinal Brenard and Monsignor Hasler?'

'The private airline company that Cardinal Brenard is using have filed flight plans for a flight scheduled to leave Dublin for Rome.'

'Should we intercept their plane?'

'I would advise against that. I think we should get them both back to the Vatican. If you give the order for our plans, then that will be enough to see them both silenced for good.'

President Cleary took a moment to think it through. Once the command was given there would be no turning back. Feeling the threat growing by the minute, she had to do something. Powerless to stop her nation from being attacked, she was not powerless to end her problem with the Vatican.

'I've taken the decision, Virginia.' The President finally spoke up. 'I want you to proceed with your plans for the Vatican. I can't take the chance of this truth ever getting out. I've let it run on for far too long.'

'I'll get onto it right away.'

'You're convinced it'll look like an attack from the Islamic States?'

'Absolutely Ma'am,' she insisted, knowing that her operation was fool proof.

'I need it carried out today, will that be possible?'

'Everything is already in place, I've just been waiting for your command.'

'Make sure you keep Cardinal Guarducci alive. We'll need someone on the inside who'll be of use to us in the coming days. Plus, he'll back us on our version of events and he'll be best suited to control the aftermath of the attack. The last thing we need to worry about is some other maverick cardinal or bishop latching onto the truth that we're involved in this.'

'We'll make sure Guarducci is spared,' she insisted. 'Is there anyone else?'

The President thought about it for a moment. 'No. I want this problem to go away once and for all.'

'You've nothing to worry about, Ma'am' she replied. 'It will be a successful operation.'

'Thank you, Virginia.' The President said, as she hung up the phone.

As the most powerful woman in the world, she'd never felt so powerless as her plane flew somewhere over a country she could not protect. In a matter of hours the world would be reeling in horror with the terrorist attack on the Vatican. But, she could see no other way out. Lifting a blanket from the end of the couch, she fixed the pillows before lying down. There was nothing else she could do but hope that sleep would come. She flicked the switch beside her, turning off the lights in the room. Closing her eyes, she listened to the drone of the plane's engines. Her mind turned to prayer as she sought an absolution, not just for what she was about to do, but for the unspeakable wrong she had already committed.

49.

As punctual as ever, General Durkin arrived at his office at Rawlins' Air Force Base at six in the morning having had less than three hours sleep.

'Good morning, Sir.' His secretary greeted, as he stood to attention behind his desk.

'At ease, Lieutenant,' he replied, handing him his coat and military cap.

'Would you like your coffee now, Sir?' He asked, taking the items from him.

'Yes, bring it through.'

'The morning report is already on your desk. You have a meeting with the senior base staff at six-thirty.'

'Thank you, Ryan.'

His day was starting out like any other, structured with precise routine and calculated with military planning and precision to prevent the unexpected from happening. Except, he knew with the current security situation facing his nation, his day was going to be long and the unexpected could well happen.

Standing beside his desk he opened the report, his ears picking up the news that was coming from the television. As usual his staff had not disappointed him, they had prepared the bunkers and the operation facilities for the possible military evacuation that afternoon. Operation Freedom Hawk, as it was aptly named by the chiefs in the Pentagon, had Rawlins' Air Force Base designated as the location to house the Members of the Senate and their families.

'Come in,' he shouted, hearing his Lieutenant knocking at the door.

'Your coffee, Sir,' he said, as he carried the mug which bore the crest of Rawlins' military base on its side.

'We'll all be living off this stuff in the coming days,' Durkin said, as he sipped the strong roasted coffee.

No sooner had he set the cup down on his desk, the phone began to ring.

Durkin picked up the phone and listened intently before clicking his fingers at Ryan to fetch him the remote for his digital security system.

'Negative! You're not to enter that room, until I've assessed the situation. Are you sure he set off the panic alarm?'

Holding the phone to his ear, he took the remote from Ryan and pressed the green button, changing the signal on his television to the security link up within the base. Flicking through his menu he located the camera he was looking for. An empty room appeared on the screen.

Using the sensor on the remote he made the cameras scan the room. He saw something. He zoomed in towards the door.

'Shit! Captain, you have permission to enter the room,' he gave the order down the phone. 'Our prisoner has collapsed beside the door and looks to be in need of urgent medical attention. Call for the medical team. I'll be there in five minutes.'

Taking his security pass from his pocket, Captain Larry Barton pushed it into the security lock and entered his password. The doors opened, giving him access to the room where the prisoner was held in solitary confinement.

'Stand aside,' he ordered the two soldiers, as he approached the main door to the secure room.

'Sir, we have direct orders from General Durkin to allow no one into this room.'

'I've been given clearance,' he spoke firmly to them. 'General Durkin is on his way. I'm ordering you to stand aside.'

They knew better than to resist. So standing aside, they allowed Barton access to the security lock, and typing in the authorisation code he unlocked the door.

He went to push it open, but the body of the prisoner was wedged against it on the floor where he had collapsed. He looked down, noticing the legs of the prisoner's orange jumpsuit. With his shoulder pressed against the door, he slowly pushed it open to give himself enough room to get inside.

Lying face down on the floor, the prisoner was unconscious. So pulling him away from the door, Barton turned him over onto his back.

He knew the prisoner was not dead. He had seen death many times before and this was not one of those times, but he knew the prisoner was close to it. Placing two fingers to the prisoner's neck he felt for his pulse. It was weak, but he was still clinging to life.

Grabbing the pillow from the bed he lifted the prisoner's head.

'Jesus Christ!' he cried out, when he looked at the prisoner's face.

He felt his own heart begin to pound. *It can't be him?*

He heard footsteps running towards the room.

'You'll be alright,' Barton said to him, as he gently placed his head onto the pillow. 'Help is on the way.'

'Is he okay?' Captain Brad Mueller, the base's chief surgical doctor asked, as he arrived at the door.

'I don't know,' Barton replied, as he stood back to let Mueller have a closer examination. 'His pulse is very weak.'

'It looks as if he's suffered a heart attack,' Mueller replied, as he knelt down beside him.

Mueller suddenly stopped his examination. He had to look twice.

'Is this who I think it is?' He asked Barton.

'I don't know Brad, but it sure as hell looks like him.'

Arriving at the secure room, General Durkin stood outside the open door as he watched the doctor work on his prisoner.

'Is he going to pull through this?' Durkin asked.

'He's in a stable condition for the moment,' Mueller replied. 'I think he's suffering a heart attack. All his vital signs are good, and he's starting to respond to us.'

'What medical treatment do you think he needs?'

'We need to get him out of this bunker and up to the hospital.'

‘Can’t you treat him here?’ Durkin asked, not too keen with the thought of him being removed from the secure cell, in which his identity had been kept hidden since his arrival.

‘Sir, he could die without the necessary medical treatment’, Mueller insisted. ‘He may need to be operated on.’

‘A bypass?’

‘More than likely, but I’ll need to put him through a series of tests to get a true picture of his condition.’

‘Fair enough,’ Durkin replied, knowing he had no other option.

With his clearance granted, Durkin could only watch as his classified prisoner was lifted onto a medical stretcher.

‘Right, let’s get him up to the wing,’ Mueller said, as he fastened the last strap around his patient’s legs.

‘Just one thing before you go,’ Durkin said, as he blocked their path. ‘I take it you know who this man is?’

‘To be honest, it’s none of our concern,’ Mueller replied. ‘We just need to get him to the medical wing so we can treat him.’

‘Well, it’s a matter of National Security and classified,’ Durkin insisted. ‘Do you both understand?’

‘Yes, Sir!’ they replied in unison.

‘Let me see him,’ Durkin ordered, as he walked over to look at him.

‘We are going to give you the best treatment there is,’ he said. ‘Try to relax.’

The patient could only look back up at him, his eyes heavy with the trauma his body had just gone through.

Leaning forward, Durkin took hold of the prisoner’s frail arthritic hand and whispered into his ear, ‘You’re in safe hands, Your Holiness.’

50.

'What is so urgent?' Guarducci snapped, at his private secretary.

'There is a phone call from The White House waiting for you on your secure line,' Tardini replied, shocked to hear the anger in the Cardinal's voice.

Knowing that this was the call he had been expecting, Guarducci walked into his office, closed the door behind him and lifted the phone. 'Jean Guarducci speaking.'

'Your Eminence, I have the Director of the CIA on the line,' the male operator said. 'I'm putting her through to you now.'

Moving around his desk he took his seat as he waited for her to come on line.

'Jean,' a female voice said, 'this is Virginia Moore, Director of the CIA. We haven't had the pleasure of speaking to one another before now, but I thought it right to give you a call. I've just spoken with the President and she's made a decision.'

Guarducci gripped the phone tightly as he straightened himself up in his chair.

'The President isn't prepared to hold off any longer. We appreciate that you have tried your utmost best, but we now feel that we need to bring this to an end.'

Guarducci closed his eyes and took a deep breath as he waited to hear her plan.

'Cardinal Brenard and Monsignor Hasler are currently flying back to Rome on a chartered jet. When they land I need you to ring them, get them to attend a meeting in the Vatican. Once there we will silence them.'

'Are they to be murdered?' Guarducci asked.

There was a moment of silence on the phone before Moore replied, 'Yes!'

Guarducci knew it had to be done. 'How?'

'We plan to stage a terrorist attack right in the heart of the Vatican.'

'What?' he asked, nearly dropping the phone from his hand. 'How are you going to do that?'

'Once they are in the Papal Apartment one of my agents will execute them, before setting off an advanced explosive device within the Apostolic Palace.'

'A bomb?' he asked, as he stood up behind his desk. 'Is there no other way?'

'It's the only way we'll be able to mask this,' she explained. 'The blame will be placed on the Islamic States. Plus, it will also deal the Clement problem.'

In that moment Guarducci felt a sadness of heart, not for the deaths that were about to take place but for the fact that when he finally inherited the papacy, he would never get to live in the beauty of the Apostolic Palace.

'You seem a little quiet!' Moore pointed out, not reassured with his silence.

He stood looking around his room, knowing that by the end of the evening it would all be turned to rubble. It was a high price to ask of him to achieve his destiny.

'So Jean, are you with us?' she asked, pushing him for an answer.

He could feel his hour coming to hand. It was a painful decision to make, but then again there were many palaces within the Vatican that he could reside. Yet, what mattered most of all was the fact that he would be the bearer of the fisherman's ring.

'I know this is happening much sooner than we had planned,' Moore continued. 'And, yes, the means to achieving the end have changed. But, allow us to do this and by the end of the day the Holy See of Rome will be vacant. This is your moment, Jean. We need you.'

Guarducci smiled. 'You have my complete trust and support.'

51.

General Durkin arrived back in his office, having just left the Holy Father to the medical tests Captain Mueller was putting him through. 'Get Admiral Lyman on the phone as quickly as possible.'

'Yes, Sir,' Lieutenant Ryan replied.

Durkin took his seat behind his desk, anxiously waiting for the phone to ring. He knew that Pope Clement's illness was going to throw the whole evacuation operation completely off course. He looked at his watch. He had already missed the senior officers' briefing. He made a note to reschedule it for later on in the morning.

His phone rang. He picked it up.

'I have Admiral Lyman on the line for you, Sir.'

'Put him through.' Durkin ordered Ryan, straightening himself up in his chair to take the call.

'Hello,' the voice came through on a crackled line.

'Morning Sir, this is General Durkin from Rawlins' Air Force Base.'

'This had better be good General,' Lyman said. 'This isn't a particularly good time.'

'I understand, Sir,' Durkin replied. 'But, I thought I should inform you that we've a situation here at the minute.'

'Has something happened to our operation plans?'

'No Sir, we have a situation regarding Prisoner P.'

Lyman didn't respond, it was not the news he wanted to hear.

'Are you still there, Sir?'

'What's the situation, Durkin?'

'About an hour ago Prisoner P collapsed in his quarters.'

'Is he alright?'

'We've had to move him to the base hospital for some urgent tests.'

'What sort of tests?'

'The chief military doctor suspects that he's suffered a mild heart attack.'

'I take it his identity is now known throughout the base?' Lyman answered, more fearful of the real truth being exposed than the Pope dying.

'No Sir,' Durkin insisted, wanting to show that he was still containing the situation. 'Apart from the doctor and the officer who arrived first on the scene, no one else in the base knows that we have him here.'

'What about the nurses in the hospital and other medical staff?'

Durkin hadn't thought about them until the Admiral mentioned it.

'You'll need to keep him well isolated, and make sure everyone who comes into contact with him is made aware of their need to keep his identity and presence at the base strictly classified.'

'I've already taken the appropriate measures.'

'Good.'

'There is one more thing.'

'What's that?'

'He might need to go through emergency surgery.'

'Well, the President did give very clear orders that she wants him kept alive and well at all costs. If an operation is what it takes to keep him alive then put him through it.'

'Thank you, Sir.'

'One more thing Durkin, make sure the operating team know that they must tread very carefully. We can't have the Pope die on one of our operating tables.'

'Will do, Sir.'

'Keep me posted on his treatment.'

Before Durkin had the chance to reply, Admiral Lyman terminated the call.

Having been granted the permission needed to carry out the necessary medical treatment on the Pope, he lifted his cellphone and headed for the medical wing.

52.

As their taxi pulled up on the edge of Saint Peter's Square, Brenard ended the call and placed the cellphone back into the inner pocket of his suit jacket.

'Well, there's no such a thing as coincidence.' He said.

'Was that Cardinal Guarducci on the phone?' Hasler asked.

'Yes. He wants us to join the Holy Father and himself for lunch.' Brenard replied, as he looked at his watch. 'Obviously, they know I took you out of the abbey.'

'Are you afraid?'

'Yes,' Brenard replied, as he turned to look at him; his face drawn with worry and his eyes burdened with a fear of the unknown. 'I just don't know what's going to happen once we enter the Apostolic Palace.'

'In the end we should have nothing to fear,' Hasler said. 'With the Lord on our side, who can truly be against us?'

Paul Brenard managed to give him a smile, but Hasler's reassurance failed to settle the tangible fear he now felt.

Getting out of the taxi they walked across the square. Reaching the Bronze Door, the Swiss Guards gave a visible look of surprise the moment they saw Gustave Hasler.

'The Holy Father is expecting us,' Brenard said.

'Yes, Your Eminence,' the main guard replied. 'Cardinal Guarducci has just contacted us, he is on his way down to meet you. Please take a seat inside. He will be with you shortly.'

As a Prince of the Church, Brenard found it humiliating to have to sit and wait, especially when passing Vatican staff looked at him, and then in a mixture of shock and disgust when they saw Hasler sitting beside him.

After a few minutes, Brenard saw Guarducci walk towards them. In his regalia he held the Palace like it was his own court, and for the first time Brenard could see something about him that he had never seen before.

The closer Guarducci came towards him, the more Brenard's blood boiled within him.

'Paul,' Guarducci said, as he stretched out his hand.

'Why did you lie to me?' He finally spoke up, standing to his feet and refusing to shake his hand.

'Be careful!' Guarducci insisted, not wanting people to hear Brenard raise his voice and call him a liar to his face. 'Let us go upstairs, have lunch with His Holiness and all will be revealed there.'

'Everything?' Brenard asked, determined not to move until he had his reassurance.

'I will tell you everything,' Guarducci promised him. 'Even the reasons why we silenced the encyclical.'

Once in the security of the Papal Apartment, Guarducci stopped outside the door to the Pope's private study. 'Do you have a copy of the encyclical with you?'

Brenard hesitated for a moment, before he tapped his briefcase.

'Have you read it?'

Brenard nodded.

'In that case, let us go in,' Guarducci said, as he opened the door and led them into the Pope's study.

'Gustave, close the door,' Guarducci requested. 'Please, take a seat.'

'Where's His Holiness?' Brenard asked, surprised not to see him in the room ready to receive them in audience.

'He will be with us shortly, now please take a seat.'

'So, why did you lie to me?' Brenard asked again, as he sat down.

'Paul, you should have left it alone!' Guarducci replied. 'You should have come to me with the encyclical.'

'Innocent people have been killed!' Brenard said, raising his voice in justified anger.

'I know. They also wanted to kill both of you to stop the truth from ever getting out. If it were not for me, both of you would now be dead. Paul, the Holy Father told you his wishes in person, and still you disobeyed him. That is the reason why so many people have been killed.'

'Don't blame me for their murders,' Brenard replied, angered by the very suggestion. 'I want to see the Holy Father.'

Guarducci's moment had come. Taking a deep breath, he tried to calm the adrenalin that was pulsating through his body.

'Very well, that is what you are here for,' Guarducci said, as he walked over and opened the door that led into the Pope's bedroom.

Brenard and Hasler stood up from their seats and waited for His Holiness to arrive. Slowly, Guarducci pushed him into the room in his wheelchair.

For Hasler it was a moment of great shock to see the man he had served and loved for years so frail and so near death. Walking over to him, Hasler could not believe how different he looked. Suddenly, his instinct took hold and he sensed something was not right. Then it dawned on him, the moment he saw the old man's hands.

Guarducci smiled knowingly. The game was up. He knew he would never have fooled Hasler.

'That is not him!' Hasler spoke up, as he walked closer to the old man in the wheelchair.

'What do you mean?' Brenard asked, as he followed him.

Sitting in the wheelchair, the old man looked nervously at them all. It was not the reaction he had expected. Guarducci had told him that it was just going to be an informal meeting with two junior cardinals.

'This is not the Pope!' Hasler said in horror, as he looked into the old man's eyes and saw the dark truth gazing back at him. 'Look at both his hands, there is no sign of arthritis.'

'What is it, Paul?' Guarducci asked Brenard, taking great pleasure in the fear he could actually feel coming from his body. 'You look like you have just seen a ghost!'

53.

'What have you done with the Holy Father?' Brenard asked.

'As far as I am aware he is safe and well?'

'Where is he?'

'To be completely honest I do not know,' Guarducci replied, as a matter of fact. 'Your government is looking after him.'

For Paul Brenard it was the final blow of betrayal, the final piece of the puzzle he had spent the last few days trying to piece together. Looking at the imposter before him, dressed in full papal pontificals, he genuinely passed for the real thing. Brenard mind struggled to fathom the enormity of what was unfolding before his very eyes.

'You need to relax yourself Paul,' Guarducci smiled, knowing he now had nothing whatsoever to lose. 'Sit down and let us talk this through.'

Slowly, Brenard turned and looked at Guarducci. 'Jean, what have you done?'

Guarducci laughed.

'Jean, tell me this isn't true.' Brenard said, hoping against all hope that Hasler was wrong.

Guarducci looked into Brenard's very soul. 'He is not the Pope.'

'Then who is he?' Hasler asked, who unlike Brenard wanted to know.

'His name is Giorgio,' Guarducci answered. 'He is an old friend of the powers that be.'

'I'd like to go back to my room,' Giorgio said, not wanting to listen to Guarducci.

'You will stay right where you are!' Guarducci told him.

As Brenard watched Guarducci's manner change, he knew there was going to be a price to pay for being told the truth.

'Our contact with the CIA brought him on board,' Guarducci explained. 'He has worked for the agency all his life. When we suggested that Pope Clement needed removed from office, they came up with this plan. Giorgio had nothing to lose. Tell them about your illness.'

'I have only weeks to live,' Giorgio spoke softly, struggling for breath. 'I have terminal pancreatic cancer.'

'We needed someone willing to take on the role,' Guarducci took over. 'Giorgio fitted our profile well. He was the same age, same build and had similar facial characteristics as Clement. Three weeks ago, we had a plastic surgeon work on him to refine the detail on his face. That is why we had to get rid of you Gustave and the nuns from the Papal Apartment, for you would have worked it out the moment we brought him home from the Gemelli.'

'What's he getting for all of this?'

'Apart from his one way ticket to hell?' Guarducci joked, much to Giorgio's displeasure. 'We are going to make sure that his daughter is looked after financially once he passes away.'

'How much?'

'A few million. The modern day equivalent to the ancient thirty pieces of silver.'

'Jesus!' Brenard said, as he ran his hands through his hair, still trying to come to grips with the enormity of it all.

'You need to start looking at it from a different angle, Paul.'

'There is only one way to look at it Jean!' he argued back. 'You've broken every vow that you've ever made.'

'Nonsense! I've taken every decision with the best interests of the Church in mind.'

'More like your own!'

'For crying out loud, Paul! Clement had lost the plot. He was delusional in the end. I could not sit back and allow him to bring everything we hold dear tumbling down around us. I had no choice but to do what I did.'

'Come off it, Jean. Look around you and what's happening. Everything he'd written in that encyclical, every vision he'd ever witnessed is all starting to be fulfilled. He was right and you were wrong, but then again it's all to your advantage.'

'Why do you say that?' Guarducci asked, as a knowing smile crept across his face.

Brenard, felt a fear like he had never felt before in his life. He knew the moment he uttered the words that the price to pay would be his very life.

'I know who you are!' Brenard finally said. 'You are the Antichrist!'

Guarducci stood motionless before them all. For the first time in his life someone had named him for who he truly was. In his mind he felt a peace like he had never felt before, because the truth had set him free. Something within him, in that very moment, changed. The darkness which he has suppressed all his life began to take hold.

'My time has come, when I must be glorified for all the world to see,' Guarducci revealed. 'I was destined for this moment from the moment of my creation. For many years I have had to hide the truth of who I am, remain silent and serve until this very hour came to pass.'

'What about your priesthood?' Brenard asked him, looking him straight in the eye. 'Does that mean nothing to you?'

'There is nothing of substance within it to believe.' He coldly replied, his very eyes burning with the truth he held from them all. 'Sure, what is it all about? Stone and precious ornaments? Designer vestments that cloak the power we have over people lives? For over forty years I have had to graft this path to get to where I now am. But, it has been worth it for the glory that the world is going to bestow on me when I will lead them to their destiny. You are a man of great potential, Paul. Come follow me and I will make you complete in every way.'

Amid the outside clamour of midday Rome, an unsettling silence permeated the room.

'No!' Brenard finally replied. 'My soul belongs to the One who will in the end destroy you and everything that you stand for!'

Guarducci looked at him and nodded his head in understanding. With nothing else to be gained he turned, walked over and opened the door.

Brenard felt his body tighten as Mode entered the room.

'Answer me this, Paul,' Guarducci said, as he walked into the middle of the room with Mode. 'There is an old belief that light will always overcome the darkness. But, what would happen if the light was extinguished forever?'

'You'll never be able to silence the light of truth,' Brenard argued. 'It is far greater than you will ever be!'

'Let us see, shall we?' Guarducci replied. 'Execute these two men.'

Brenard stood frozen in horror as he watched Jean Guarducci point his finger towards Giorgio and then to Hasler.

'Stop Jean, this isn't right.'

'It is the only way Paul,' he replied, as he watched the agent lift his pistol from his jacket and screw the silencer onto the end of the barrel. 'Nothing will stop me from achieving my destiny.'

'No!' Giorgio cried out, as Mode raised his gun towards him.

'Let him live, Jean,' Brenard pleaded.

'Why? His existence is no longer of use to me.' Guarducci replied. 'Kill him!'

Without a second's hesitation, Mode released the safety on his gun and fired.

'No!' Brenard cried out, as he watched the old man jolt back as a trickle of blood emerged from his heart, flooding his white cassock as he slipped away into his own death.

'Now the other one,' Guarducci ordered, looking directly at Gustave Hasler. 'We should have done this a long time ago!'

Brenard pulled Hasler behind him to protect him.

'Please, Jean, this is not right.'

'Shoot the priest but keep the cardinal alive,' Guarducci ordered Mode.

Suddenly, in a desperate last second chance for his life, Hasler pushed Brenard towards Mode and ran for the door.

The gun went off.

As Paul Brenard fell to the floor, clutching his bleeding stomach, Mode turned around and placed his focus entirely on Gustave Hasler as he ran towards the door.

He pulled the trigger, bringing Hasler down.

As Hasler, lay choking in his own blood, Mode walked over and slammed the sole of his boot down onto his back, pinning him to the floor. Then aiming his gun to the back of Hasler's head, he pulled the trigger.

Paul Brenard heard the dull slump of the bullet, but his own pain was enough to force him to defend himself. Pulling himself onto his side, and in great agony, he rested against a chair. He could feel the coldness of death coming over him, while warm blood flowed through his hands as he covered the wound over his stomach.

Gasping for air he looked around the room, only to notice Mode walk towards him with his gun aimed at his head. Closing his eyes he waited for the trigger to be pulled.

'Wait!' He heard Guarducci's voice cry out.

Slowly, Brenard opened his eyes, only to see Guarducci looking down upon him.

'Leave us for now!'

Slipping his gun inside his jacket pocket, Mode followed Guarducci's command and left them alone.

54.

'I want you to understand this before you die,' Guarducci said, as he knelt beside Paul Brenard.

Struggling for breath, and choking with the pain, Brenard looked at him knowing that his life was quickly ebbing away from him.

'You should have followed my instructions and left this to lie,' Guarducci continued, ignoring his suffering. 'You were never destined to win this battle. Look at you. You have failed. Your soul now belongs to me. Everything you ever believed has been lost, because the power I am about to unleash throughout the world will see to it that everything will be placed in the right order.'

'You will burn in hell,' Brenard replied, his pain and uncontrollable fear growing by moment.

'It is a pity you will never live to see the full manifestation of my power. Had you followed my way you could have held great power and influence, and no harm would ever have come to you. Not now, not ever!'

As his breathing shortened and became more rapid, Brenard could only look at him, knowing that his faith in the light was stronger than the darkness Guarducci possessed.

'Look I will show you,' Guarducci replied, as he reached out his hand until it touched Brenard's wound.

Brenard suddenly felt the pain of something being driven deep into his wound. He cried out in agony. But, Guarducci silenced him by placing his other hand over his mouth.

'Shush!' Guarducci whispered softly into his ear.

Brenard could not stop his cries. The pain was growing too deep. It felt like his very flesh was being torn open as his insides burned with an agony of fire.

'I have total power,' Guarducci continued to speak softly to him. 'I know you can feel the power.'

Writhing in agony, Brenard struggled as the pain tore deep into his heart, while his head convulsed in the anguish of the torture.

'I have the very power over life and death itself,' he continued. 'I used and played everyone to get where I am. No one can stop me. I know you can feel it.'

Unwilling to give into him, Brenard prayed into the light to be taken from his suffering.

'There is no use in praying,' Guarducci said, reading his mind. 'He has forsaken you and left you in my hands.'

Suddenly, Guarducci pulled his hand away and the pressure of the pain sharpened, leaving Brenard twisted in agony and gasping for breath as his heart pounded inside his chest.

'I will rule everything and everyone, Paul. Just like it has been prophesied. Yet, still you cling to the hope of salvation, why?'

Brenard couldn't reply, as his pain was too overwhelming.

'For two thousand years, people like you have been fooled by this,' Guarducci said, with utter disgust, as he ripped his own pectoral cross from around his neck and flung it at Brenard. 'The salvation of Calvary that was meant to have conquered sin once and for all? The biggest lie ever told in the history of the world. What Salvation? What victory? Look around you Paul, my Master's power was never defeated by some Jew on a cross. He has always ruled the world and no one has ever stopped him. I have played the game well, and very soon I will hold everyone in the power, and in the majesty that my Master will clothe me.'

'You're wrong,' Brenard replied, still not willing to submit his own soul to Guarducci's darkness.

'This is your last chance,' Guarducci said, as he leaned in closer to him. 'Renounce it all, come follow me and I will give you back your life!'

'No!' Brenard cried, his pain making it nearly impossible to get the words out. 'Today I will die…' He struggled to find the breath that he needed. 'But… come the morning… It will… be… beautiful!'

Guarducci smiled, 'Then I have no further need of you.'

Walking over the door, Guarducci brought Mode back into the room.

Brenard knew that this his end. Reaching up he grabbed hold of his own pectoral cross. Suddenly, his pain died away and the room fell silent. A peace like he had never felt before in his life graced his spirit. Even though he could see Mode aim the gun at his head, he did not fear the terror of his plight. Taking one last breath, he surrendered everything to the One he professed.

55.

Striding over to the Pope's desk, Mode cleared everything off it with one swipe of his hand before setting down Brenard's briefcase. He opened it and handed Guarducci the fourth and final copy of the encyclical.

Holding the document which had become the lodestone of his life, Guarducci's qualms evaporated. He was no longer subject to the power of exposure the encyclical held. In that moment every concern about his future evaporated. Standing beside the desk, he looked around the study and the price that had been paid. To his left lay the dead imposter with his white soutane stained red with his blood. To his right lay the lifeless body of Gustave Hasler with a pool of blood congealing around his head. And at his feet lay the brother cardinal who had died believing in Christ and a Church that Guarducci had spent a lifetime strengthening to achieve his final aim. His transfiguration was almost complete. He had climbed the mountain and the tents had been pitched at his feet. His time had come.

'I want it destroyed in the explosion,' Guarducci instructed, as he set the encyclical down beside the briefcase. 'So, what happens now?'

'I'm activating an advanced thermobaric air explosive,' Mode replied, as he retrieved a much larger case from the Pope's bedroom. 'When I trigger the detonator it'll ignite a supersonic explosive wave. It'll have the same effect as a two-thousand pound warhead. There'll be very little left of the Palace once it goes off.'

'What about the bodies?'

'They'll be incinerated to a handful of ash.'

Closing the case carefully, Mode placed the detonation trigger into his pocket. 'Are you ready?'

'I need to wash the blood from my hands. Give me two minutes.'

Walking from the study into the Pope's bathroom, Guarducci began scrubbing his hands under the running warm water. As the water mingled with Brenard's blood, and spiralled into the drain, Guarducci recalled the years of ritual when his hands were washed at the altar before he said the words to consecrate elements the people deemed sacred. The pointless blood sacrifice of Calvary. Pointless words spoken over tasteless bread and bitter wine which transformed it into nothing of substance. From the moment he was ordained he felt nothing. There was no anointing of his soul. The chrism oil of majesty, anointed on the palms of his hands left no indelible mark. But, the moment he was sealed by the Church he knew that he had been given a power few men had. For those who believed in him he held a power beyond life and death, a power that reached into eternity. For this he owed the Church everything. Now on the verge of absolute power he knew that the world would fall before him and follow him into its true destiny.

'We need to get as far away as we possibly can,' Mode said, as he walked into the bathroom. 'Somewhere that'll shelter us from the direct explosion.'

'Would the rear of Saint Peter's Basilica suffice?' Guarducci asked, as he dried his hands on a cotton towel, before brushing back his hair with his hand and adjusting his red zucchetto.

'Perfect.'

Following Mode, Guarducci went to leave the apartment. Stopping at the door he turned back the moment he realised that his pectoral cross, which he had ripped from his neck, lay beside Brenard's body. Lifting the golden cross from the floor he wiped the splattered blood from it onto Brenard's sleeve, before looking at the broken chain. Tossing it to one side he knelt beside Brenard and removed his pectoral cross and chain from his body.

'Wash and dry this,' Guarducci ordered Mode, as he handed him the pectoral cross and chain.

Reluctantly, Mode took the blood soaked cross and went into the bathroom knowing that Guarducci needed it to avoid suspicion.

'Damn fool!' Guarducci whispered, as he looked into the open but lifeless eyes of Paul Brenard. 'I would have given you anything you desired if you had followed me. Now, you face an eternal darkness. Your life extinguished forever. I do not know if you can still hear my voice, but if you can I want you to know that you have given up everything for nothing. The beautiful morning will never come for you, but come tomorrow I will unite the world against everything you lived and died for. No one can stop me now.'

With nothing more to say, Guarducci leaned forward and kissed Brenard on the cheek.

Mode saw the moment.

'There is one more thing that I want to take,' Guarducci replied, as he took the pectoral cross and chain from Mode, placed it around his neck and walked over to the fixed bookcases that lined the wall opposite the Pope's desk. In the middle sat the icon of Rublev's Saviour of Zvenigorod, gifted to Pope Clement from the Patriarch of Moscow during his first ecumenical visit to the Vatican at the beginning of his Papacy. 'I like the symbolism of Christ's decay,' Guarducci said, as he removed it from its niche. 'It would be a shame to see it destroyed so soon. I want to keep it as a reminder of what is to come.'

'We need to get going,' Mode said, as he watched Guarducci wrap the icon in a linen cloth he had removed from the coffee table.

Taking one last look around the study, Guarducci nodded that he understood Mode's request. Then, with absolute assurance he turned and left.

Taking the Pope's private elevator, Guarducci and Mode arrived at the ground floor of the Apostolic Palace a few minutes later. Following Guarducci, Mode was taken through a series of less ornate corridors and rooms before entering the vast sacristy of Saint Peter's Basilica. Surprised that no one was there, Guarducci opened one of the large vestment drawers and placed the icon inside for safe keeping. Then exiting a side door, that led them outside to the eastern gable wall of the basilica, they approached the boundary of the Vatican gardens. Upon seeing the Secretary of State, the Swiss Guards opened the gate and allowed them through.

'It will be quiet here,' Guarducci explained, as he led Mode through the majestic beauty of the gardens.

Reaching the rear of the basilica, Guarducci stopped and turned to Mode. 'Will here do?'

For a moment Mode stood emotionless. With his eyes locked with Guarducci's, he understood that the cardinal was not the man the world believed him to be. Gently, he took the detonator from his pocket, flicked open the lid and handed it over.

In a fluid motion, Guarducci took the detonator and pressed the button.

56.

Saturday, 12th April.

Through a corridor window, General Durkin stood looking into a side room of the medical wing as Pope Clement, who sat on a chair beside his bed, recovered from his operation.

What will become of him? He wondered, knowing that the Pope would either spend the rest of his days in solitary confinement, or face an executive order to have his life terminated to prevent the truth from ever becoming public knowledge that America was involved in the terrorist attack against the Vatican. Either way, he felt sorry for the old man. But, he had his orders to follow and he was determined that once the Pope was well enough to leave the medical wing that he would be going straight back to the bunker until his fate was decided.

'Morning, Sir.' Captain Mueller, said as he approached the door to examine the Pope's progress.

'I can't believe that he's recovering so well,' Durkin replied, genuinely amazed at the turn in the Pope's fortune.

'He's doing very well, but he will need some physiotherapy.'

'What for?' Durkin asked, irritated that more people were going to be having access to him.

'He needs to carry out a few breathing and coughing exercises, to prevent pneumonia from setting into his lungs. That's why I have him sitting up in the chair.'

'Is he in much pain?'

'Quite a lot of discomfort. It'll take about four to six weeks for his breastbone to completely heal and for the swelling in his right leg to subside following the surgery to remove a vein. Yet, with all that put aside, his progress has been exceptional for a man of his age.'

'Good.'

'Would you like to speak with him?'

'No. It's more important that he rests.'

'No problem,' Mueller replied. 'If you'll excuse me Sir, I'm going to need to examine him.'

'Don't let me hold you back,' Durkin replied, as he took his cap from under his arm and put it on his head. 'Continue to keep me informed on his progress.'

Mueller acknowledged with a smile that he would, and then waited until the General turned to leave the wing, before he opened the door to walk into the room.

'How are you feeling?' Mueller asked Pope Clement, as he walked into the room. 'Are you in much pain?'

Pope Clement could only manage to nod his head. It was too painful to lift his arms to remove the oxygen mask, let alone find enough breath to say a few words.

'Okay,' Mueller replied, as he walked around the room closing the vertical blinds to give him complete privacy. The whole time he was doing so, he was aware of the security camera in the corner of the room watching his every move.

'Now, let me see this scar of yours,' he said, as he pulled a chair up before the Pope with his back to the camera, before he started to unfasten the buttons of his pyjama shirt.

Slowly, he peeled away the surgical plaster that covered his breastbone, watching the Pope's face the whole time to make sure he wasn't causing him too much discomfort.

'That looks good,' Mueller continued, as he checked the wound for swelling, gapes, oozing fluid and early signs of infection. 'Excellent,' he said once he finished his examination and put on a new sterile plaster.

'Has anyone explained what happened?'

Pope Clement shook his head.

'Two days ago you suffered a heart attack. Do you remember?'

Again he shook his head.

'We had to carry out a few tests on your heart, only to discover that you needed emergency bypass surgery. I performed the operation myself and it went well.'

In grateful appreciation Pope Clement mouthed the words, *thank you.*

'Hopefully you'll make a good recovery.' Mueller replied, reassuring him with a warm smile.

Lifting the chart from the end of the bed Mueller looked through the notes. 'Your Holiness, I'm a Catholic and my brother is a priest. Why are you here?'

For a moment Pope Clement looked deeply into his eyes, to see if he was a man he could trust.

'Let me help you,' Mueller said, as he removed the oxygen mask from his face.

Despite the pain of breathing, Pope Clement managed to speak.

'They have silenced me.'

Mueller could see the struggle it was for him to talk. Still, it was enough to confirm his own suspicions.

'Why?' Mueller asked, as he took his pulse.

'That the world is soon going to…' he went on to explain, before he had to stop with the shooting pain that came from his chest.

'Take your time,' Mueller replied, holding his hand firmly to reassure him.

'… See the second coming of Jesus Christ!' Clement finished saying.

Mueller stopped what he was doing.

'What is it?' Clement asked, seeing the fear deep in Mueller's eyes.

With trembling hands Mueller placed the oxygen mask back over his face.

'I need you to trust me, Your Holiness,' he said, as he flicked through the medical records. 'I'm going to tell you something that they've been keeping from you, but I don't want you to react in any way. Do I have your word?' He looked up to see the Pope nod his head in agreement. 'If they find out that I've told you, or that you know, then I fear that the consequences will be severe.'

As Pope Clement sat and listened, he became more aware of the security camera that watched his every move and he sensed the risk the young surgeon was taking.

'Two days ago, there was a terrorist attack in the Vatican,' Mueller began, as he placed a stethoscope under the Pope's shirt. 'The world is placing the blame for the attack with the Islamic States. I don't know the full story, but you were apparently murdered in the attack along with a hundred and fifty workers inside the Apostolic Palace and over fifty tourists in Saint Peter's Square. They are planning to hold your funeral tomorrow morning.'

Placing the stethoscope back around his neck he looked up at the Pope, only to see silent tears rolling down the old man's face.

'I brought this in to show you,' he continued, as he slipped out his cellphone from the pocket of his white medical jacket. 'I think you should watch this.'

Sitting in his chair, Pope Clement watched in silence as Mueller continued to examine him. There was no sound from the cell phone, but the images said it all. His Apostolic Palace lay in ruins. The top two floors had been completely destroyed. His photograph was in the corner of the screen, as Cardinal Guarducci explained something to the assembled media from the steps of Saint Peter's Basilica. They had a terrorist suspect they claimed was responsible, and the Italian police had him in custody.

Holding the phone in one hand, Mueller continued to write until the two minute news report finished. Then slipping the phone back into his pocket, he continued to explain. 'At the moment we're also trying to track down terrorists from the Islamic States, who have smuggled chemical weapons into America.'

The whole time he spoke, Pope Clement recounted the vision he had experienced, knowing that they it was starting to be fulfilled.

'I can't talk too much at the moment,' Mueller explained, as he placed his seat back over into the corner of the room. 'I'll call back in later to speak with you, and hopefully by then I'll have more information.'

Unable to say anything, Pope Clement could only close his eyes and pray. He prayed for those who had lost their lives. He prayed for the American government and leaders of the world. But, most of all, he prayed for tomorrow.

57.

Sunday, 13th April.

'If you would like to follow me, Madam President,' an assistant to the Papal Master of Ceremonies said, as he stood beside her.

With a gracious smile, President Cleary got up from her chair and along with Debra Conway, walked across the outdoor sanctuary on the steps of Saint Peter's Square.

As the Vatican's choir sang the communion hymn of the requiem mass, the President queued for communion with the other Heads of States, who had answered Cardinal Guarducci's call to unite together in peace and love against such evil.

Reaching into a silver ciborium, Cardinal Jean Guarducci, who presided at the Mass, lifted out a small Host and raising it up he offered it to the President. 'Corpus Christi.'

'Amen!' Cleary replied, before she placed out her tongue to receive it.

'Thank you for coming,' Guarducci said, as he placed his hand onto her left shoulder.

Knowing the world's media was watching the moment between them, President Cleary bowed graciously in appreciation, blessed herself and walked back to her seat.

'What was all that about?' Conway asked her, when she sat back down.

'Don't ask,' she replied, as the Prime Minister of the United Kingdom, Harold Downs sat down beside her.

'So how's the operation progressing back home?' Downs asked her.

'We're getting there,' Cleary whispered, through the side of her mouth. 'After the attack here, the Caliph of Baghdad has publicly called off the planned attacks against us.'

'Have you been able to find the chemical weapons?'

'No.' Cleary said, with a polite smile not wanting to sound discourteous.

'They caused some damage here,' Downs went on, looking across the square to the ruins of the Apostolic Palace.

'They certainly did,' Cleary replied, looking at the devastation she had caused.

'You know certain things don't add up,' Downs continued. 'MI6 can't seem to corroborate your intelligence reports that this was carried out by terrorists from the Islamic States.'

'Well, our intelligence is pretty certain, Harold.'

'I was briefed on their findings this morning,' he continued. 'Did you know that the security is tighter within the Apostolic Palace than it is around Number 10?'

'What's your point?'

'Well, from the tourist footage and intelligence gatherings two things are quite clear. Firstly, the explosion took place from within the heart of the Papal Apartment. Secondly, the Islamic States don't have the capacity to create a thermobaric bomb.'

For President Cleary, his point sat uncomfortably close to the truth. Ignoring him, she opened the funeral book and started to read through it.

'Such a bomb could only have come from one place,' he added.

'Enough, Harold,' she said empathically. 'We can talk about this at a later time.'

'Well, let's just pray this terrorist attack doesn't trigger something we won't be able to control,' Downs added, eliciting no response.

Not lifting her eyes from the booklet, the President was determined not to raise her head until the communion had been distributed and Cardinal Guarducci was about to conclude the mass.

Returning to his presiding seat, Guarducci sat and waited until the Master of Ceremonies instructed him to proceed with the concluding rite; once he was sure all the dignitaries, cardinals, bishops and priests had received the sacrament.

As he sat looking across the sea of mourners gathered in Saint Peter's Square, Guarducci had to stop himself from smiling with pride at the sermon he had delivered. Were it within his power, he would have canonised Clement there and then. He knew he had done enough to place himself front in the race to be his successor, and with control of the conclave in his hands as Dean, he knew it would not be long before he would be sitting back on the same spot for his own coronation to the papacy.

'Your Eminence,' the Master of Ceremonies whispered into his ear. 'It is time to say the concluding prayer.'

With that Guarducci stood up, as the servers came across the sanctuary with the microphone and lectionary.

'Oremus,' he spoke into the microphone, bringing the millions gathered in Rome to silence.

As he went to raise his arms, he suddenly noticed several men running towards the altar from his left hand side. He stopped and turned to look at them. For a moment an almighty terror seized him when he thought they were running towards him. But, they ran across the sanctuary, and made straight for the American President. Without explanation, they escorted her from the congregation and started to run towards the main door of the basilica.

As the crowd watched the large televisions, their silence turned to murmurings of desperation when they realised that something big was happening.

'What's going on?' The President demanded, worried that her agents had their guns drawn, ordering clerics out of the way as they ran through Saint Peter's Basilica.

'We don't know Ma'am,' an agent replied. 'We've been ordered to get you airborne.'

'Jesus!' Conway replied, fearing the worse. 'We shouldn't have come here.'

Exiting the rear of the basilica they ran at full speed towards Marine One; its rotor blades already in motion. Pushing the President up the steps the agents stood aside to allow Conway to board. Then with great urgency, the Marine guarding the helicopter stepped onboard, pulled up the steps and sealed the door.

Sitting into her seat the President quickly strapped herself in as the rotor blades roared into full throttle, 'What's going on Debra?'

'I'm finding out Ma'am,' she replied, as she lifted the phone and got herself connected to the Chairman of the Joint Chiefs.

As the helicopter lifted off the ground, the President looked out the window as the multitude of people gathered for the funeral came into view.

'We'll be touching down at the end of the runway where Air Force One is waiting for immediate take off,' the Secret Service Agent informed the President of the news he'd just received through his ear piece. 'We should be there in four minutes.'

'Thank you,' Cleary replied, loosening the buttons of her suit jacket. 'Any word Debra?'

Conway raised a hand to silence the President. 'Admiral Lyman, explain the situation again?'

As her stomach tied itself in knots, she could only watch on nervously as Debra received the information. The look on her face said it all.

'No!' she shouted down the phone. 'No, no, no, no, no!'

'What is it Debra?'

'We've failed to stop them Ma'am,' she replied, tears welling up in her eyes. 'Less than five minutes ago sensors simultaneously detected high quantities of VX in the heart of New York, Dallas, Los Angeles and DC. We are under an orchestrated chemical attack.'

'Sweet Jesus!'

'Give me the phone Debra,' the President ordered. 'Admiral, this is the President.'

'Madam President, we are now at DEFCON one!' Lyman said, loud and clear. 'It is the opinion of the Joint Chiefs that the United States of America is now at war!'

58.

The doors of Marine One opened the moment the aircraft landed beside Air Force One. Immediately, President Cleary disembarked the aircraft along with Debra Conway and made her way towards Admiral Lyman who stood waiting on the tarmac.

'Everything's in order Madam President,' he shouted, above the roar of Air Force One's engines and the rotating blades of Marine One.

President Cleary said nothing as she climbed the steps to board Air Force One. Once inside she made her way towards the conference room, where all her staff stood to attention around the table.

'At ease gentlemen,' she ordered, as Lyman picked up the phone to the cockpit and gave the Colonel permission for immediate takeoff.

Taking her seat, the President sat back as the noise of the engines roared into life, before she felt the thrust of the plane as it made its way down the runway. No one said anything during the takeoff, but sat waiting for the jet to begin its ascent. The aircraft seemed to take longer than normal to travel the runway, but they all knew the procedure. In the event of an evacuated lift it would take Air Force One less than ten minutes to reach its altitude of forty-thousand feet, but it needed to use the full length of any given runway to gain as much speed as it could in order to give it maximum lift. Finally, they all felt the lift of the aircraft as it took to the sky as steeply and as fast as it could.

'What's the update?' Conway asked in a raised voice to Lyman, as the plane vibrated with the turbulence of its climb.

'At 07:35 Eastern Time, our intelligence agencies confirmed that they have detected VX in the atmosphere.' Lyman explained. 'At the concentrated levels it has been detected, we believe it has been released into the atmosphere in high amounts.'

'What's the cost of life?' The President asked.

'At the moment it's minimal, Ma'am,' Lyman stated. 'But, in the coming hours we will see those infected quickly begin to show signs of blindness, painful lacerations and burns to the skin, loss of bodily functions, extreme tightness of chest muscles as breathing slows and lungs begin to fill up with the burning effects of VX, ending in a slow and painful death by asphyxiation. By the end of today we will have lost around ten million American lives, possibly far more. Depending on the amount released and wind direction that number can be expected to multiply in the coming days, months and years through the effects of chemical poisoning and related cancers.'

As the scale of the devastation sank in, everyone in the room took a moment.

'Madam President, we need to strike back, now!' Lyman said.

No one spoke but waited for their Commander in Chief to take command.

Moments later, the President nodded.

Across the conference desk a Colonel of the Armed Forces passed the doomsday briefcase to Lyman who placed it in front of the President.

'What do you recommend?' The President asked.

'The Joint Chiefs believe we should take three approaches. Firstly, launch an all-out nuclear attack on all countries and major cities with sworn allegiance to the Islamic States, along with targeted strikes at remote military facilities, bases and runways throughout the Middle East and North Africa. These will stop short within five hundred miles of Israel. Secondly, we protect Israel, by assisting her in the bombing of every major city and town close to her borders that cannot be attacked with nuclear strikes. Thirdly, we cripple Russian cyber networks and strengthen our defence systems. Let the Russians have time to think, but if they launch an attack against us then we hit them with everything we have.'

'What will be their success rate in an attack against the United States?'

'A complete annihilation.'

In that moment, everyone in the room knew that they could lose everything and everyone that they loved.

'Speak to the Russian and Chinese Presidents,' the President said. 'We do not wish to attack them nor their interests. This is a war between ourselves and those loyal to the Caliph in Baghdad.'

Reaching into her jacket pocket, she took out the plastic launch code wallet, broke the seal and removed the code.

Taking the code from her, Lyman entered the first code: ZJE374H829K0.

The screen inside the briefcase confirmed the code.

'Who's going to verify the two man rule?' Lyman asked.

Breaking her own launch code wallet, Debra Conway handed her code over to the Admiral.

Lyman entered the second code: 7HS3KOW248L3.

With the code authorised it was time to proceed with the final verification.

'Ma'am,' Lyman invited her, as he pulled the briefcase closer to her.

Resting closer to the screen, President Cleary waited until the retina of her right eye was scanned.

'The launch codes have been recognised and confirmed,' Lyman informed her. 'With your permission Madam President, I would like to authorise a two minute countdown,'

'Confirmed.'

Lifting the secure phone to Strategic Air Command, Lyman gave the order for the two minute countdown.

From the day she took the oath of office and was given her first security briefing, President Cleary had prayed that a day, such as she was facing, would never come to her. Now that it had, she felt her inner body shake with the tension and the fear of what she was about to do.

'What happens now?'

Lyman took the briefcase and with his launch key placed it inside the terminal, turned it and opened the launch button, as the flashing red light illuminated the growing tension within the room. 'The countdown is waiting your final command.'

With her moment of truth before her, Cleary looked around at her joint chiefs and members of her staff. Placing her finger over the button, she stopped.

'I do this for the innocent lives I failed to protect and to protect the rest of the American people who have survived.'

Without further hesitation she pressed the button, which stopped flashing once activated. Looking up at the screens surrounding the room, she watched the live information fed from Strategic Air Command and the countdown that was ticking the seconds away until the wrath of liberty would strike those who'd taken it from so many.

In the final moments no one took their eyes from the screen, knowing that hundreds of millions from North Africa to the boarders of Pakistan, right through the Middle East to the European border with Turkey, were about to die.

Three. Two. One. Zero.

There was no turning back.

59.

As he removed his vestments in the sacristy, everything felt surreal but normal. Yet, every cardinal knew that the world was at war. America had been attacked. Nuclear strikes had taken place against Nigeria, Mali, Algeria, Tunisia, Libya, Egypt, Somalia, Yemen, Saudi Arabia, Iraq, Sinai Peninsula, Syria, Turkey, Afghanistan, Pakistan and even Iran. While ground and air offences were underway involving the United States and Israel against Palestine, Jordan, Lebanon and southern Syria.

Guarducci knew he had to act fast.

Walking towards Saint Martha's House, with Cardinal Oliveri, Guarducci used the moment to propose his idea.

'I doubt Cardinal Pascual would agree,' Oliveri replied. 'Just by bringing the funeral forward we denied most of the cardinals the opportunity to travel to Rome in time.'

'Well, they are unlikely to make it now, are they?' Guarducci insisted. 'You are the Vice Dean of the College. As the Dean I think it is in the best interests not only of the Church, but the whole world, to bring the Conclave forward and to elect a successor to give the necessary spiritual guidance that is going to be needed in the coming days. We cannot afford to sit around, following protocols and stagnant traditions for fifteen days before the conclave is convened.'

'Then you should speak to him about it.'

'It cannot be me,' Guarducci replied. 'The cardinals would not look too favourably on the Dean bearing pressure on the Camerlengo. It would look like the Curia influencing the College and they would not stand for it.'

'I do not know,' Oliveri replied, as he stopped outside the main door to Saint Martha's House, where all the cardinals would be staying until the conclave ended.

'We have no choice. We need to appear strong and decisive. Look at what is happening. Apart from being attacked ourselves, America is at war and has already destroyed most of the Islamic world. As the largest Christian Church we cannot go through the coming days and months without a Bishop of Rome. Only twenty-three of the one hundred and twenty voting cardinals were unable to attend the funeral. Our voting College is not going to change from the number we have now.'

'The Camerlengo would have to put it to a vote among the College.'

'The Camerlengo is a weak man. If you were to speak to him he would go along with you.'

'Why me?' Oliveri questioned, not wanting to step into the spotlight.

'You were the Prefect to the Congregation of Doctrine and Faith, Fernando will not dismiss the suggestion if it came from you. Furthermore, you know it is something that we must do.'

For a few moments Oliveri pondered the proposal. 'I will talk to him before lunch.'

'Good,' Guarducci said, as he touched his shoulder. 'You are doing the right thing.'

As they walked into Saint Martha's House, one of the priests directed them to a reception room where the cardinals had gathered for lunch.

'There he is,' Guarducci said, pointing out Fernando Pascual to Oliveri.

As he watched Oliveri walk over to Pascual, Guarducci knew his suggestion would work. It would only be a matter of time.

Walking over to the drinks table Guarducci lifted an orange juice and ignored the wine, then he started to mingle among the rest of the cardinals whose conversation was not about the excellent sermon he preached, but the nuclear attacks that were taking place across the globe. Never one to miss a moment, Guarducci used it to his advantage by listening and agreeing with everything most of them said; even though he personally only had time and respect for a few of them. Yet, in a conclave the vote of every single cardinal was as strong as the next.

'Your Eminences,' the Chief Steward announced. 'If you'd like to make your way into the dining room, lunch is about to be served.'

Carrying their drinks, the cardinals started to file into the modest dining room.

'What did he say?' Guarducci asked Oliveri, as he walked alongside him.

'I'm not the first to approach him about the matter,' Oliveri replied. 'Other Cardinals have already spoken to him.'

Taking a sip of his drink, Guarducci hid his pleasure. He knew they would all blindly carry out his request. Everything was in the palm of his hand.

Discretely, Guarducci took a seat in the corner of the room with five cardinals from Africa. He could have sat alongside the Camerlengo, but he knew what was coming.

It was only when all the cardinals sat down for their lunch to be served that Pascual rose to his feet and lifting a knife gently tapped the side of his glass to gain their attention. Once the hall fell silent, he turned to the household staff and asked them to leave the room and to secure the doors. He had the cardinals' undivided attention.

'My brothers,' he began to speak, in a soft Roman brogue. 'As you are aware, the world has slipped into unprecedented peril. So far we have seen a deadly chemical attack against America, followed by retaliatory nuclear strikes against every country that aligned themselves to the Islamic States. It is a situation that as Christ's Church we must represent before the crisis spirals further out of all control. God only knows what the forthcoming hours and days will bring.

'Therefore given the current circumstances, and the fact that the Holy See is vacant, I have been asked by several cardinals to put aside the Apostolic Constitution Universi Dominici Gregis, which stipulates that we wait for fifteen days until we elect a successor.'

It was clear from where Guarducci was sitting that many within the room agreed, although a few cardinals were visibly unnerved by the idea.

'I know this is going against all tradition,' Pascual continued, 'but we must face this world crisis with true leadership. God Himself only knows what will happen to the stability across the world if we wait for fifteen days. It is no longer a luxury we can afford to take.'

Getting to his feet Cardinal Olasky of Krakow had to make his objection.

'With all due respect Fernando, as the Camerlengo you must be aware that the full electoral body has yet to make it to Rome for the election.'

'You are right my brother,' Pascual agreed, 'but with the impossibility of world travel it is going to be impossible for the rest of the cardinals to make it here on time, even if we did allow fifteen days.'

Looking across the room Guarducci locked eyes with Cardinal Boyer, and gave him the approving nod he'd been waiting for.

'May I address the College Fernando?' Boyer asked, as he rose to his feet.

'Of course.'

'I wasn't one of the cardinals who made this proposal to the Camerlengo, but I believe that it is something that we must do. Having served as a cardinal in Washington I know from my contacts that the threat within the world is growing by the minute. Unless the Church elects someone to unite the world in true peace, we could see the rest of the world dragged into this conflict. Repercussions will hit the world within a matter of days; potential further wars, uprisings, food and water shortages, reduced production in oil supplies and the inevitable collapse of worldwide banking markets. How can we allow this to happen without a Pontiff and a spiritual voice for peace? Whereas, there is someone here in this room who can lead us and the world away from the brink of catastrophe. My brother Fernando, you have my support in your proposal, because I know that if we do nothing we will have failed in our duty. The Spirit of God isn't restricted by a deceased Pontiff's constitution, and if we back this proposal unanimously then that same Spirit will stir not only us but the effects will be felt throughout the world.'

Brilliant! Guarducci thought to himself, knowing that Boyer had sold it to the College.

'Is there anyone else who'd like to say something?' Pascual asked.

This was his time, pushing out his chair Guarducci faced his brothers.

'As Dean of this most Sacred College, I do not object. As our good brother Warren has just said, we are facing the biggest crisis the world has ever seen. More people will be killed today than the totality of all the wars throughout the history of civilisation. As we sit here debating this issue, billions across the world, whether Christian, Muslim, Jew, Buddhist, Hindu or whatever religion they profess are praying to their Higher Power for an answer. It is easy for us to sit here in the Vatican and to debate these issues, but we cannot afford to remain idle. As the true Church of God, we must be His voice of reasoning against this growing threat of evil that is taking hold across the world. If you have fear and caution then you are right to do so, even the apostles experienced that fear. But, once they opened the windows to the Holy Spirit on Pentecost Sunday, the Spirit moved their hearts and they were changed men before the whole world. It is clear to see that the same Spirit is moving here today, so please do not close your hearts or lock the doors of this election to him. Let us be united for the sake of the world.'

Sitting back down on his chair, Guarducci knew from the attentive silence that his words had touched them. So folding his hands together, he placed them under his chin as if lost in deep prayer.

'We can only do this unanimously,' Pascual broke the silence. 'What I propose to the College is very simple. We have two options. The first is to adhere to the Apostolic Constitution and allow fifteen days to pass before we elect as successor, and the second option is to move swiftly to provide a voice for the world in this troubled time.'

'How swiftly?' Cardinal Kristof from Berlin asked.

'With the damage caused to the Apostolic Palace the Sistine Chapel is structurally unsafe, so any election will have to take place within the apse of Saint Peter's Basilica. I will speak to staff within the Vatican and have a temporary partition erected to give us the privacy we need. If this can be done in eighteen hours, I see no reason why the Conclave couldn't sit tomorrow morning for the first round of ballots.'

His words had left all the cardinals with a lot to think about, but Pascual knew their decision had to be made promptly.

'Like I said, we must be unanimous. Shall we ballot after lunch?'

'There is no need to hold a ballot,' Oliveri spoke up. 'I stand because I am backing your proposal Fernando.'

One by one the cardinals rose to their feet. Guarducci waited a few seconds to make sure he was not seen as one of the first to back the proposal. But, when he stood his African brothers stood up alongside him, along with most of the College, and their support did not go unnoticed. A few cardinals lingered, torn between the rubric and the spirit of the moment, but not wanting to be seen as objectors they rose to their feet to give the full unanimous support that was needed.

'Very well my brothers,' Pascual concluded, his proposal secured. 'We will begin at eight o'clock tomorrow morning with our opening mass and will start balloting from ten o'clock onwards. From now on, no cardinal is permitted to leave this house until our body has chosen its successor to our departed Holy Father. I will inform the world's media of our intention.'

60.

'How are you?' Captain Mueller, asked as he walked into the room.

'They have no need for me now,' Clement replied, as he opened his pyjama top to allow the doctor to carry out his assessment. 'How many have died?'

'It's hard to say,' Mueller answered, as he checked the Pope's chest wound. 'It's estimated to be around several hundred million.'

Clement took deep and painful sigh.

'There will be many more, this is only the beginning.' Clement said. 'Make sure you keep your faith in these coming years, for it will be the only thing that will see you through the horror that is about to be unleashed.'

Mueller could see the spiritual anguish deep within the Pope's eyes, but there was nothing he could do for him.

'Thank you for all that you have done for me.' Pope Clement said, as he took hold of Mueller's hands. 'Promise me that you will never lose faith in the Lord.'

As Mueller sat beside him, he knew the footsteps coming down the hallway were coming to get the Pope.

'Do not worry for me. I am not afraid of the end,' Clement replied, sensing Mueller unease.

As the doors to the room opened, a senior officer walked in followed by six armed soldiers.

'Secure him!'

Immediately, two young soldiers approached the Holy Father and as he offered his hands to them they cuffed him.

'Come off it, there's no need for that!' Mueller said, as they wheeled the Pope out of the room. 'He's just come through major heart surgery.'

Muller turned to the door to see an unknown Air Force General taking control of the situation.

'Who are you?'

'I'm General John Lechner, and I'm here under orders to escort this prisoner out of Rawlins.'

'Well, I'm afraid that's not going to be possible. As the senior medical officer of this base I'm the only one who can discharge him, and as long as he's under my care he'll be going nowhere.'

'That's why you are going with him!' The General replied. 'Bring with you what you need.'

Grabbing the Pope's medical notes, Mueller followed them out of the room and into the main medical wing.

Everyone in the medical wing stood looking on. Now they all knew who their patient was, but like Mueller they were powerless to stop his transfer.

Once outside, the Pope was wheeled across the tarmac towards an awaiting chinook helicopter.

'Get him in quickly,' Lechner ordered, when they approached the aircraft.

Struggling for breath, Pope Clement was lifted onto the Chinook, and strapped into his seat.

'Hurry up!' Lechner shouted, his impatience growing by the second.

Climbing on board, Mueller attached the portable oxygen tank to the Pope's breathing line, and immediately increased the flow to help him settle more quickly.

'You've nothing to fear!' Mueller said.

With his troops and more importantly his prisoner onboard, Lechner ordered the main doors of the chinook to be closed.

As the rotor blades started to increase in velocity, the General sat opposite the Pope and gave a sigh of relief before turning to Mueller and smiling.

'That was nerve-wrecking!' Lechner said, as the chinook took to the sky, unnoticed amid the escalating buildup of military activity at the base.

'You did well bro!' Mueller said, giving him a high five.

'What is happening?' Pope Clement asked.

'Do you remember I told you that my brother was a priest?' Mueller asked the Pope. 'This is him. He's a Catholic chaplain to the Armed Forces. I told him about your situation and he put together this plan to rescue you.'

'Please to meet you, Holy Father!' Fr. Mueller said, as he reached over and removed the handcuffs from the Pope. 'I'm sorry about the way we had to evacuate you from Rawlins, but we had to make it look like your evacuation was ordered by the top level of command within the government. Today was our only chance of getting you out. With the military buildup taking place in Rawlins, we knew that this was the only chance we had while the attention of the Armed Forces is on other matters. Had we left you there, I reckon they would have killed you.'

'And who are these men?' Clement asked.

'They're going to be looking after you, Your Holiness. They are men I can trust. We took possession of this aircraft this morning to carry out the operation.'

Now aware of the pain he was in, Clement sat back and closed his eyes. 'Will they come after us?'

'Your disappearance will cause a certain level havoc, but this country is quickly spiralling into turmoil and soon you'll become the least of their problems. We're going to be touching down relatively soon. Let's hope we have time on our side before someone works out that you were kidnapped instead of transferred. We have arranged a military convoy to take us to the Canadian border. With the military movement that is taking place we just hope and pray that it won't be noticed too soon. It will be a bit of a journey, but we aim to have you in a safe house by the morning. The main thing for you to know is that you are safe. With a little help from above, we will protect you.'

61.

As Dean of the College, Guarducci had an important role officiating over the conclave. As such he was given one of the largest rooms within Saint Martha's House. Following the lunch it had been a busy day, but as the evening closed he invited Oliveri to his room.

'A glass of wine would be nice,' Oliveri replied to his offer.

'So, within the next few days we should have a successor elected,' Guarducci said, as he took a seat.

'I think it might be a lot sooner than that!'

'Why?'

'The cardinals are already talking about the papabile candidates and your name appears to be top of their list.'

Guarducci didn't reply to what he already knew, but sipped his wine nonetheless heartened by Oliveri's words.

'I think we need someone like you who knows the real truth,' Oliveri continued. 'We cannot afford to allow someone outside the three of us to succeed, and then to discover the truth of what we have done.'

'It does not have to be me,' Guarducci played along. 'It could be Warren Boyer or yourself.'

'Never in a million years would the College elect an American. As for me, I've rubbed too many of them up the wrong way over the years. It has to be you.'

'What about all I have done? Do you have no problem with that?'

'Jean, I took the decision with you. We both know that it was for the right reason.'

'But it looks as if Pope Clement was right, maybe we are entering the end of times.'

'We have discussed this,' Oliveri defended. 'What we did was for the best interests of the Church. Now that we have seen it through, neither of us can afford to let this control slip out of our hands. I know once you become elected that you will do the right thing by us all, and through your actions you will receive the necessary absolution that you need.'

Guarducci smiled at him. 'It is good that I have your unquestionable support. I promise you, if I am elected I will seek to do what is right and you will have an honoured place alongside me.'

'I will be honoured Jean,' Oliveri replied. 'There is one little obstacle that haunts my mind.'

'Clement?'

'Yes. What if word gets out that he is still alive?'

'You need not worry, the American Government have him well secured. They cannot afford to see the truth coming out any more than we can. As long as I can unite the world in peace then they will never reveal the real truth of what we have done.'

62.

Monday, 14th April.

After mass the following morning, the cardinals gathered together in the nave of Saint Peter's Basilica to begin their conclave. As the bells of Saint Peter's Basilica tolled the tenth hour, the Papal Master of Ceremonies started to lead them up the empty nave towards their temporary conclave chapel.

Chanting the Litany of the Saints, they walked in steady procession; their red robes trailing the ground as they made their way to perform the most sacred of duties that any cardinal has to undertake.

Following the ninety-seven cardinals eligible to vote, Guarducci as the Dean followed them at the rear, just behind Oliveri the Vice Dean and Pascual the Camerlengo. As they processed around the high altar, under Michelangelo's majestic dome and his final gift to the world, even Guarducci felt the symbolism as diagonal beams of light shone through the windows of the dome directly onto sanctuary that stood over the tomb of Saint Peter himself.

Guarducci had no doubt that the other cardinals were trying to experience a feeling of the spiritual as they walked, trying to see the light as the touch of God reaching down upon them. But, for Guarducci he saw only the folly of man who needed to create such a building to experience the wonder in its creation.

As the cardinals filed under the temporary partition and into the apse, they started to take their seats behind the tables that were set out for them. Standing near the door Guarducci waited until they were all seated before he instructed the Master of Ceremonies to seal the doors.

With the conclave in session, Cardinal Guarducci made his way to the foot of the altar under Saint Peter's Chair. Piously, he genuflected before turning to address them.

'It falls on me as the Dean of this Sacred College to address you before you make your selection. I will not take long. I know you are all aware of the seriousness that the world faces and the urgent need for us to elect a man strong enough to fill the shoes of our late Holy Father. Christ tells us not to be afraid. My brothers, do not be afraid. In your hearts you know the man Christ is calling to wear the ring of the Fisherman. Trust your conscience and the light of this election will shine for all the world to see.'

Walking back towards his allotted seat, he stood behind it.

'In front of you, you have your single ballot to elect the man you believe the Lord Jesus Christ is calling to lead this Church. Do your sacred duty.'

Sitting behind his own table, Guarducci lifted the pen, and under the Latin words, *Eligo in Summum Pontificem,* he wrote his own name. GUARDUCCI. Then folding the rectangular ballot he waited for all the other cardinals to finish.

It took less than five minutes for the cardinals to make their choice. Seeing they had all set down their pens, Guarducci stood up holding his ballot up in the air for all to see.

'In turn you will now all process to the altar, swear your oath and place your ballot into the chalice.'

As the cardinals left their tables, Guarducci led them towards the altar. Then stopping before the altar, he held his ballot up for them all to see and he read out his oath. 'I call as my witness Christ the Lord who will be my judge, that my vote is given to the one who before God I think should be elected.' Then placing his ballot onto the paten that covered the chalice, he used the paten to drop his ballot into it. With his sacred duty performed he returned to his seat, knowing that it would take some time for the other ninety-six cardinals to go through the same process.

Closing his eyes, Guarducci did not want to make eye contact with any of the electors, but as each one read out his oath before dropping his ballot into the chalice, Guarducci kept repeating the same mantra over and over again in his mind. *At last all powerful master, it is time for your power to be glorified through me, your servant!*

It took forty minutes before the last elector, Oliveri as the Vice Dean cast his vote, and as he returned to his seat Guarducci stood up and invited the three nominated scrutinisers to come forward.

As the first cardinal shook the ballots within the chalice he handed it over to the second cardinal who emptied them onto the table and started counting them. When he announced that he had the required corresponding ninety-seven ballots Guarducci breathed a sigh of relief that they would not have to start the process over again.

Taking a seat behind the election desk to the side of the high altar the three cardinals were prepared to announce the result. As the first cardinal took each of the ballots and unfolded them he handed it to the second cardinal to note the name down before the third cardinal announced the name to the assembled College.

At first Guarducci sat uneasy as the cardinal of Westminster's name was declared in the first four ballots. Then his own name was drawn, and for the duration of the vote it was a two horse race between Tindal and himself. At the end of the processes the result was read out. 'Guarducci, fifty-nine. Tindal, thirty-two. Hiro, three. Olasky, two. Fruchtenbaum, one.'

Guarducci opened his eyes only to feel the eyes of every elector looking at him. He had failed to meet the sixty-seven votes to give him the two-thirds plus one majority that he needed to be elected. As the ballots were burned, sending black smoke into the sky above Saint Peters, it now fell upon Oliveri as the Vice Dean to take over control of the Conclave as Guarducci was a very strong contender.

'My brother Cardinals,' Oliveri addressed them from his seat opposite Guarducci. 'In the light of the closeness to electing a successor I think it would be unwise to proceed with another ballot so soon. Therefore I propose an adjournment, to give us time to contemplate our next vote. All in favour raise your hands. Those against. The adjournment has been agreed unanimously, so we will convene at two o'clock after lunch.'

With the morning session of the conclave drawn to a close the doors were opened and the cardinals silently left the basilica and made their way back to their rooms in Saint Martha's House.

Staying behind Guarducci waited until they had all left before he walked over to Oliveri.

'That was a good result Jean,' Oliveri commented.

'It is too close. Now that Tindal is in the race many of the College will think that I do not have enough support and they could switch to him.'

'Leave it with me Jean,' Oliveri reassured him. 'Go back to your room and I will sort it.'

'How?'

'I am going to bring Tindal crashing down.'

63.

Oliveri walked along the empty corridor, and when he reached Cardinal Tindal's room he stopped outside it and gently knocked the door.

Opening the door, Tindal was surprised to see him.

'Is everything alright?'

'I need to talk to you urgently,' Oliveri replied, as he walked into his room. 'Close the door!'

'What is it?' Tindal asked, sensing something was wrong.

'If you get the vote will you accept the Papacy?' Oliveri asked him.

'If it is the Lord's will that my brothers should elect me, then yes.'

'I see!' Oliveri replied, as he walked over to the window.

'What is it you want?'

Turning to him, Oliveri spelt it out as clearly as he could.

'You are not to become Pope. You are not the man we need.'

'Excuse me?'

'It is very simple Anthony, you will cause a scandal if elected.'

'What do you mean?'

'I am talking about your trips to male masseurs in the Soho area of London. I have letters in my office regarding the more unsavoury aspects of those encounters. In fact, had we known about this before you were elevated to the episcopate, then your promotion would never have taken place.'

As Tindal sat down on the edge of his bed, it was clear for Oliveri to see that he had taken the wind from his wings.

'Is it true?'

'It's in my past,' Tindal insisted. 'I haven't engaged in such activity in over thirty years.'

'But you can see the consequences if the world found out?'

Tindal could only lower his head in shame.

'If it has been kept this quiet for so long, then there's no reason why it can't remain so. However, if you proceed with your nomination then I'll have no choice but to inform the College.'

'Why would you do that?' Tindal asked, as the emotion of his past filled his eyes.

'I cannot allow them to elect you. You would be discredited before the whole world. What we need is someone strong like Cardinal Guarducci to lead us. You know what you have to do.'

'No, I don't!' Tindal replied.

'During lunch you will announce to the assembled College that you do not wish to be elected Pope, and publicly throw your support behind Cardinal Guarducci.'

'And if I don't?'

'Look at it from this angle, if you do this, your name and reputation will remain intact. I will leave you to ponder it over.'

Having done his duty, Oliveri left and went back to his own room, knowing that he had secured the Papacy for the one who could lead them out of the darkest days they faced towards the light of hope.

64.

Gathered together for the second ballot, Oliveri looked across to Guarducci who sat calm and collected. Oliveri, however, felt his blood boil with rage that Tindal had failed to instruct the cardinals during lunch of his intention that he did not wish to be nominated. Then looking to the far end of Guarducci's row, Oliveri clocked eyes on Tindal who sat like a troubled soul. He knew the Englishman was wondering if he had it in him to out him.

Oliveri rose to his feet.

Expecting Oliveri to direct them in the voting, the College was surprised when he asked them to allow him the duty to address them on an issue of grave importance, but his calculated move was enough of a threat to force Tindal to his feet, fearing that he was going to be exposed.

'You have something to say, Anthony?' Oliveri asked him.

Walking into the middle of the aisle, Tindal took the floor to address them.

'My brothers I would like to thank all of you who have placed your confidence in me, but I want to inform you that I do not wish to succeed Pope Clement as the Bishop of Rome.'

His declaration to withdraw sent murmurs of disbelief amongst the College.

'My brothers,' he spoke out loudly and clearly to them, bringing them back to silence. 'I'm not the man who has the strength needed to carry this cross during this difficult time. So if you vote for me I will not accept your election. However, there is one here among us who has the necessary strength, conviction and spiritual zeal to lead us and the Church. Therefore, I am declaring my support for Cardinal Jean Guarducci, and for those who backed me I would ask you in conscience to consider doing the same.'

No sooner had he spoken, Cardinal Boyer rose to his feet. 'I declare my intention to elect Jean Guarducci too.'

Having surrendered his chance, Tindal could only go back to his place, as one cardinal after another rose to his feet declaring his support for Guarducci. Within five minutes the only one sitting was Guarducci himself, as the wave of support grew throughout them all.

Finally, Oliveri turned to him once all the other cardinals had declared him, and with a smile on his face said, 'Cardinal Guarducci I declare my support for you as well.'

Each member of the College sat back down in silence, waiting for Guarducci to speak, but he continued to sit on in silence with his eyes closed.

'Cardinal Guarducci you have been unanimously declared by your brother cardinals to succeed Pope Clement as the Bishop of Rome,' Oliveri spoke out loud. 'According to the Apostolic Constitution, Universi Dominici Gregis, a unanimous declaration is enough to forfeit any further election by ballot. Could the Camerlengo please inform the Papal Master of Ceremonies that we have arrived at our decision.'

Rising to his feet, Guarducci turned and bowed to them all. Then joining his hands he waited for Pascual to inform the Master of Ceremonies.

As the locked doors to the conclave were opened, the Master of Ceremonies, Bishop Boris Guishar, walked in carrying the decree that was required to certify the acceptance of any newly elected Pope. Standing alongside Oliveri, Guishar smiled when he saw that it was Cardinal Guarducci that the College had elected.

'Are you ready to proceed?' Oliveri quietly asked Guarducci and Guishar. When they nodded their heads, he cleared his throat to ask the most anticipated question of any conclave. 'Do you, Cardinal Jean Guarducci, accept your canonical election as Supreme Pontiff?'

'By the power from on high, I do.'

'By what name do you wish to be known?'

'Christopher.'

Placing the decree onto the table before Guarducci, Guishar wrote in the new Pontiff's name; which in Latin said everything about the man they had just elected - *Xpofer.* When he had completed the task, he rolled up the decree and placed it inside the ringed holder before handing it to Oliveri.

Turning to the College, Oliveri ceremoniously showed them the decree, and then officially announced their decision.

'My brothers behold our new Supreme Pontiff, The Bishop of Rome, The Vicar of Christ, Servant of the Servant's of God, and Pontifex Maximus, His Holiness, Pope Christopher.'

As the cardinals applauded in congratulations, Pope Christopher, as he was from now on to be known, stepped out from behind his table and walked into the middle aisle, and with staged piety he humbly bowed before them all before lifting his eyes to heaven as if in prayer. Except Christopher acknowledged the one greater than him, the one whom he truly served. Having spent his life securing the ultimate and unquestionable power, he knew that his time had come when his true power and authority over all the dominions would be shown to the whole world in a short matter of time.

65.

Led by Oliveri and Bishop Guishar, Christopher followed them over to one of the smaller sacristies that had been set aside as a temporary room of tears. Opening the door for him, Guishar reverently stood aside as Christopher walked into the room alone.

In the room of tears, so named because previous Pontiff's cried following their election, knowing that once they dawned the Papal white robes their lives would never be the same, Christopher stood alone looking at the three different sizes in the white soutanes that were hanging from the dressing rail in the middle of the room. He could only smile, somewhat in disbelief that his election had been so quick and relatively painless.

Then he heard the rear door to the room being opened as Marco Gammarelli, the papal tailor, walked in. Christopher reached out his hand to greet him, but Gammarelli in his traditional way didn't shake it, but knelt before him and kissed his ring.

'It is good to see you old friend,' Christopher replied, as he helped the old man to his feet.

'Likewise, Your Holiness,' Gammarelli replied. 'Would you like to vest now or would you prefer to be alone by yourself for a while?'

'The world is in need of a Pope, so let us proceed.'

'Yes, Your Holiness. If you'd like to stand behind the partition.'

Smiling at him, Christopher took off his red Zucchetto and handed it to Gammarelli following the tradition. And while Gammarelli placed the Zucchetto into the case he had brought with him, Christopher walked behind the screen and started to take off his red pontificals.

'Your Holiness what size do you take in a shirt?'

'Sixteen and a half.'

'Your waist measurement?'

'Thirty-six.'

'Shoe Size?'

'Eleven.'

As Christopher stripped down to his underwear, Gammarelli opened the large chest he had brought with him and took out the white grandfather shirt and the breeches he knew would fit him. Then when he saw His Holiness place his clothing over the top of the partition he asked him if he was ready.

'Yes,' Christopher replied, before he saw a small silver dressing trolley appear around the corner of the partition; containing the black breeches, white linen shirt, white linen stockings and red shoes.

Giving the Pope time, Gammarelli started to fold his old robes and clothing away, before placing them into the case he had with them. Apart from the Zucchetto, everything else was to be incinerated.

Having finished putting the clothing on, Christopher stood out from behind the partition.

'They look fine Your Holiness,' Gammarelli commented, as he slipped the gold cufflinks into his cuffs. 'I will call by your residence later on this evening, to measure you and to make sure you have a perfect fit for tomorrow.'

'You are most kind,' Christopher replied, as he lifted the white clerical stock and attached it to his shirt.

'Now, let me see,' Gammarelli said, as he walked over to the three papal soutanes. 'I would say, like the majority of popes, that the medium sized soutane should fit you.'

'That looks fine.'

Taking the soutane from the hanger, Gammarelli opened it up like a coat and held it out for Christopher, before walking in front of him, and then on bended knee he started to button it up.

'How does that feel?' He asked, as he stood back.

'I think it is a perfect fit,' Christopher commented.

'I think Your Holiness is right,' Gammarelli replied, quite pleased at how well fitting it looked. 'If Your Holiness would lift his arms for me please.'

Lifting his arms, Christopher allowed Gammarelli to place the white silk woven fascia around his waist, and like the soutane it fitted him well.

'Now, for the pectoral cross,' Gammarelli said, as he walked over to the chest and took out the golden cross and chain. 'It was designed by one of Rome's top jewellers, but if Your Holiness does not like it we can arrange to have another one made.'

Taking the cross Christopher looked at it.

'It is beautiful Mr. Gammarelli, but I would prefer to wear the one I wore when elected Pontiff.'

Handing the cross back, Christopher walked over and lifted Paul Brenard's pectoral cross and chain, placed it around this neck and attached the little hook of the cross to the fourth buttonhole on his soutane, close to his heart.

'Now would Your Holiness like to wear a mozzetta and stole for the announcement?'

Christopher thought about it for a moment.

'No, I think it will be enough to wear the traditional white.'

'Good choice. We only ever use the mozzetta to hide the fact the white soutane either hangs or is too tight, but in your case it fits perfectly.'

'You have done an excellent job Mr. Gammarelli. You always do,' Christopher said, as he admired his new image in the full length mirror that was beside him.

'Now, for the last thing,' Gammarelli said, as he lifted one of the little black leather boxes and opened it. 'The white zucchetto.'

Bowing his head, Christopher allowed Gammarelli to place it on his head. Then rising up to his full height, his investiture complete, he walked towards the mirror for one final look.

'Near perfection, Your Holiness,' Gammarelli said, as he walked over to him to make some small adjustments. 'Now, would Your Holiness like some time alone, or will I ring the bell to summons the Master of Ceremonies.'

'I am ready,' Christopher replied.

66.

All the cardinals rose to their feet as the Master of Ceremonies appeared, leading Pope Christopher back into the basilica's apse. For the second time they began to applaud him.

'If you would like to stand here, Your Holiness,' Bishop Guishar directed him, once they arrived at the foot of the altar. 'Would you like to sit?'

'I'm fine, thank you,' Christopher declined, as he wanted to stand to greet his cardinals.

One by one they came forward and knelt in homage before him. To each one Christopher offered his right hand for them to kiss and to swear their loyalty to him. Yet, before each of them rose, Christopher placed both his hands onto their heads, and while all the cardinals thought they were receiving his first blessing, Christopher quietly imparted his own power onto them knowing that in their homage they were subjecting themselves to everything he desired.

When Cardinal Anthony Tindal stepped forward, it was a bitter sweet moment knowing that he was so close to achieving the sacred office. Pope Christopher whispered into his ear, 'I will award you greatly for your loyalty.' Upon hearing the words Tindal grabbed his hands and kissed them before falling to his knees.

Last to approach him were Cardinals Boyer and Oliveri, whose smiles were larger than the rest knowing that they had covered themselves well by electing Christopher. Boyer received the same blessing from him as all the rest of the Cardinals received, but as Oliveri rose after receiving his blessing, Christopher took a firm hold of him. 'You have served me well my most loyal friend.'

'And I always will, Your Holiness.'

'I need you to remain close by me,' Christopher said to him, as he looked deeply into his eyes. 'Will you become my Secretary of State?'

'It will be my greatest honour.'

Smiling warmly back at him, Christopher let his grip on him go as the Master of Ceremonies approached with a microphone.

'My brothers, we are still grieved after the death of our most beloved Holy Father. Now you, the eminent cardinals, have called me to be the Bishop of Rome in these the most difficult of days.

'I will not hide behind any smoke screen, because we all know that we need to seek a way forward within the world. It will require us to step out beyond our limits, and act as true peacemakers, because only then can we be accepted as the sons of men.

'My plan is very simple, and it is one that I will ordain from this moment onwards. I will do everything in my power to secure the world in stability and peace. If it means walking through unknown lands, then I will go there. If it means reaching out to those who are against us, then I will. What the world needs now is a man of peace, a man of vision and a man of courage. I know that I am that man, and I expect you as my brothers to follow me and to make my vision the mission for the rest of your lives.

'There is no other way forward. We cannot bury our heads in the sand. Instead, we must do good for all, and as the world calls out in this hour for salvation, we must be seen as the way and means to that salvation.

'Unity among ourselves is essential, because if we stand united we can achieve the impossible. Now who is behind me?'

One by one the cardinals stood in support. Christopher looked at them all. His true mission had begun.

'I never doubted you for a moment,' he joked with them. 'Where is the Cardinal Protodeacon?'

'Here Your Holiness,' Cardinal Nouwen replied, as he walked towards him.

'You may announce to the world that the College of Cardinals have elected a new Pope.'

About The Author.

Damian North was born in Ireland and lives in County Antrim. *Pontifex Maximus* is his debut novel. It is the first instalment of a papal trilogy.

www.damiannorth.com

@damian_north

Acknowledgements.

'Every book is the wreck of a prefect idea.' Iris Murdock.
Without the following, it would have been a complete disaster:

Special thanks to my family for their constant love and support - I finally got there in the end. In particular, a special thanks to my late uncle and beloved Godfather - John Rogan, who taught me to love a story since I was a young boy.

To all my amazing friends for their years of encouragement, constructive criticism and for never doubting that I'd achieve my dream, especially: Joan Campbell, Philip Smyth, John O'Kane, Patrick Buckley, Kevin and Carole Tierney, Graham Colby, Joanne and Mark Flynn, Christopher Smallwood, Donal McKeown, Aiden McCroy, Fainche Craig and Maura McCann.

I could not have completed this work without the help of two remarkable people who read the manuscript and made many insightful suggestions. Many thanks go to two great friends: Roisin Deighan who encouraged me when I doubted myself. To Paul Creaner who came on board and with an eagle's eye made all the difference. Their help saved me from many inaccuracies and helped to trim the fat. The errors that remain are now my own.

Great thanks to Jay Ahere who designed the cover for the novel. How you did it from the drawing I sent you I will never know. But, it blew my mind it was that good.

Even though she cannot read it, because she is a beagle, thank you to Downie who has been my constant companion in the dark early mornings and as I burned the midnight oil. The first to hear the story before you all.

Ultimately, this book could not have been written without the rock that is Daniel Cunningham, to whom this book is dedicated. Thank you Daniel for everything.

Thank you, the reader for buying the book. Writing a novel has been a dream I have held close to my heart for many years. Publishing is a tough industry in which to make your mark. I hope you enjoyed my debut novel and that you will continue to support me beyond this first step. Until next time ...

Damian North.

Facebook code

~~046535~~!

008376

Password.

Printed in Great Britain
by Amazon

44815907R00158